CROWN OF THUNDER

TOCHI ONYEBUCHI

RAZORBILL

RAZORBILL

An Imprint of Penguin Random House LLC
Penguin.com

RAZORBILL & colophon is a registered trademark
of Penguin Random House LLC.

First published in the United States of America by Razorbill,
an imprint of Penguin Random House LLC, 2018

Library of Congress Cataloging-in-Publication Data
Names: Onyebuchi, Tochi, author.
Title: Crown of thunder / by Tochi Onyebuchi.
Description: [New York] : Razorbill, [2018] | Sequel to: Beasts made of night. |
Summary: "Taj has escaped Kos, but Queen Karima will go to any means necessary—
including using the most deadly magic—to track him down"
— Provided by publisher.
Identifiers: LCCN 2018013400 | ISBN 9780448493930 (hardback)
Subjects: | CYAC: Magic—Fiction. | Guilt—Fiction. |
Monsters—Fiction. | fantasy.
Classification: LCC PZ7.1.O66 Cro 2018 | DDC [Fic]—dc23 LC record available at
https://lccn.loc.gov/2018013400

Printed in the United States of America

1 3 5 7 9 10 8 6 4 2

Interior design: Eric Ford

To Mom,
as always.

And to Chinoye, Chibuikem, and Uchechi,
who, without fail, turn darkness to light.

CHAPTER 1

THE SETTING SUN cuts ribbons of red and blue across the sky. Night's on its way, which means so are the inisisa sent to kill us.

The rebels say that after I peeled back the shadows of that boar, that sin-beast I called forth from myself, I passed out. Makes sense that I don't remember it. But it makes it all harder to believe. Not remembering makes it easier to question things—to wonder if it's all really true. Maybe I never called forth my own sin—this sin that turned into a sin-beast that glowed. Maybe the battle at the Palace was a dream. Maybe I could say the same for the arashi that flew out of the sky and set the city of Kos—my city—on fire. Maybe I dreamed up Princess Karima's betrayal too. And Bo's.

It's easy to wish things were different.

It's hard—it feels impossible, even—to go back and make things better.

I'm right on a cliff's edge, and valley spreads about beneath me. There's more green down there than I've ever seen in my entire life, so different from the browns and reds of Kos. Whenever I close my eyes, I see those streets, and I see the jewels of Gemtown sparkling in the sun, threatening to blind you if you look at them directly. I see Kosians wandering that part of the Forum where jewelers sold their wares, everyone in bright-colored robes and wraps, shouting to be heard over one another, arguing prices, examining gems, turning canes or necklaces or earstones over in their hands. Then I open my eyes again, and all I see in front of me is strangeness.

An explosion sounds in the distance. I don't even need to squint to know it's coming from Kos. It's not the continuous roaring of the arashi, that enormous mythical monster that had come out of the sky, drawn by the army of sin-beasts Karima and her Palace Mages had summoned. It sounds more like a Baptism. Like a dahia getting demolished, a whole neighborhood quarter turned to rubble. My chest warms with anger. Things were supposed to be different. I can't believe that Karima's as callous as the previous rulers of Kos. I still remember her touch. I can feel her fingers running along the sin-spots on my arms and shoulders.

Leaves rustle in the tree branches overhead, and I turn around just in time to see Noor leap down and land behind me as gracefully as any Kos street cat. White-pupiled eyes shine out over the black cloth pulled up over her. I trained this young sin-eater once, in a forest just like this. She joined us in the battle to save Kos. And she fled the city with us when all was lost.

"Oga," she says, by way of greeting. I still can't tell if she's calling me *boss* as a joke or if she really means it. I'd be surprised if she still looks at me as a leader.

"What's the news, Noor?" I sit down by the ledge. She steps next to me, fists balled at her sides. She's constantly coiled now; whenever I see her, she's ready to knock out someone's jaw or gouge out someone's eyes.

"It'll be time to eat soon."

"All right." I grunt as I get back to my feet. I should count myself lucky I got even that tiny slice of time to myself. I almost want to ask Noor to stay with me a little bit and watch the sun set, but some of the rebel Mages have been making noise about airborne inisisa. Scouts, they say. In the form of birds and sometimes bats. And if I were to sneak out from under the cover of the forest and one of those things were to see me, Karima would know exactly where to send her army. If I were the only one I had to worry about, it wouldn't be a problem, but I know as soon as I step out and get spotted, every loose sin-beast in Kos will be sent straight for me. Noor and Ras and the others would try to get in the way, the rebel Mages would try to shield me, and by the end, there'd be a bunch of dead bodies everywhere just because I wanted to catch a sunset. Under those circumstances, it seems like not being late for supper is the least I can do. No need to make everyone's job harder than it already is.

Even though we're all equals in the forest, the aki and the Mages still dine apart. Once upon a time, we worked for those same

Mages. For a few ramzi, we aki would go where the Mages sent us. They would call forth some rich Kosian's sin, and, once we killed and Ate it, they would get a purse heavy with money. Then they'd hand us barely enough of the ramzi inside to feed ourselves.

A few of the sin-eaters keep me company. They are my bodyguards. I'm not sure how to feel about it. When I was in charge of these kids, training them under the watchful eye of other Palace Mages, their skin was unblemished. No tattoos. No marks from battling inisisa. Then I had to train them how to fight, how to Eat sins. Now they sit or stand or lounge around me with bowls of egusi soup, and I see the mark of a sin-bird's open wings on one of their arms. A sin-lion rears up on its hind legs along another aki's thigh. One aki girl has a sin-sparrow tattooed just beneath her left eye. They chat with one another, but they mostly do the silent, stoic thing that serious bodyguards are supposed to do. It's a thing Bo used to do.

As soon as I think of Bo, my heart sinks. Sometimes, when I sleep, I dream of our fight. I remember standing on the steps to the Palace and Karima telling me to come rule Kos with her. I remember telling her no and seeing Bo come up the steps. I remember feeling glad to have him back. But even in the dream, I know something's wrong, and all of a sudden Bo is on top of me with his daga aimed at my heart, and it takes all of my strength to keep him from cutting it out of my chest.

Some of the Mages currently eating on the other side of the campfire were there to watch the whole thing. They saw Kos in its final moments. The one with the silver braids, Miri, is the one all the rebel Mages listen to, but sometimes Miri and Aliya head off together into the darkness, and it's usually pretty soon after they get back that we have to get up and get moving again.

The urge sometimes bubbles up in me to go to Aliya, but it always evaporates a second later. I don't know what I'd say to her, or what exactly I'd ask her. Maybe something about the inisisa I supposedly called from myself or maybe something about the fact that I can't remember it. Maybe I would ask her if all those things she said to me on the steps to the Palace were real, all those things about me staying true to myself and not being seduced by Karima and the power she offered me. Maybe I'd go to her just to be near her. She's different now. She's not the same girl I met at Zoe's all those months ago, so eager to learn about sin-eating and equations that she would spill tea all over me, but there's still some of that curiosity there—some of that hopefulness. I see it at night when I catch her sneaking out to stargaze, her eyes bright and wide, just like they used to be all the time.

She's chewing on some goat meat, and she's got her head cocked to the side while another Mage whispers to her about something. She finishes, licks her fingers, then tosses the bones into the fire. Grease stains her robe, but she either doesn't see it or doesn't care.

I don't notice that I've been staring directly into the fire until she nudges me.

"Taj, are you OK?" she asks.

I shake away the dizziness. "Yes. I'm fine." But I'm not. I'm thinking about those explosions again, imagining houses crumbling in a Baptism, whole dahia demolished. I find myself replaying all those conversations Karima and I had. About sin and about Eating and about the Unnamed. I remember how her eyes lit up when she saw me. She didn't sneer at my sin-spots. She didn't wrinkle her nose the first time she saw me in the Palace. When she looked at me, I felt loved. And now, under her command, dahia are crumbling. Was she lying to me the whole time?

Aliya's gaze softens. "You're thinking about Karima."

I shrug and hug my knees. "What did I even mean to her?"

"I am probably not the right person to answer that question. Better you ask me about the tau function or the etymology of *al-Jabr*, but I . . ." She trails off. "I don't know if you can love someone and want their head separated from their body. In all the ancient texts I've read, I have yet to come across that circumstance." She smiles and puts her hand on my knee.

People shuffle behind me, and I turn around just in time to see everyone breaking down camp. Not again.

Ras, with sin-snakes ringing both biceps, appears behind me, hand on my shoulder. "Time to go, Chief. Spotted some patrols to the north and to the east."

"All right. Let's move."

Aliya and I get up. Aliya heads to the front of the group with the other Mages, and I lag behind. I break into a jog with Ras, and we catch up to some of the other aki as we reach a patch of dense forest. I look over, and Ras is smiling.

He catches me, tries to stop smiling, but can't, which only makes him smile more. "Before my eyes turned and I became aki, I cleaned houses," he says in between breaths. "With Mama. We cleaned houses in our dahia for money. All the other kids

were running around, exploring the city, having adventures."
His eyes don't stray from the path he's cutting ahead for us with
his daga. "This is my adventure."

The other aki have gathered around us so that I'm at the
center of a protective diamond formation. I have no idea what
book they spun to learn that.

I'm grateful for them—this group of aki and Mages, young
and old, thrown together by rebellion. They are risking everything to protect me. But running around from forests to fields
to hillsides, constantly surrounded by Mages and aki who don't
seem to know any more about what's going on than I do, is getting old. Yet they move with purpose. They know what to do.
Sometimes it feels like this is everyone's adventure except mine.

Either way, I'm running on a full stomach, which means I've
come a long way from being a lowly aki in the streets of Kos
scrounging for sins to Eat. For some reason, the thought of how
much life has changed and how quickly makes me chuckle. All of
a sudden, I'm smiling right alongside Ras as we dart through the
forest toward safety, just as night washes all of us into darkness.

CHAPTER 2

THUNDER CRACKLES IN the sky as we reach the cave. The rain waits till everyone's inside before it starts pouring down. The Mages watch in silence. Some of the aki—my bodyguards—take up posts at the cave's mouth. A few of the others, the younger ones, sit nearby in a circle and laugh at something. Ugo, a kid with a single dragon spiraling up his leg, snaps his fingers at Nneoma and points to something he's drawn in the mud.

"My favorite meal from home," Ugo is saying while a few of the others hold their own side conversations. "Fresh fish." He gestures at the drawing he's made in the ground. Squiggles mostly, with a few lines around to suggest a table. "With kwanga surrounding it and makembe on the other side. What you call plantain. Or what the northerners will call plan*teen*." He swipes at the air as if to disregard that word.

The others get raucous, and Nneoma smacks his hand away. She has the hard, broad shoulders of a northerner, someone used to working the mines to farm gemstones for the royals. "That's because that's the right way to say it. I don't know no plant*ain*. We say plan*teen*." The others roar with laughter. Plan*teen*. Plan*teen*!

But Ugo barges through the protest. "You've got it wrong. Main*teen*. Plan*teen*. Enter*teen*."

The others start rolling on the ground. "Are you trying to enter*teen* him?"

Nneoma tries to stay serious, but even she's starting to crack. "Fine, have it your way. Plan*tain*, main*tain*, enter*tain*, re*main*!" The group erupts into another fit of laughter. "You southerners talk like your mouth is full of suya wrap anyway," she says.

They were probably there for the Fall of Kos. It sounds weird in my head to think of what happened to my city like that. The Fall of Kos seems like something you read about in a book, or a story your mama or baba tells you during the fasting period before the Festival of Reunification, or something the Ozi talks about in his sermons. It sounds ancient and faraway. But it's not. I see it almost every time I close my eyes to sleep. The inisisa rampaging the streets of Kos, the hundreds of Forum-dwellers sprawled out in the streets or in their homes with their eyes glazed over, Eaten by the sin-beasts that had been unleashed. The aki who Crossed, fighting to keep everyone safe. The others who died. These aki probably saw it all too. The sins they're wearing they probably earned saving Kos. And here they are arguing about how to pronounce "plantain." And protecting me.

Miri finds me standing at the mouth of the cave, staring into the forest. The rain has started to come down in sheets. It's as though I'm looking through curtains made of water.

"Taj." She smiles. "How are you feeling?"

"To be honest, I feel like a housefly trapped in a jar. Do we have a plan?"

"That is just what we were discussing." She nods to the other Mages.

"And?"

Her smile tightens. "We are waiting."

That conversation was about as satisfying as I expected. No new information. No plan. No direction. "Those explosions," I say finally. "Were those Baptisms?"

Miri frowns. A shadow has come over her face. "Dynamite."

"Dyna-what?"

Nneoma walks toward us. "It's what we use in the north to open up the earth for mining. Thunder sticks. You put flame to the string attached, then it BOOMs." She mimes the blast with her hands. "Earth everywhere, and then there is a hole in the ground for you to dig into."

Another tool in Karima's hands. She's tearing Kos apart.

Just then, I check movement out of the corner of my eye, and we all turn to see a group of aki carrying something large over their heads. From far away, they look like ants that found a giant gray leaf to shield themselves from the rain. Backs bowed, they enter the cave, then toss the thing to the ground. It makes a loud *thunk* that revereberates around the cave.

A bunch of the other aki crowd around it. By the time I get there, Aliya's there too. She pulls down her spectacles and crouches over it, examining it in silence while the others whisper around her.

The hunk of metal has a rounded center with sharp edges. It looks like a shield. Something Palace guards would have, but bigger. Nobody can tell where it comes from, but somebody murmurs about how they bang metal up north of Kos. It's too big and simple to be auto-mail. Auto-mail has gears and hinges. It is shaped like arms and legs and has mechanisms to mimic the movements of human limbs. For a second, I envision someone trying to fit this to a stub of an arm or to where a leg used to be. Nneoma taps the thing with her foot, then leaps back, like she's been bitten by a snake.

Another Mage, Dinma, hovers over my shoulder, peering at the thing. His snakeskin eyes flicker blue before glazing over again. "There are no attachment slots on it."

Aliya nods in agreement. "There's nowhere for straps to fit in. And its geometric structure is odd. What could this have been fitted to?"

I shove my way forward next to her. "You think it was attached to something?"

It's been flipped over like a turtle shell upside down. She points at its inside. "You see? There are streaks of black inside." She crouches and gets even closer to it. "And the Fist of Malek." She gasps. The faded insignia of the Palace Mages has been written in dried blood. "Mages made this."

The Mages huddle together and whisper while some of the aki take to kicking the metal and testing its durability with their feet. Despite being around all these people, I feel alone. Trapped. No one seems to notice me walking away.

With my back against the cave wall, I hold my head in my hands. On my wrist, a dull blue stone dangles from a thin piece of string. The last time it glowed, I was standing on the steps to the Palace, fighting my best friend. The stone had belonged to Zainab, an aki girl with sin-spots covering every inch of her body. I remember when we were both children, a Mage brought her in to heal Mama of the sin that had crippled her. The Mage had led her around with a chain attached to a collar around her neck. Then, the next time I saw her, we were grown, and she was watching over the aki I trained in the forest just outside the Wall. I remember carrying her limp body after she had Crossed and died. After she had Eaten too many sins. Aliya and I had buried her somewhere in this mess of trees and bushes. I have no idea how near or far her grave is from here.

I look at Aliya and wonder if she's thinking about Zainab too. Maybe Zainab's inyo—her uncleansed spirit—haunts that patch of forest.

I'm so lost in the daydream that at first I don't even notice everyone scurrying around. And that's when I hear it. A noise that sounds like grinding metal. It sounds like something groaning.

We all get to the mouth of the cave, and a few of the aki move forward to peer through the sheets of rain. The rain falls so hard we barely see anything, but we can still hear the noise, and it's getting closer.

Ugo's at the front, and he takes a few more steps out of the cave.

"Ugo! Get back!" Nneoma screams.

Ugo keeps walking out until we can barely see him turn to look over his shoulder. Before he can turn back around, something massive leaps out of the forest and crashes onto him.

Through the sheets of rain, I see the metal plating covering whatever it is that's crushing Ugo. I barely take a step forward before Ras grips my wrist and pulls me back.

Ugo's struggling to cry out, but the beast on his chest chokes all the breath out of his lungs.

"Ugo!" Nneoma races out of the cave with her daga at the ready. She jumps into the air to get a good angle at the beast's neck, but she hits the metal, and her daga spins out of her hand. She falls to the ground, gripping her wrist.

The beast rears back on its hind legs and lets out a roar. Wisps of black smoke curl out from between the plates of armor.

Miri gasps. "It's . . . it's a sin-beast."

"But how?" Aliya's between me and Miri, and everyone stares in shock while the inisisa covered in armor stares at all of us. "It's . . . it's impossible."

"The armor is fused to the inisisa." Dinma sounds like he's in a laboratory ogling chemicals and not like we're all about to be eaten by a metal sin-lion.

"We have to save Ugo!" It comes out of my mouth before I realize it. My daga is ready in my hands. I break away from Ras, and I can't remember the last time I ran this fast. The sin-beast barely flinched when Nneoma struck its metal plating, but I can see small spaces between its shields. One opening right by its shoulder. The inisisa shifts on Ugo's chest. I run up to it, gripping my daga, and slice right through its shoulder.

It bucks up off Ugo, throwing me off balance. I recover, move to strike its underside, but I realize too late that it is also covered in armor. Nneoma crashes into me, shoving me out of the way just as the sin-lion's paw slams down where my head was. We aki all circle the beast.

Tree branches above us shift, and something drops straight out of the sky and lands on the inisisa's back. Noor!

I remember she'd been out scouting and hadn't returned before we found the cave. Her fingers find a gap in the armor on the lion's back. It tosses its head, trying to throw her off, but she manages to hold tight with one hand. Noor stabs at the unprotected nape of its neck until finally the lion's legs buckle. Noor jumps off.

As the beast dissolves into an inky black puddle, its armor slides off, falling to the forest floor.

The pool of ink where the inisisa had been splits and jets past Noor, bouncing off the ground in front of her before flooding into her mouth. She staggers back, coughing and sputtering. Then the Eating is over. We don't have time to see the new beast that has been etched into her skin. Nneoma leads the way, and Noor and I hook Ugo's arms around our shoulders and guide him back into the cave.

"We have to go. Now!" Noor shouts. "More are coming."

Aliya's eyes go wide. "There are more?"

"Many more."

We don't make it more than ten feet out of the cave before a group of more armored sin-beasts barges through a thatch of bushes. A bear, another lion, and several wolves. We all hurry in the opposite direction, but another squadron of inisisa is waiting for us.

"There are too many of them," I hiss as the semicircle pushes us closer and closer together. We have our backs to one another, Mages and aki. I lean in close to Aliya. "Follow me," I hiss. "When I move, don't slow down. Stay right on my back."

"Wait, but—"

I run as fast as I can right toward the sin-lion in front of me. If I guess right, I may make it out of this alive. I keep running, and when I'm only a few feet away, it crouches, ready to leap.

I time my steps perfectly, plant my foot, and jump. It jumps right after me, but I'm a little bit higher, and just as I arc over its back, I throw my daga out at the nape of its neck. The cord attached to the knife wraps around it, and I pull the inisisa with me on the way down so that it lands on its back. The line almost snaps under the pressure, but I glance behind me to see Aliya frozen right where she stands.

"Come on!" I shout.

The inisisa stirs, then dissolves into a puddle of shadows on the ground.

Aliya runs through it, ink clinging to the hem of her robe, and I grab her hand and swing her behind me. The pool of sin turns into a single stream in the air and rushes into my open mouth.

My eyes shut reflexively. My body spasms. The sin knifes through me like a river made of thorns, but eventually it passes. I fall to one knee. I have to get up. The clash of stone dagas against metal armor rings through the forest. Everyone's still upright. Suddenly, the inisisa stop and all turn in my direction. They're after me and only me.

Aliya turns and sees the pride of inisisa charging toward us.

"Run!" I shout. I catch up to her and take her hand, and the blood pounds so loudly in my ears that I hear nothing else. Not the soft patter of rain on the leaves in the trees overhead. Not the rumbling of a herd of sin-beasts that want nothing more than to eat my soul. Nothing.

At least the others are safe.

CHAPTER 3

"COME ON!" I shout at Aliya. She's falling behind.

Creaks and moans. That awful groaning sound.

They're getting closer.

"Taj . . ." Aliya whispers, pointing toward the rustling leaves of a bush a few feet to the right of us.

Before I can answer, black shapes launch themselves out of the shrubbery and gallop toward us. More inisisa. Aliya stumbles toward me. I grab her arm, and we run as fast as we can. A shadow glides through the sky overhead, blotting out the sun. Even from down below, I recognize the griffin. They're going to get us.

Memories flash through my mind, blurry and out of focus.

The memories don't belong to me. They're from the sin I just Ate. Still, the guilt makes my chest so tight, I can hardly breathe.

Roots trip me up, and I fall hard. My daga comes loose. I see people in front of me. They look so real. Mages, cloaked in black. And other figures in brown robes, heads shaved. Men and women arranging tiles on the floor. They're in a circle, and someone is chanting.

I shake away the vision. I can't get lost in my head. Not now.

Aliya helps me up. The inisisa are gaining. The grinding is louder now. Closer.

Wind bows some of the tree branches in front of us. I muster as much strength as I can and leap for one. Thistles cut into my palms, but I maintain my grip. My arms burn. Slowly, I pull myself up. My feet scrape against the wet tree trunk. After a few moments of struggling, I manage to get all the way up and take a breath, leaning my back against the tree trunk.

Aliya's below me.

"Here, grab my hand."

She chances a glance behind her. The inisisa aren't tall enough to get all the way up here, not if we climb higher. She leaps, grabs my hand, and I struggle with all my strength to haul her up. She scrabbles up, and we both make it onto the branch.

"We have to get higher," I huff. The visions dizzy me. I know they're someone else's sins, but guilt bubbles up in me like bile, burning the inside of my throat.

"Taj? Taj!"

My eyes shoot open, and that's when I realize I'd gone unconscious. The effects of sin-eating aren't supposed to last this long. I haven't been this sick since I Ate my first sin as a child. "How long was I out?"

"Just a moment." Aliya has that worried look in her eyes that I haven't seen in a while. It warms my heart to see her look at me like that again. Last time she did, she was begging me to leave my home and follow her into this cracked forest. "I just need . . ." I put my palm to my forehead.

The sound of scratching draws my attention to the ground, where a small group of inisisa paws at the tree we're trapped in.

"Come on, we have to get farther up." The rain has stopped. The thunder is gone, but still, I can barely hear myself talk.

"Taj, you can't move right now. The sin—it's making you sick. We have to figure out what it did to you, if it's different from other inisisa."

"There's no time," I hiss through gritted teeth. I stumble to my feet, then sway. Aliya grabs me and pulls me back down.

"Taj, what do you see?"

I close my eyes. For a moment, the dizziness stops. "Mages. And people . . . in brown robes." My eyes grow wide. "Algebraists."

"What else?"

The scratching gets louder. The inisisa are jumping on top of one another, trying to scramble up. They're able to stand on one another's metal backs. We don't have much time. All at once, the feeling that I'm going to throw up goes away. I can breathe again. "I think I can stop them. Like before."

"No, wait. Taj, what are you going to do?"

Before she can finish, I jump to a nearby branch, then hop onto the ground. My landing isn't as soft as I would have liked, but now at least I have all the inisisa in front of me. My mind is still hazy. Each flash of memory is like lightning under a cloud.

But I think back to that night on the balcony with Princess Karima, and I think of the inisisa that swarmed through the streets of Kos. I think of the chaos that swallowed my city, and I try to think of what was happening inside me when I did what I did.

I hold my hands out.

They've stopped trying to climb up the tree and instead stalk toward me. A wolf, a lion, a bear, and a lynx. Their armor grates and creaks with each movement. I can see them tensing. Then, in one movement, they burst toward me.

"Taj!" Aliya screams.

I expect it to be the last thing I ever hear. I squeeze my eyes shut. All at once, the metal screeching stops. I hear birds chirping. I hear wind whistling through tree branches and rustling pine needles. I hear insects buzzing. I open my eyes.

The inisisa all stand in front of me. They stopped.

I almost can't believe it. They stopped!

"Aliya, I don't know how long I can hold them like this." My arms and legs tense. The whole inside of my body burns.

She scrabbles down the tree and stands close to me.

"We need to get going." It's creeping back into me. That dizziness, that feeling like I'm going to vomit every meal I've ever had. That guilt. Someone else's guilt. Someone else's sins.

She looks at the beasts in awe, breaking me out of my trance. "It's like at the Fall of Kos. You did it."

"OK, OK. I did it, sure. But we have to get moving!" I'm worried more are coming. There were a lot of them when they first cornered us. We have to get to safety.

The inisisa bow their heads, then sit on the ground. They don't make a sound.

Aliya looks up at the sky, shielding her eyes with one hand from the sun. The clouds have parted. Then she spins in a slow circle. "OK, this way," she says, pointing west. She grabs my hand and pulls me along.

I don't even dare look behind me. I have no idea how long it'll all last. I try not to think of what would have happened if they had caught up to us in that tree. More guilt latches on to my heart. Will the inisisa go back for the others? As we're running and we see a break in the forest with sunlight shining through, Aliya turns and smiles at me, and in that moment, her face is glowing. My heart feels lighter.

We leave the forest with such suddenness that the sun's brightness stops us in our tracks.

The land dips beneath us into a small valley with a river at the bottom.

"OK, let's go," I tell her.

This is new for both of us. It's most likely the farthest either of us has been from home.

It finally feels like an adventure.

We set off down the hillside just as I hear the clatter of metal behind us. Inisisa emerge from the forest, pause at the top of the ridge, then charge after us. I grab Aliya's hand as we sprint down the hill.

"Maybe if we can make it to the river, we'll be safe," I say, breathless. I have no idea how we'll cross it, but the alternative is getting eaten.

The river flows with more force than any body of water I've ever seen before, but neither of us slows down. We run straight into the water. It's up to our waists, and the current is strong.

"We have to keep going!" I don't look behind us. It's so cold that chills run up my back. The deeper we get, the less I can feel my feet.

"I don't know how deep it gets," Aliya tells me, worry thick in her voice.

"Have faith," I say. I give her hand a squeeze and lead us farther into the water. The same rush of adrenaline I felt when I leapt across rooftops in Kos dodging Palace guards or raced through the narrow streets trying to lose the Agha Sentries surges in me.

"They stopped!" Aliya shouts.

I take a glance behind me. There they are, lined along the shore. I whoop with laughter. "The metal. It's the metal! It'll sink them." I start laughing and don't care that I sound cracked when I do. But my joy is short-lived.

I turn around just in time to see a massive tree branch swing toward me and knock me straight in the head.

The last thing I feel is my body spinning, flipping over and over as the current takes me. Aliya yells my name, and her voice grows fainter and fainter. Then darkness.

Blacker than the flank of an inisisa, nothing but darkness.

CHAPTER 4

WHEN MY EYES open, Aliya's mouth is on mine.

"Taj," she says. "Taj, wake up." It sounds like she's yelling underwater.

I feel something bubble in my stomach, then my chest, and I throw up water so hard it comes out of my nose.

It takes me a minute or two of feeling like I'm coughing out every single organ in my body before I can sit upright. Everything's white, then Aliya's face comes into focus. The sun's still out. But I'm dripping wet and shivering.

"Wh-where . . ." I look around. It's all green shoreline. Water laps at my ankles. One of my flats is gone, never to return. The river is so wide here that I can't see to the other side. "Where are we?"

Aliya slaps my back. Hard. "The river took us down for a while. You were unconscious the whole time. But I managed to drag you to shore."

"What hit me?" My hand goes to my forehead. The lump feels like it would fill my palm.

"A tree branch. While you weren't looking." She's smiling, joking, but I can tell in her voice that she's grateful I'm alive.

"Branch didn't give me a chance to fight back." I try to get to my feet, but the ground's too soft underneath me, and I slip and land hard on my backside. Now that hurts too. That's when I notice it. On my right forearm. A single, solid band of black. No lion or bear or dragon. Just a stretch of solid black covering the sin-spots that were there before. The armored inisisa. My mind replays the battle again in flashes.

"The others?"

She sees the expression on my face and looks away, toward the riverbed. "I don't know."

"They're OK," I say, more to myself than to her. I force myself to my feet and do a few stretches. Satisfying cracks echo up my spine. I feel limber again. Dizzy, but limber. "Trust me, they are." I have to believe it. It hurts too much to think otherwise. Aliya's still crouched, so I reach down and help her up. "At least now we're out of that cracked forest. Uhlah, I was starting to get claustrophobic."

She arches an eyebrow at me.

"Yes, I know what 'claustrophobic' means," I say, and she smiles. I was hoping for a laugh, but I'll take it.

"Let's get going. I'm hungry."

The ledge isn't too steep, and I scrabble up to get to a grassy plain. I figure if we follow the river long enough, it's bound to lead us somewhere. Either way, I know I just need to move.

I don't really care which direction it's in, just as long as we're moving.

Aliya climbs up after me. "Hungry?"

"Yeah, there's gotta be berries or something around here, right?"

The sun's still high in the sky when we hit the first patch of fruit trees. A bunch of them line the river, and more stretch out so far I lose track of the rows. I don't mind walking in the sun, as it dries me out faster than expected. The sight of the kiwis on those trees has me drooling. My stomach is speaking to me. Loudly.

"Taj, slow down!"

But I can barely hear Aliya as I run toward the trees. I pick up a stick lying on the ground and swat at the first branch. Kiwis cascade down on me. They're so ripe they practically burst open in my fingers. The first bite brings me so much bliss it feels like I've died the most peaceful death possible and joined Infinity. It feels like a blessing. Juice streams down the sides of my mouth, and before I know it, empty kiwi skins litter the ground.

"Taj!"

My mouth is bulging when Aliya catches up to me. My hands are full. I can't stuff my pockets fast enough.

"Taj! This is someone's orchard."

I try to ask her what the problem is, but it comes out all garbled.

"Taj, you're stealing."

I swallow hard, then burp. The look on her face gets me chuckling. "You see all these trees? They're not going to miss a few kiwis."

"A few?"

That's when I look at the graveyard of kiwis at my feet. I've cleaned out almost a whole tree. "OK, just a few more for the road. You should get some too. We don't know how much longer we'll need to go without food."

As we turn to head back along the river, I spot motion up ahead. Figures emerge from a shack in the distance. It looks like they're wearing umbrellas for hats. In their hands are staffs as tall as they are. They're heading straight for us.

"Taj!" Aliya warns.

"Here!" I toss her a bunch of my kiwis, and she catches a few just in time. The rest fall to the ground. I jump and snatch a few more from the trees and hold my shirt out to catch them, then we're off. We skid back down the ledge to the riverbed and run, and I can't help but laugh. Feels like when I was a kid and raided foodcarts in Kos, then had to outrun the fishmongers and butchers as they chased after me through the Forum. "Catch up!" I shout to Aliya. Kiwis fall out of my shirt, but eventually we run far enough that the cries of the people wearing the wide-brimmed straw hats fade away.

By the time Aliya finds me hidden behind a boulder along the shore, she's laughing too. It takes us both a second to catch our breath. Aliya settles down beside me and holds the first kiwi up in front of her face. Her robe is smudged and stained with mud. The golden Fist of Malek embroidered over her chest, faded. Some of the threads have come loose. But when she takes a bite of the kiwi, her wide eyes and big grin transform her back into that girl I first met at Zoe's all over again.

She looks up, sees me staring, then cuts a look my way. "Are you watching me eat?" she asks, mouth full.

I try not to laugh, fail, give up, and laugh anyway.

Hairy kiwi skins litter the ground around us. Without warning, she snatches one of the kiwis out of my lap. In my scramble to get it back, I drop a bunch more, but Aliya is up before I am and already out of reach.

"You dropped your fruit," she tells me, smiling, as if I didn't already notice. She looks toward the riverbed, then back at me like an idea has just occurred to her. "Come here, I want to show you something."

"Sure," I tell her with a smile. I wipe my palms on my shirt and get up to follow her.

Her gaze searches the shoreline for something. Her eyes settle on a twig, and she picks it up. For several moments, she holds the kiwi out in front of her, right between her eyes. I watch her concentrating. The sun's setting over the water, and the waves shimmer behind her. Strands of brown hair flutter around her face. Her eyes remain completely focused. She glances my way, breaks her trance, then starts scribbling in the sand with her twig. Brow furrowed, back bent, she looks like she's digging for treasure.

I step closer and peek over her shoulder. "What is that?"

I lean closer and try to decipher the string of letters, numbers, and arrows she's drawn in the earth.

"It's a proof." Aliya beams.

"A what?"

"A proof."

I look at the scribbling, then at her, then again at the scribbling. "A proof of what?"

"Of the kiwi, stupid! I drew a picture of the kiwi."

I squint. Maybe there's something I'm not seeing. I don't even see a crude drawing of the fruit we were just eating. "You're going to have to help me here."

"Uhlah." She's about to throw up her hands in frustration, but she stops herself. "OK, so you have a straight line, you see?" She draws a straight line in the ground. "And you can extend that line indefinitely in either direction, yes?"

I nod. "Sure."

"And you have a circle." She draws a circle so that the line starts from its center and cuts through. "And this right here?" She points again to the line. "This is the difference between the center and the end. The radius." She draws another line, this one perpendicular to the first. "And you have a right angle, and assume that all right angles are equal, yes?"

I shrug. "Sure, why not?"

"Now, if a line segment intersects two straight lines forming two interior angles on the same side . . ." As she's speaking, she draws another series of lines that form some weird, misshapen triangle, and she writes letters on the inside of it. I recognize some of them in her "proof," but other than that, it's all gibberish. "Also, remember that these are models of objects and not the objects themselves. Now, it's all down to angle and distance; those are the only two components you need—"

I'm starting to get dizzy. I start backing away slowly.

"—and then you can extend that to a different plane and measure the volume of a parallelepipedal solid and from there . . ." She looks up finally and sees that I've walked back to where we were sitting before. "Taj!"

"I'm sorry, but all of that is a picture of a kiwi? I haven't seen a single kiwi in all of Odo that looks like that."

"It's the kiwi in a different form." She points to the mass of letters and arrows and other markings she made earlier. "This is its algebraic form. The equation that describes the kiwi."

I look at the hairy fruit in my hand. "So that's what we've been eating all this time?"

She smiles. "That's what I see, yes. Every time I eat a kiwi, that's what I see." Her smile broadens. Deepens, even. She tosses the stick down, then walks over and scoops up the remaining uneaten kiwis. "Come on. It's getting dark. We should keep heading south."

I follow her lead. "What's south?"

"I don't know. But it's away from those metal monsters, at least." She turns on her heel and starts walking along the river's beach. I catch up, and we walk side by side.

"Hey, can you do that with everything?" I ask.

She looks at me. "What do you mean?"

"You think you can write one of those things for me?"

"What, like a Taj proof?"

I bite into a kiwi. Juice dribbles down my chin. She reaches out like she's about to wipe it from my chin, but at the last second, her hand goes to her hair, brushing it out of her face. I feel my cheeks heat up. But Aliya doesn't miss a beat.

"There's not enough mud in the whole kingdom to write a proof for you, Taj."

"Is that 'cause I'm so special?"

She laughs. "Well, I prefer the word 'complicated.'"

I grin. "I'll settle for that."

CHAPTER 5

AT NIGHT, THE wind picks up.

We've slowed down only a little bit, but I notice it. Aliya hugs her robe a little tighter. Her teeth chatter. The tips of her hair that frame her face under her hood glisten, still damp from our trip on the river. Or, rather, in the river. And it looks like her robe hasn't dried out all the way either. I wish I had a coat or a blanket or something to give her, but the only thing I've got is my tattered shirt, and that won't help any. So we just keep walking, and the wind keeps blowing.

"Maybe we should head away from the river?"

She doesn't respond, just keeps putting one foot in front of the other. Almost mechanically, like her legs are auto-mail.

Almost getting killed by armored inisisa, nearly drowning in a river, then being chased by people in large hats, and now shivering in the dark. I'm starting to get tired of this "adventure."

Things were easier when the Wall was the farthest I'd ever gone. When I was younger, Kos seemed like the entire world. I could wander and wander and wander and still not see everything worth seeing. I could get lost for days in the different dahia. I could walk up and down the Forum all day for weeks and not see the same thing twice. Then there were times when I would wonder what was outside of Kos. It seemed like the world ended after the Wall. I would see people come and go through the Wall, but most were going, and once they left, they never came back.

I think of Arzu. My sicario, the one charged with protecting me when I was a servant in the Palace. The one whose mother brought her here from the west. She'd told me of things I couldn't believe. Aki who aren't spat on or slapped around. Aki who are revered for their ability to Eat sins. The last time I saw her, she'd pinned my best friend to the steps of the Palace with a knife to his throat. To keep him from killing me. Then an arashi came out of the sky and set the city on fire. Set my home on fire.

I'm lost in thought when Aliya nudges me with her arm.

"Taj, look!" She points to the sky, toward the horizon.

I don't even need to squint to see it.

Red glows over the hills. Dark, purplish red. Like a bruise on the sky. It rises in rays and sways. Stars shine through the waves of light, but the silhouette of the hills shifts. Small changes at first, but enough for me to notice. Like a wildfire dripping from the clouds.

"Is that a fire?" I ask her. I can hear the distant sound of snapping and popping.

"Falling red flames," Aliya says, breathless.

"What?"

"That's what the scholars of old called it. In the Great House of Ideas, scholars would study the sky at night and say these lights were what happened when the sun kissed us. Before they knew what the lights were, they would call it *ụtụtụiụ n'abalị*. Morning at night." Her voice is thick with wonder. "The Unnamed moves the stars and the planets around us even while we sleep. Always in patterns. I never thought I would live to see it." She breaks out of her trance and leads me closer.

As we get closer, I can feel the heat of the flames.

We start running with newfound strength. When we crest the hill, we slow down. There's an entire community in the valley below. People sit around fires, others walk in and out of tents and small homes with thatched roofs that look like they were put together quickly. It's like a small city. In the distance, I can hear kids giggling as they run around while their mothers and fathers shout after them to be careful. Someone's kicking a leather ball in the air, bouncing it off their ankle, then their shoulder, then their head. And jewels. Everywhere I look, gemstones in ear studs, opals attached to toe rings, hands that shine with the light of so many sapphires. They glow brighter than the stars. And then I look up and see the curtains of color above us and realize that the stones have something to do with it. These people, they're from Kos. Refugees from my city, and they brought their beautiful gemstones with them. They brought their world with them.

I wonder briefly how much coal the people of this small makeshift city carry, how much of the dull stuff to remind themselves of the dead left behind. Since these are people from Kos, they'll have news. They might know what has happened over the past few weeks. They might know what's happened to Bo. If all of these people survived the arashi attack, then maybe some of the aki who fought alongside me during the Fall of Kos survived as well. I have to believe that they did. I'm tired. Exhausted and broken down. But I'm still strong enough to hope.

"It's gorgeous," Aliya says in a whisper, like she's afraid that if she talks too loudly, she'll mess up the whole vision. "The stones . . . they're causing the light." I look and see that the gemstones refracting off the fire are making the sky look like it's changing colors: blue and green and red. "It's unclear how the light waves are interacting with the solar winds, though that may indicate our current longitude and—"

My stomach grumbles loud enough to silence her. She shoots me a look, and I shrug guiltily. "I ate our last kiwi hours ago," I confess.

"Well, we should head down, if for nothing else than at least to gain news of Kos and learn of the current state of affairs."

"What's the likelihood any of the others will have made it here?" I don't specify whether "others" means the aki and Mages we left behind in the forest or those we couldn't take with us when we first fled Kos during the arashi attack.

"Low," Aliya replies.

It's strange how Aliya alternates between being able to pull a sense of wonder out of something as boring as a kiwi and acting like a hardened general. I try to school myself into not expecting to see Ugo or Nneoma or Miri down there.

Aliya skids down the hillside behind me. "More than zero."

"What?"

"The likelihood that we'll see any of our friends down there." She catches me out of the corner of her eye, as though telling me it's OK to hope. "Still more than zero."

As we get closer, Aliya sticks out a hand, stopping me. "Wait," she says as she shrugs off her robe. Underneath, her dress hangs damp over the belt cinched at her waist, and I realize that this whole time she's been colder than I'd even imagined. Slowly, delicately, to keep from dropping it, she turns the robe around. She's reversing it, hiding the golden Fist of Malek embroidered on the front. I reach out and help her turn the sleeves inside out.

"We don't know who's down there or what they might want, what they might be looking for." She slips the reversed robe over her shoulders. "Better not to announce our presence."

"And what about these?" I ask, pointing to my sin-spots.

"We'll think of something."

Our problem—well, my problem—gets solved by a young woman, older than me but younger than most adults, who's been handing out blankets to what look like new arrivals. I quickly wrap one around myself like a cape.

Aliya and I didn't see where they might have come from, but people appear in a steady stream at the booth set up on the outskirts of the camp at the bottom of the hill. And this woman smiles at each of them as she hands them a folded woolen blanket. Some of them even get their own rolled pallet. I notice there aren't many families. Mostly adults without children and children without parents. After we get our blankets, Aliya and

I wander a few steps away into one of the larger walkways, and for a while, I watch the people come through.

"Who are you looking for, Taj?" Aliya asks me.

Mama. Baba. Bo. Anyone I might recognize.

The faces of the refugees darken in the night. Here, no one wears jewels. Instead, they're adorned with coal. Coal in the rings on their fingers. Coal in their ear studs. Coal hanging around their necks, their ankles, their wrists. Some of them have bundles, but many of them don't, just the clothes on their backs. There's no obvious trail leading here. We got lucky being swallowed up and spat out by the river. How do people find this place?

"Taj, let's go." Aliya turns to walk away. "Maybe we can find someplace to sleep before we figure out what to do next."

I thought seeing the refugees would depress me, make me slower and sleepy, but angry energy runs through me. It's injustice that has sent these people here. Their faces are gray. They've suffered. I remember those looks, seeing them every time a dahia was Baptized by the royal family, every time Wreckers and Hurlers were sent to cleanse those neighborhoods of sin, of sinners, raining down boulders of stone and enflamed wood. The royal family and the Mages that served them would watch while houses crumbled beneath the onslaught, claiming that the Baptism was merely to cleanse various parts of Kos of the sin that had been building up. But really all they were doing was punishing us. For bothering to live.

I see it again now. These people have lost their homes. Many of them, their families. No matter how clean their clothes were when they left the city, they're all gray and brown and splotched with dried blood now.

Turning to follow Aliya, I see the camp humming with life before me. Someone here can tell me about what's happened in Kos since we left. As we walk, I drape my blanket around my shoulders and over my neck. These people don't need to know I'm aki. Not yet.

Suddenly, I freeze where I'm standing. There, in the middle of the trail, almost swallowed up by the moving crowd, is Sade. Sade, who had battled inisisa alongside me during the Fall of Kos. Sade, who hadn't made it out of Kos in time to escape the arashi attack.

"You're alive," I murmur.

Her dark purple robe is tied at her waist by a belt. Both her arms are sleeved, and she wears leather breeches. This is the fanciest she's ever dressed—it looks like some sort of uniform. Where did she get those clothes? She sees me and heads straight for us. Too fast. She removes rope from the belt at her waist. "Put your hands out for binding."

"Wait, what?" I look to Aliya, but there isn't a trace of emotion on her face. "Sade, what's going on? It's me!"

"Shut up, smuggler. Do not make me say it a second time." Her daga is unsheathed and pointed right at my chest. She's close enough that I can't leap away. I can't move in any direction without her slicing me open.

"What are you doing?"

"You're coming with me."

I try to call out for Aliya, but before I can, I feel a bag cover my head. It's pulled tight at my neck.

Darkness.

CHAPTER 6

"SADE, IF YOU don't undo these ropes, I swear by the Unnamed . . ." I shout as the bag comes off my head.

I've been dragged into a large tent. There's a desk with a mess of papers scattered on it. Books are coiled tight in their cylindirical shapes and piled up on one side. Boxes cover the floor. I blink as my eyes adjust to the dimly lit room. I can still hear the muffled noises of the camp outside. Aliya stands off to one side, arms crossed, and in front of me, leaning against the desk, is Sade, still in her fancy robe. Her eyes look tired, but she's smiling like she's happy to see me.

"You're just going to leave me tied up like this?" I say, raising my bound wrists above my head. Their smiles burst into laughter. "This is not funny-oh!" I settle down. I've barely spent any time with her, and already my accent has returned. "You haven't tied up my feet, so I can still run."

Sade raises an eyebrow. "We can fix that." She's still smirk-ing. Then she relents and comes before me and undoes the ropes.

My wrists burn. "OK, will someone explain what's going on? Sade, what is this?"

"I had to pretend you were a smuggler. There's a bounty for your capture. I had to pretend like I was arresting you," Sade explains.

"What?"

"Karima wants your head," Aliya butts in.

"And she doesn't care if it's attached to your body or not," Sade finishes.

My stomach drops. "Wait, do they know?" I nod toward the tent flap. "If my face is all over, then they all must know they can collect."

"No. Most of the refugees don't know about the bounty. It wasn't announced until later." Sade goes behind her desk and sits down. "After the arashi attack, Kosians fled the city en masse. And camps like these sprung up. Karima, when she took charge, sent me out here to monitor the camps and bring back criminals who were trying to undermine her rule. Rebels," she adds ominously. She glances at Aliya, who doesn't seem to notice. "There are many criminals trying to make quick and easy coin by smuggling people out west. So she sends people like me to restore order. Routes to the north have been closed. Her troops invaded there soon after closing off Kos. That's when the armored inisisa appeared."

Aliya and I lock eyes. "It was a gamble bringing you here. The rebels are scattered. The left hand sometimes doesn't know what the right hand is doing."

I start. *She knew about this place?* I want to ask if the other rebel Mages and aki know to come here, but I can't tell if Sade is someone to count on just yet. Still too many questions.

"Others have passed through here," Sade says, and cuts her eyes at Aliya, as if to say, *You should have known to trust me.* She fiddles with her gauntlets. "Word travels. Often, it has to go through here." She pauses. "I'm glad you're both OK."

There are so many things I want to ask her. If she's been at the Palace, then she can tell me if any of the others survived the attack. She can tell me what happened to Omar and Tolu and the aki who fought alongside me to try to save the city when Karima and the Mage Izu unleashed the inisisa. She can tell me what's happened to Bo.

"A lot happens here. As you can probably tell, I keep records. Karima's big on keeping records. But it helps me assist individual refugees. Many people come here without families, and sometimes I can reunite them with their lost loved ones. It's the least I can do." She looks away. "Anyone who tries to leave is thrown into prison."

All of this makes me dizzy. So much to process. It's still tough to believe. I thought I loved Princess Karima once. Well, Queen Karima now, I guess. It feels like it happened a lifetime ago, but I know that if I close my eyes, I can still feel her lips on mine. I was so close to being accepted by her, being a part of that life, living among rulers. I could have changed things. But then I remember the Karima who killed Izu and let the inisisa run free through Kos. The same Karima who threw her brother, King Kolade, in prison after telling all of Kos that he'd tried to have her murdered.

"Taj, it's not safe for you here," Sade says.

"Is it safe for me anywhere?" It comes out harsher than I mean it to.

"If the rumor gets out that you're here, it'll spread like plague." Sade turns away, as though remembering something. It is like a shadow has crossed her face. "They may be too frightened to try attacking you themselves. Some of the refugees come from faraway villages. There've been reports of aki rampaging through those villages, killing everyone, leaving almost no survivors. Nobody knows who they are or what they're looking for, but everyone who escapes tells of the markings on their bodies."

"Sin-spots," I whisper.

Sade nods. "They're looking for you, Taj. And the refugees—they speak of one aki in particular, whose body is covered in markings . . . the one with no mercy."

"Bo." I know it as soon as his name leaves my mouth. "It's Bo." It has to be.

"He is changed," Sade says solemnly. For a moment, her eyes cloud over, and I wonder if she too is thinking of an earlier time, when we were all aki who watched out for one another, who cared for one another while sleeping in a cramped room in a shantytown and serving at the behest of Palace Mages. "You can't stay here, Taj. It's too dangerous."

"I know that."

"Not just for you. Karima will stop at nothing to get to you, even if that means razing a refugee camp to the ground." Sade's face tightens in a frown. Her light-brown eyes smolder. She really has changed, become older. I see it in the way she moves too. Like there's a weight on her shoulders. She's so far from the little aki I used to run through Kos with, the one I shared a room with along with a bunch of others in our old shanty house. "We have to get you out of here."

"Where would I go?"

Aliya steps forward. "West." She and Sade share a long look, like they're speaking with their eyes or something. Not knowing what it is they're planning makes me even more frustrated.

"What route do the refugees use?" I ask.

Sade turns and looks at some of the papers on her desk. Then she pulls one sheet out. A map. "Osimiri. It's an obodo not far from here. Not a town, really. More like a . . . community. It's on the river, and you should be able to find passage to the west from there."

"It's a trading hub." Aliya speaks up again, and it seems like she knows more about this than she's letting on. I wonder how much she knows of the land outside Kos. And now I feel even smaller. There's an entire world out there, and all I've ever known is Kos. As free as I might have felt, I was completely caged in by the Wall.

Sade puts the map back on her desk. "There will be a raid there tonight. Lots of chaos. It should be easy to sneak through. I will be busy with the guards, bringing the prisoners back to Kos. The camp will be unguarded during that time."

"Why will there be a raid?" I ask her.

"Camps like these are a haven for smugglers," Sade replies. She takes a moment to gather herself, then lets out a sigh. She's readying herself to go to work at a job she hates. "You're safe hiding here for the night, Taj." On her way to the tent's entrance, she puts a hand on my shoulder. "I knew you were still alive." Her smile is small and soft and a little mischievous. "Nobody's as lucky as you." Then she walks past me and leaves.

She was smiling when she said that, but the more I repeat her words in my head, the more they sound like an accusation. *Nobody's as lucky as you.*

Much of the camp is quiet by the time Aliya sneaks me out of the tent. It seems like everyone's asleep. A few kids run around, trying to keep their voices down. All the bustle of the camp earlier in the night is gone. Older refugees, men from different tribes, it looks like, sit across from each other on wooden boxes and share a shisha pipe. From afar, it looks almost like they know each other. They both wear large keys around their necks. Aliya leads me through the winding paths, and we stick to the shadows. By the time we make it to the camp's edge, the sky's starting to turn blue over the mountains. The falling red flames have dimmed. It'll be morning soon.

We get to the crest of a hill, and Aliya's eager to push on, but I take a moment at the top to look back at the camps spread out beneath us. All those displaced people brought together here, trying to find their families again or just trying to find safety. Just like me, they have to leave their city behind. I realize that the keys I saw those older men wearing must've been keys to their old homes. How many other people are wearing their keys around their necks or holding them in their pockets? I ball my fists at my sides.

Then I hear the clanking.

In the distance is a wide path, and I see a large, dark column rise over a ridge. From this far away, it looks like a centipede. But the sky brightens, revealing the mass to be a line of horses and wheels and what turn out to be men sitting on carts. First there's one, then another, until I see all five rumble past us. Wheels roll against the ground, and the only other sound I can hear in the early morning is the rattling of chains. Sitting back to back in each car are men, grizzled and bearded. Around their necks are metal collars attached by chains to their wrists and, in another direction, to the collars of the prisoners behind them. At the front of each cart sits someone in the same outfit I saw Sade wear earlier. A new uniform, from the Palace.

The carts all keep to the middle of the road, and Agha Sentries, the chief law enforcers of Kos, march alongside them, their cutlasses slapping against their thighs.

I don't notice how cold it's gotten until I see the men on the carts shivering in the morning chill. It's tough to say whether or not any of them were ever wealthy enough to own gemstones, but some of them probably had, at one time, a ring on every finger. Some of them probably had ears studded with gems. And now all they wear are torn linen tunics and threadbare trousers. They all jostle along in silence.

The sun rises on the other side of the camp, and when the glare hits the caravan of prisoners, it makes the collars around their necks look like fire that swallows their heads. I raise my hand to shield my eyes. Aliya and I watch them pass. They look so mournful. I tell myself that Queen Karima did this. I can feel my heart hardening against her. Guilt seeps into my bones. This is happening because of me. Because I fled.

"Taj, let's go." Aliya tugs my sleeve. I wrap my blanket tight over my shoulders and follow her down the other side of the hill.

As the sun rises, people start to emerge from their tents in the camp. I can hear the place coming to life with water boiling for soup and mothers washing the children that might or might not be theirs. Families are coming together, readying themselves for the day. We're going to survive this.

That's the thought that runs through my head as Aliya and I start out toward Osimiri.

She holds my hand all the way down the hill.

Chapter 7

We haven't gone too far before we see it: a tiny town along the same long, winding river I almost drowned in. Then, suddenly, the river widens.

At first, it looks like some of the shantytowns in Kos. But as we get closer, it looks like the houses are floating, moving and swaying in the breeze. The houses aren't along the river—they're *on* it. I squint, and we see that they're all boats. So many of them and so close together that I can barely see the water underneath. I thought the part of the river I'd almost drowned in was the biggest body of water I'd ever seen, but it's an alleyway stream compared to this. Past the town, the water stretches on forever. There's no end to it.

Small riverboats huddle close to the shore. They look like they're made of bamboo, and some of them have two planks of wood overhead with covers rolled back. When it rains, I imagine they can just unroll them and stay dry. Some of the riverboats move back and forth across the small stretch of water to Osimiri. In many of them, gangly kids about my age hang out and joke and laugh. I can't understand any of what they're saying, even as we get closer.

The whole place is buzzing with activity. Somebody's making something that smells so good—peppery and a little sweet. The odor wafts all the way to where Aliya and I stand. I hear dogs barking and chickens clucking. I hear singing, pots sizzling, and people shouting at each other—not angry, just trying to be heard over all the rest of the noise.

We inch closer, and I can see there are small lanes of water between some of the bigger boats for smaller ones to pass through. Planks of wood connect some of the bigger boats. People run and leap back and forth over them, some of them carrying heavy pots, some of them holding chickens by their legs; nobody seems to be worried about falling in. It's like they're running on any old street. As we get closer, I see a workshop of sorts. Someone making shoes. Another man hammering on bits of material. Metal? Gemstones?

"We made it," Aliya breathes.

"It . . . it looks like the edge of the world." A part of me is scared, but a bigger part of me is shaking with excitement. There's so much world out there, so much to see. It's like every single day promises a new thing, some wonder I couldn't even have dreamed up. Cities floating on water. And boats that can go anywhere. This looks like the edge of the world. I can only imagine what lies beyond.

Aliya squints at the shoreline. Then she gasps and leaps into the air, smiling and waving her arms. Before I can ask what she saw, she takes off toward Osmiri. I stumble to catch up to her, searching for what's gotten her so excited.

A small black speck silhouetted by the sun breaks away from the shoreline. The person gets closer. Aliya's already halfway there. I squint to make out their features.

It's her.

I let out a whoop and start running as fast as I can, faster than I ever thought I could run. I feel like I'm flying, practically gliding over rocks and brambles and weeds, knocking aside reeds, breathless until the three of us smash into one another and collapse onto the ground in a tangle of limbs and laughter.

"Arzu," I whisper through tears as we all hug one another as hard as we can.

"You're alive," she says as tears run down her own face. We all lie on the ground, rolling around and trying to wrap our arms around too many people, all the while laughing and crying and looking like we've lost our minds.

I know I'm eating too fast, but I can't stop.

Arzu has led us to one of the houseboats, and we sit around a steaming pot of food. The food is a little different here, but the spiciness is familiar. I taste pepper and cloves and coriander and mint and tomatoes and garlic. My tongue is alive with flavors. May I be struck dead by the Unnamed before I say anything tastes better than Mama's jollof rice, but this . . . whatever rice and stew this is fills me with joy.

Incense mixes with the smell of the food, and it sounds like someone's praying nearby. This place buzzes with activity. There's so much going on. It reminds me of the Forum in Kos. All this noise and all these smells and people. It's the same. I take a huge bite of rice and chicken. The food is just as spicy too. I'm lost in thought but can still half hear what Aliya and Arzu are saying to each other over cups of hot tea. We're on the second "floor" of the houseboat. It's more like a roof than anything else, with tarp hanging overhead to protect us from the sun. Over the railings of the boat, the sprawling city bustles underneath us. Osimiri surrounds us completely.

I pause. My chest is on fire, and I let out a soft burp behind my fist. Let me at least try to be polite.

"The inisisa are armored now," Aliya says into her cup. She's spent a lot of time staring into it, and I can only wonder at how fast her brain is moving, trying to put all the pieces together. I realize this is the first real chance we've had to settle down and catch our breath.

"More of Karima's new weapons, no doubt," Arzu says, shaking her head.

Aliya's eyebrows draw together. "But how? It doesn't seem possible—"

I'm swirling my last piece of bread in the sauce on my plate, but I stop mid-motion. "The vision."

Both of their heads turn my way.

"When I killed the sin-beast with the armor, the sin was. . . different. And I saw Mages. And people in brown robes. They were in a circle, chanting." I stare at my plate, trying to remember it all amid the swirl of colors and muffled whisperings. The black band on my arm, the mark of that armored beast, itches. I try to flex feeling back into my fingers. "They were arranging tiles on the floor."

"Palace algebraists," Arzu says. She still has that terseness I remember from our time in the Palace together. "Karima has made them part of the Palace order; they work with Mages to create new weapons." She tips her cup back toward her mouth. As she raises her chin, her scarf slips, and I see a vivid scar around her neck. Pain pinches my heart. Where did that come from?

"That has to be it," Aliya replies. "Equations." She's still staring into her cup. "They've found a way to bind metal made north of Kos to the inisisa with algebraic geometry."

Then Aliya slaps her hand on the table. "A proof. They were writing a proof. Taj, you remember that proof I wrote out in the sand by the river?"

"The kiwi."

"Every item in the universe can be described with a proof." Her hands move like they're looking for something to do or hold, but eventually she just folds them in front of her. I bet she was looking for dates to rearrange or a stick to scribble onto the wooden table with. "Even the inisisa. Hardened metal is easy to describe. Its nature and components don't move. But the inisisa . . . how did they do that?"

"I don't know," Arzu says. "Everything is a weapon in Karima's hands." She coughs into her fist. Her hands shake for a few moments, then stop. She grips her cup.

I move to pour her some water and catch another glimpse of the scar on her neck. Just a portion of it shows above her scarf. She sees me staring and quickly moves the cloth to cover it. I open my mouth to ask her about it, but the look on her face stops me from speaking.

When we saw her on the shoreline, she had a wide-brimmed hat on her head to shield her from the sun, but other than that, she wears loose-fitting clothes. A shirt that billows around her wiry frame and loose cotton breeches that whip in the wind. I have so many questions for her. How did she escape? Was she in prison? Who gave her that scar? Instead I say, "And Bo? Is he a weapon too?"

Arzu looks my way and nods. "She has sent him after you."

"We know," Aliya tells her. "We passed through a refugee camp that had survivors of some of his massacres."

"Kos as we knew it is dead," Arzu says. "There is nothing there for us."

Their faces flash before my eyes. Tolu. Ifeoma. Emeka. Omar. Noor. Ugo. Ras. All left behind. And then there are those twisted by Karima. Bent to fulfill her will. Those like Bo. And how many others? I refuse to believe it's over. That they're all gone. That the city can't be saved. I refuse to believe that Mama and Baba will be trapped forever in the prison Karima has made out of my city. I refuse to believe that she has won. But I can't find anything to say to Arzu. I want to tell her she's wrong, but I can't bring myself to say the words. I leave the last piece of bread on my plate, uneaten.

"Iragide," Aliya says suddenly.

Arzu and I blink in surprise and wait for more.

"It's the art of binding. It's what algebraists used to do in the Before. To change the physical property of things. They would use it to bend metal, to build statues, to break them down." Aliya looks at her hands. "Ka Chike, the Seventh Prophet, was the most adept practitioner of Iragide. He could pull water out of thin air. But the power overwhelmed him. It was considered heresy. An affront to the Unnamed because it sought to remake the pieces of the world." She looks up at both of us. "If used in a certain way, it could shatter mountains. It could break the world. That's what they're doing in the Palace. That's how they're able to bind metal to inisisa." She shakes her head in amazement. "It was supposed to be banned. All his notes and proofs were burned with him."

"And Karima has that knowledge again?" Arzu asks.

Aliya shakes her head, still thinking. "Not all of it. Ka Chike knew the Ratio. The one equation that could describe everything. That would mean complete and total control of not just Kos but the entire Kingdom of Odo." She looks up at me and Arzu. "She's trying to find it."

Quiet falls over us. The rest of Osimiri bustles beneath us, people living their lives, all seemingly oblivious to what's happening a half-moon's journey eastward. But Aliya's words give me hope, strangely enough. She's still thinking of Kos. She's still thinking of the troubles its people face. She's still thinking of a way to fix it.

Arzu rises to her feet. Stains dot the front of her shirt. Food. Ash. Dried blood.

"Where are you going?" I ask her. "What are you going to do now?"

"I'm going west." Arzu smiles. "I'm going home. To be with my people."

"But—"

"Taj, my mother may be there."

I feel my eyes go wide.

"Your mother?"

Arzu nods slowly. "After she left Kos, the only place where she could have been cured of her sin is back home. Among the tastahlik. If she survived the journey, that's where she will be."

"Her sin?"

Arzu looks to me with a sad smile on her face. She has the same gray tinge to her skin as the refugees. "She dared to love a Mage. And he dared to love her."

"You were born in the Palace," Aliya says.

Arzu nods. "My mother used to say that restlessness had brought her to Kos. She tired of life with the tribe. One day, in the street, she met a man. Fell in love. And that man found her a job in the Palace so that they could be near each other. My mother was still new to her job when I was born. My mother's position meant that I was cared for, even though my mother had birthed me unwed.

"Children notice everything. And of all the people in the Palace who tended to me, there was one man who spent more time with us than anyone else. He was a Mage. A kanselo—a lawmaker. Sometimes, he and my mother would look at each other strangely. She saw him differently from the other Mages. Treated him differently. There was no way I could have known back then, but he was my father. I didn't discover until much later that he had tried to change the law so that what he and my mother did would not be illegal." She shrugs. "I'm the result of a crime."

I almost can't believe it. The Kayas, in my mind, are so far apart from the rest of Kos that the idea of anyone in the Palace having a child with a regular person is unfathomable. And I remember how I used to think of Mages. I remember the Mages who used to round up aki after every Baptism, scouring the dahia for the newly orphaned or, in some cases, ripping them from the arms of their parents as soon as it was discovered that their eyes had turned. And I remember the Mages who would come to the slum where we aki lived and would call on us whenever someone in the Palace or some rich person up on the hill needed to have a sin removed and could afford to pay for it. I used to think all Mages were the worst kind of ruby-lickers, that all they cared about was money and using aki to get it, draining us dry until we Crossed and couldn't Eat any more sin, then tossing us into the rubbish bin. Then I'd met Aliya and, after that, the Mages who had tried—and failed—to rebel against Izu and the Kayas and save Kos from the planned invasion of inisisa.

Now a Mage in love is no longer so astounding a thought. Maybe they are just like the rest of us.

"What was his name?" I ask.

"It does not matter." When she sees the question in my eyes, she says, "He is dead. The Kayas had him murdered when his crime was discovered. He tried to escape with my mother but was hunted down and killed. They did not even give him a trial."

And Arzu's mother was given a reprieve only as long as her daughter was stripped of her ability to have children and made to serve Karima for the rest of her days, ending their family line.

So, just like that, Arzu's family was scattered. Ripped apart, then thrown to the wind. Her father dead, her mother disappeared. And now here she is, stranded in a land not her own.

"We'll come too!" It's not until I hear the words that I realize I'm the one who said them.

"Wait, what?" Aliya can only blink at me.

"There's a bounty on my head. Eventually, word will arrive in Osimiri. Or, worse, Bo will come and turn this whole obodo into ashes on the river." I turn to Aliya. "We were heading in that direction anyway, right?"

"Yes, but—"

"There's a ferry leaving tonight," Arzu says. "I've already booked passage. The smugglers know me; there will be no problems getting you on board."

I get to my feet. "Done," I say, and that settles it. After Aliya glowers at me for a few seconds, she and Arzu get to talking, and I wander to the edge of the roof and look out over Osimiri. I stuff down that lingering shame that bubbles up whenever I remember Noor and Miri and Nneoma and Dinma and all the others I left behind in the forest. *It's not my guilt*, I say to myself.

It's just the sins I've Eaten doing their job. Even as I think those words, I know it's a lie.

In Arzu's homeland are the tastahlik, people just like the aki with their sin-spots and their ability to consume the sins of others. But over there, they're revered. Respected. Every time I think of Kos, I feel pain. I can't go back. I want to. For the chance to see Mama and Baba and know that they are safe. For the chance to know for certain that Karima never loved me, had only meant to use me. For the chance to talk Bo out of whatever lahala Karima has convinced him to do. But what good would I do just dancing back into Kos after all of this? At least by doing this, helping Arzu find her mother, getting far away from the people I may put in harm's way, I can feel useful again.

Water runs like a scar at the horizon, just beyond the city. Arzu's home is there. Her people. Maybe my future's there too.

CHAPTER 8

"Do you still see them?" I ask Aliya as we lie on a boat deck beneath the stars. This is the ship that will take us westward. In less than a quarter-moon's time, we'll be in Arzu's homeland.

We both have our pallets rolled up, serving as pillows. It's warm enough, even with the sea breeze, that we don't need blankets. We're on the outer edge of Osimiri. Most of the noise and bustle of the city is behind us. Here, boats large and small are docked, tied to moorings that stretch around the city and touch the shore.

"The equations," I elaborate. "Do you still see them when you look up at the stars?" I point at the scattered bits of light in the blue-black sky. I like talking to her. It keeps me from thinking about the band of black ink on my forearm, all my other markings, and the people back home.

"Of course I see them," she replies, smiling.

Young men and women, bare to the waist except for cloth over their chests, work on the ship, tightening and testing ropes, moving crates, lounging about, chatting or drinking, some of them quietly gazing at the stars just like us.

Her smile widens. "Every child is told about the constellations and the stories we make out of them."

"I wasn't."

She gets quiet, and I can tell she's realizing the mistake she made. Aki aren't like regular kids. We don't grow up with our parents and go to school. We're not told stories about the stars at bedtime. As soon as our eyes change, we're snatched up by the Mages and taken into indentured servitude, Eating other people's sins for next to nothing. "I'm sorry," she says at last.

I snort. "I don't care for that lahala anyway. I'd much rather make up new stories. I bet the old ones are pretty boring." We grow quiet. "You lot are trouble, you know."

"What?"

"Apparently, according to Arzu, making a child with a Mage is a capital offense."

She squirms a little next to me. "I've heard that, yes."

"That would never be me. Aki and Mages, we are two different things," I say.

For a long time, neither of us says a word.

"Are we?" Aliya says, breaking the silence with her whisper. "You've also seen Mages and aki fight alongside each other—sacrifice themselves to save a city." She turns toward me and looks me in the face. "And you've seen a very kind, helpful, and, I must say, quite intelligent Mage console you while you

58

were busy pining over an evil queen. Frankly, I think that one's the more noble effort. Certainly the tougher out of the two."

I let out a laugh. "That's true."

"Which part?"

Our eyes lock for a second. I'm not sure who looks away first, but our gaze breaks, and we settle back into the night's tranquility. Eventually, the only sound we hear is the soft rolling of the sea beneath us.

"They come to me in my dreams too," she says, so softly I don't know if it's to me or to herself. "The equations." She's still staring at the stars. "They build on each other."

"What do they show you?" I ask after a few seconds of silence.

She's quiet for a long time. Then she says, "Kos. But not Kos as we left it. A Kos that's beautiful and bright and Balanced."

CHAPTER 9

THE JOURNEY IS a blur.

Arzu, called a lascar by the others, bounds back and forth across the boat, pulling on ropes and scaling masts and peering out over the water. She shouts words and commands I can't understand in a language that seems like a stew made of a whole bunch of other languages. Watching her is weird, because she moves with a freedom I never saw before. In the Palace, she was all stiff and terse. The rare times I could pull a sentence of more than four words out of her were victories. Here, she barks at the other lascars, the sailors, and she challenges them to dangerous games that involve running along thin beams of wood on the ship or racing across the deck, dodging crates and barrels and the ship's mates. She sings with them too, loud songs that I'm glad I don't know the words to, because if I started singing them, I'd probably embarrass both Aliya and Arzu straight into Infinity.

It's almost like whatever sickness Arzu had in Osimiri has vanished. Maybe being on the water has cured her.

Even after what she told us in Osimiri, I know so little about Arzu's past and that she could do all these things. I feel a little bit ashamed I didn't ask about her more when we were together in the Palace. Before everything went cracked. When did she learn to fly through the air like that? Or to speak the way these other lascars speak? Where did she learn about boats and how to stay steady on them even as they rock and sway on the waves? How does someone born and raised in the Palace know all these things? Arzu had spoken earlier about what brought her mother to Kos, and I wonder if her mother felt the same restlessness I sometimes feel. That itch to be in other places, to see new and dangerous things.

Aliya spends all her time belowdecks working almost in the dark. There's a window in her room that lets the sunlight in when the sky is clear. Sometimes, at night, I peek in to see her working by candlelight. One of the mates snuck her some parchment early on, and I've barely seen her since.

I spend most of my time looking out on the water. Animals shimmer beneath the surface. Fish and bigger fish. I bet Arzu knows the names of them, even the ones that sometimes jump out of the ocean and arc in the air, all sparkles, before splashing underwater again. Some of the lascars look like darker-skinned fish themselves. The way they move about the ship, you'd think they were born on it.

Two of the masts have what the lascars call "bird's nests" on them, circular platforms near the top that ring the wooden pole.

Lascars often hang out there or sometimes sleep there. I look up and see two of them, about my age, shouting back and forth at each other. I can't tell what they're saying, but it looks like they're making fun of each other. I catch myself smiling. They remind me of Bo and myself. Racing across the rooftops of the shanties to see who could cross the dahia the fastest. Slipping on sheet metal, vaulting over balconies, crashing through people's laundry, sometimes falling through holes in a roof to land on some family's dinner. We were so fast and free.

I squint at the bird's nests. If only Bo and I had been born elsewhere. Maybe that could have been us.

I'm pulled out of my thoughts when a sharp whistle cuts through the air. The lascars in the bird's nests both turn. There, just over the horizon, a mountain peak. All of a sudden there's a flurry of activity, and as we get closer, I see the tops of other ships. Out of nowhere, other ships surround us. Merchant vessels, it looks like. Everyone's shouting commands or yelling out signals. The ship changes shape before my eyes. Sails unfurl and billow in the breeze. Someone's winding a crank somewhere, lowering one beam of wood and raising another. It all unfolds like a choreographed dance. Everyone knows exactly where to go and what to do.

I spy Arzu high on the part of the deck closest to the shoreline. She's standing completely still. I can only imagine the look on her face. She looks so stoic and imperial on that platform. The wind whips her baggy clothes around her. Her blond hair flows in waves. She looks like someone from one of the storybooks we used to spin as kids, the ones we would steal from the booksellers' stalls and peer through in alleyways or on balconies we'd snuck onto. Or the ones Auntie Sania and Auntie Nawal would give us in the marayu. Before I can walk up to Arzu, a door opens behind me. Aliya walks out of her cave and peers into the sun, hand over her eyes.

"We've made it," she says.

"How do you know? You've spent the whole trip cooped up like a hen in that dungeon of yours. I'm surprised your hands haven't fallen off yet."

She raises an eyebrow at me. "You know that this is a ship, right?"

"Of course I know that."

She crosses her arms, faces ahead, and smirks. "Then of course you'd know that there are maps on this ship." She glances at me to see if I'm blushing or not. "And navigational charts? And ways of tracking distance during our journey?"

"Well, yeah, that's obvious," I lie. "I pay attention to these things." I point to the closest bird's nest. "I know what that is." I point to some of the rigging. "And I know what that's for, and I bet you don't know how they let those smaller boats over there into the water, do you?"

She chuckles but says nothing. Shaking her head, she makes her way through the chaos on deck to where Arzu stands. I follow, making sure not to get in anyone's way, managing just barely to dodge a few lascars practically leaping through the air from one task to another.

In Arzu's clasped hands is a string of stones. Each pellet sits in a bronze clasp with rings attaching them to the string around

Arzu's fingers. They're like the prayer beads Izu and other Mages would hold, but rougher. "The sky is our ceiling, the earth our bed," she whispers. "The sky is our ceiling, the earth our bed. The sky is our ceiling, the earth our bed." Her head is bowed. Her eyes are closed. It's like a prayer, but one I've never heard before. I look in the direction we're heading and see a range of mountains. And on those mountains, little black dots are moving. We get closer, and I see that they're people. "The sky is our ceiling, the earth our bed."

Around us a few of the other lascars are doing the same thing. They clasp their hands in front of them and bow their heads, stone bracelets hanging from their wrists. And they're all reciting the same words over and over again.

The noise that blanketed the ship has quieted, and I can feel the moment weighing on my shoulders. I feel like I should be doing the same, like I should be praying with them, but I look to Aliya to see if she knows what to do, and she just stands there, silent. Instead, I look around, taking it all in. Even though Arzu's head is bowed, it looks like she's glowing. Light shines from her. Maybe it's the way the sun hangs in the sky. Maybe it's the way the sunlight bounces off the waves like shards of glass. But it looks like her hair is on fire and her body is bathed in sunshine.

"The sky is our ceiling, the earth our bed."

As we get closer, the black dots on the mountains turn into people, and I see them walking the jagged rocks and stopping every few paces to pick something up from the ground and slip it into a waist pouch.

All the people praying continue to murmur, then Arzu says beneath her breath, "May my hand and my heart find Balance." She's silent for a few moments, then she looks up and sighs.

We near the docks, where all sorts of people—merchants, lascars, pilgrims—scurry or amble about. It's like a tiny version of Osimiri.

I look at Aliya, and she glances at me, then her eyes widen. "Taj, you're glowing."

I look at my arms, and she's right. The same light that radiated off Arzu is reflecting off my sin-spots.

A cloud passes over the sun, and my skin returns to normal. Arzu and Aliya are still staring at me, and when I turn around, so are a bunch of the other lascars. I knew I should've covered up. I guess I thought that once we left Kos for good and were free of Queen Karima and the bounty on my head, it didn't matter if I was Marked or not. I can feel the shame boiling in my belly and starting to rise in my throat. But then I see that Aliya and Arzu are smiling. Arzu's eyes are wet with tears.

"What's going on?" I ask, and Arzu puts a hand on my arm.

"Olurun welcomes you," she says.

"Olurun? Is that who you were praying to?"

Arzu nods. She's still smiling.

"All these people, the lascars, they're from your land?"

She nods again. "My land and others."

I look to the sky. The cloud slides away from the sun, and everything shimmers again except me. Same old sin-spots. I look at my naked arms. "What happened?" Even though the lascars have gone back to work, a few of them still shoot looks my way. I can't tell if they're afraid of me or if they're glad I'm here. "And why is everyone looking at me that way?"

"Because you're tastahlik, Taj." Arzu claps me on the shoulder. "You are revered for what you can do."

I remember everything Arzu told me earlier about the tastahlik, aki who live among her people and consume the sins of others but are respected for it. People look up to them. When I'd first heard of them, I'd puffed my chest out at the idea of people respecting me, not kicking me aside in the street, not underpaying me for Eating the sins of the royal family. But now it feels like this massive weight on my shoulders.

Arzu and Aliya both stand next to me, and we all watch the people on the mountain, picking up what I realize are pebbles, blowing the dust off them, and putting them in their pouches to make more prayer strings.

At least, in this moment, things don't seem so heavy.

CHAPTER 10

IN THE CHAOS of the docks, Arzu finds a stablemaster, and the two go back and forth in a dialect I can barely follow. Then we're led to a small barn and each given our own horse and saddle.

I'd seen pictures of horses before, read about them in the books I spun as a child. But to see one in real life, this close, is something else. After adjusting their saddles, Arzu and Aliya mount with ease. I try to follow their movement—one foot in the stirrup, then swing the other leg over—but I swing too hard and almost fall off. I'm scrambling, and I know I'm seconds away from toppling onto my head when Arzu catches me.

My cheeks burn from embarrassment.

"The horse is your friend," she whispers, quiet enough that only we can hear. Then she's off, and we manage to leave the shoreline without my supposed new friend bucking and flinging me into the sky.

Arzu leads, and we head down the rocky trail through the valley and out into the desert plain. The land rises and dips unexpectedly. Little mountains surprise us, and sometimes when the descents get too steep, we end up having to find another way around. We try to find as much shade as we can, but the farther west we go, the more punishing the sun gets. Eventually, there are no more trees.

When we get to a small outpost, I practically fall to the ground and praise the Unnamed. With the coins we have left, we get some flasks of water and those wide-brimmed hats I remember seeing on the man at the kiwi orchard back when Aliya and I were being chased by murderous armored inisisa. I glance at Aliya, wondering if she's thinking the same thing. She's looking up at the sky from under her large straw hat, her brow furrowed in concentration. It's like she's looking for stars in the daytime.

Fog rises from over the horizon, and before long it has swallowed our horses' ankles. As the day goes on, the winds pick up. The breeze smells like it's coming from the coast, and it drives the mist off into the distance, westward. Mountainous, red-tinged sand dunes lie ahead. We climb until we can see the first traces of the burnt-up settlement: ground turned gray with salt, every blackened building like a skeleton of its former self. Our horses dance underneath us, and it takes all of Arzu's skill to quiet them down. Even though we stand at the edge of the village, our horses know something horrible is waiting for us.

When we come on the town at last, we see that every building has been burned. Some of the remaining buildings lean sideways under their own weight. A rancid smell, like when the tanners light their fires and burn whatever it is they're burning in the Forum, clings to the base of each home and runs along their upright, formerly wooden supports. On the dusty thoroughfare, I see footsteps and hoofprints; they make zigzagging formations and convoluted paths. Like people and animals frantically trying to get away.

There isn't a single living thing in this whole place.

I can feel the inyo in the air. The settlement is thick with them. I listen closely, and I can hear the uncleansed souls moaning in the wind.

I turn to Arzu. She has one hand holding her scarf over her mouth, the other gripping her reins. Aliya wipes a tear from her cheek.

Bo was here.

After we pass into a field of tall grass with brown-green stalks angled in the wind, Arzu's left arm stops working. I notice her bring it into her lap so that she guides the horse with one hand, pretending like she's letting her arm rest. But when it slips, it just hangs limply at her side. As she rides, I notice her rubbing at her neck. The scar I saw before must be bothering her.

"Arzu, let's rest," Aliya says. "There has to be water nearby, given the nature of this flora. We can find a stream and wait until nightfall, when the air will be cooler."

"I'm fine," Arzu says. It sounds like a croak in her throat.

We continue on until we make it to the stream Aliya had sensed earlier, but when we dismount, Arzu's left leg collapses beneath her, and she tumbles to the ground.

"Arzu!" I shout as Aliya and I rush to her side. We lay her on her back. She starts coughing. Blood streams down the sides of her mouth. I put my palm on her forehead. She's boiling to the touch. "Aliya, what's going on? How did she get this sick?"

Aliya's about to answer when Arzu's hand lashes out and grips Aliya's wrist, a pleading look in her eyes. Something unspoken passes between them. Then Arzu gulps a few times and seems to summon strength from somewhere deep within herself. "River water." Another gulp. "There's a blanket in my pack. Soak it in river water at dusk so that it may remain cool and sodden for as long as necessary." Aliya leans in farther when Arzu lowers her voice and whispers further instructions. We make a pillow out of my pack. Then there's nothing to do but wait anxiously until dusk to do as Arzu says.

I get Aliya's attention and nod to a patch of clear field not far from the stream, out of earshot but still close enough to keep an eye on Arzu.

I get up. Aliya follows. "What's going on between you two?" I whisper.

"What are you talking about, Taj?"

"If you know something about her sickness, tell me now."

Aliya frowns at me, almost like a parent looks at a child who's talking about something beyond his comprehension. It makes me so frustrated I want to scream. But I know that would scare away the horses, so I just grit my teeth.

"Well?" I ask.

Aliya takes a moment, then lets out a sigh. "We will do as Arzu asks. She knows her body better than either of us." She turns away and heads back to the stream. I watch as she takes cloth out of her pack and soaks it in the nearby river, then folds it and lays it on Arzu's forehead. They talk and talk, and I don't even bother trying to listen anymore.

The toughest thing in the world to do is stand by and watch someone you care about suffer. But if that's what they're asking me to do, then, by the Unnamed, I guess I have to do it.

So I rejoin our little campsite and smile at Arzu whenever she has enough energy to look my way.

Dusk arrives.

When the blanket's wet enough, Aliya and I wrap it around Arzu to make a cocoon. Arzu's face turns blue, and she shivers as nighttime washes over us. There's nothing I can do but watch her, anxious and frustrated. Every time she wakes up and we unwrap her, her eyes grow duller, more vacant. The light that once glowed under her skin is dimming and dimming.

In the nighttime, when Arzu is asleep, I inch over to where Aliya lies. I've spent much of that time in between thinking and thinking and thinking, and when I realized what was going on, it hit me like a mule kick to the chest.

"It's a sin, isn't it?" I whisper to Aliya.

She says nothing in return.

"If it's a sin, why don't you call it forth and I'll consume it? We can save her life. It's not like we haven't done this before."

Aliya shakes her head. All the while, she's been staring at the ground, at the pebbles that glow blue in the moonlight and the bugs and beetles that amble over and underneath them. "No."

"What? What do you mean, no?" I point at Arzu's body. "Our friend is dying, and if we don't do something, the guilt will eat her alive."

"No."

I feel my chest tighten. "Why not?" My voice cracks, and tears spring to my eyes. "Why aren't you going to do it?"

"She asked me not to."

My breath catches in my throat. "Why?"

Aliya refuses to look me in the face. "Whatever sin it is, Arzu is willing to wait it out until we arrive at her village and meet her people. The tastahlik can help her."

"But, Aliya, *I'm* tastahlik." I slap my chest with my hand. "You both said so on that ship! This is something I can do! I can help."

"Taj, no!" Aliya shouts. She glances over at Arzu, clearly worried she's woken her, but Arzu just turns over in her sleep. Aliya drops her voice low. "Respect her wishes."

When I realize there's no changing Aliya's mind, I head back to my makeshift bed. We all try to sleep, but Arzu twists and turns in her cocoon. I can't even imagine the visions plaguing her. Whatever she's dreaming, it must feel like it's killing her. Her teeth grind against each other in her sleep. There's no way I'm going to be able to sleep. I want to help her, to save her, and I can't deal with feeling this powerless.

I'm still awake when dawn hits. Sleeplessness has made me antsy, and my heart hammers in my chest. My fingers and eyelids twitch. I have to do something.

That's when it hits me.

In the forest, right after we'd escaped Kos. I'd called forth a sin-beast. I close my eyes and vividly remember the stew of feelings that rumbled inside of me as the pain lit my head on fire. I remember falling to my knees. I remember my head swimming with images of my betrayal: going against Karima, fighting Bo, and having to abandon the others as I fled Kos. I'd thought I was Crossing at the time, but I was calling forth my own sin.

I can do it. If Aliya won't save Arzu's life, then I will.

I sneak a glance at Aliya to make sure she's still asleep.

Then I tiptoe over to Arzu, wrapped in her blanket. I don't remember having said any incantation or having done any of the things Mages normally do when they call out a sin. And I don't remember having set myself in the middle of any pattern on the floor. It just sort of happened. So I put one hand to Arzu's stomach and one hand to her forehead, because it feels like the right thing to do. Then I close my eyes and try to bring myself back to that moment in the forest when I vomited the sin of my betrayal into the grass. If this all goes as planned, I can call forth the sin, control the inisisa, kill it easily, and Eat the sin. And Arzu will be healed. The thought excites me, but I stuff it down. It's time to concentrate.

I squeeze my eyes shut. It slams into me without warning. A twisting in my gut, then an explosion in my heart that makes it seem like my body is vanishing. I'm reaching into some other space in my mind. It's like I'm melding with Arzu—becoming her—in order to bring forth her sin.

A dark, dank space. Water dripping, chains sliding against stone. Someone counting. Then outside, wind slapping my face.

A daga, blood staining steps. The Palace steps. It comes to me in flashes. Too short and too many to make sense. Like a million mirror shards.

Then my body seizes, and I'm snapped back into reality.

I fall back. Nothing's changed. Arzu's completely still.

Suddenly, she coughs, and black ink spills from her mouth. I move her onto her side so that she doesn't choke on the sin. It flows and flows and flows from her mouth, and with each spew, her body quakes. Her eyes are closed, and I can't tell how awake she is for this or how much of the pain she feels, but it seems to go on forever. It's as though the sin is big enough that it would have ripped her apart from the inside had I not called it forth.

After what seems like an eternity, she stops. I set her head back, and when I rise, I look around me. It's dawn, so it's light enough for me to see.

I'm standing in it. I'm standing in a pool of sin that stretches all the way to the river at one end and past nearby trees at the other end. It is even leaking beneath Aliya's pallet while she sleeps, completely unaware of what I've just done.

I start to shiver but clench my fists at my sides. I know what needs to be done, so I wait for the sin to make itself into an inisisa. I've killed sin-dragons before. This shouldn't be a problem.

The puddles explode into streams that arc in the air and land in puddles around me. In an instant, each one takes the shape of a sin-wolf.

Multiple sins? I've called forth *multiple* sins?

They form a circle around me, snarling snouts dripping thick strings of saliva and hairy black hides streaked with lightning that pulses beneath the skin. I try to summon whatever it was that I had in me when I'd controlled the inisisa that trapped me and Aliya in the forest. I hold my hands out.

One of the wolves cranes its neck, sniffing at the air, then they all turn at once to see me.

They take one step forward.

Why isn't it working?

I stagger back and fall into the dirt. I have no daga, no weapon, I realize too late.

What was I thinking?

CHAPTER 11

THE WOLVES GROWL and bark. I can smell their hot breath in the air as they get closer and closer. The leader of the pack lunges toward me, and the rest follow. I raise my arms to defend myself, but just then a flash of lightning cuts through the sky. Thunder cracks, and the first wolf bursts open over me in a shower of shadows and ink. Parts of it spray the ground like rain. I turn and cover my head. Through the spaces between my fingers, I see a girl skid to a stop in front of me. She glows. Before I can get a good look at her face, she leaps over me, her blade carving straight through the second wolf, its hide coming apart as if it were a bale of straw.

I scurry back toward the campsite to wake the others if they're not up already, but thunder booms and dirt erupts into the air, hurling me back to the ground.

The warrior stands over me. Pieces of the inisisa drip from her fingers and her face. She's covered in their insides. But, slowly, they slide off her glowing form. It's like staring straight into the sun, looking at her. I can't move, and I don't know if it's from the pain shooting through me or from shock or from something else entirely. I'm frozen where I lie. Even when I hear the lone, snarling sin-wolf charging my way, I can't rise to fight back. I look up to see its fangs bared. I stiffen, preparing for an attack, but another blade of light pierces the thing's skull. The inisisa spasms before going limp and dissolving into a puddle of ink. With a flick of her wrist, the warrior casts the remains of the inisisa from her sword and onto the desert floor.

The girl extends a hand to me, and after a couple of stunned seconds, I grab her wrist. My eyes shoot open. Another sin-wolf is about to charge right into her from behind. "Look out!"

Without turning around, the girl swings her sword. The inisisa barrels right into it and falls to the ground in wisps of black. She hadn't even let go of my wrist.

Pools of sin dot the desert floor. They stir and bubble, but none of them move. None of them turn into fountains to swim down our throats. It's almost as though they're waiting.

I can't speak, can barely breathe. The girl hauls me to my feet. It is unfair to call her that. She seems like something bigger, something from the sky. She's not like the rest of us. The light engulfing her fades, and that's when I notice that it was all coming from her sin-spots. Beasts ring her arms, dragons and bears and snakes. Lions chase each other on her legs. The wings of a griffin encircle her neck. She wears a simple sleeveless robe made of light fabric. Her dark red headscarf has fallen away. Her hair shines silver in the early morning glow.

She's tastahlik.

Without a word, she sheathes her sword in a belt loop at her waist and looks around. The sin-puddles stir. She raises her arms and looks to the sky like she's preparing herself for something. She's going to Eat all of them . . .

Suddenly, it all stops. Frozen.

Against the rising sun, I see forms stir.

Night is starting to vanish, and I see them. Aliya has Arzu's arm slung over her shoulder. Arzu limps along. Sweat pastes her hair to her forehead. I can hear her breathing from where I stand. But when she sees the girl, her spine straightens, as if she's discovered newfound strength.

The girl looks squarely at Arzu. Her sin-spots have stopped shining, and all of a sudden she looks so human.

The puddles of blackness arc upward over the girl, and she cranes her neck, opens her mouth, and swallows the sins as they form one large jet straight down her throat. She doesn't move, and we all watch in awed silence. The girl's eyes are closed, her back arched so far I worry she's going to fall over.

When it's finished, the girl straightens herself, then takes a step toward us.

Arzu trembles. I can tell now it's not from being sin-sick. She recognizes this girl. "Juba," she whispers. She shuffles forward, one step, then the next, until the two are racing toward each other. Arzu trips, and Juba opens her arms just in time to catch her. Together, they fall to the ground. Arzu buries her head in Juba's shoulder as Juba strokes her hair.

Juba whispers to Arzu something I don't understand, and after a few minutes, they both get to their feet. Arzu's face is wet. She doesn't even bother to hide the tear streaks that glisten in the sunlight.

The girl steps forward and puts a hand to her chest. "My name is Juba," she says. "Apologies for that . . . spectacle. Usually my tribe is able to be more polite in our welcome."

Aliya steps forward. "I'm Aliya," she says, sticking her hand out. Juba clasps it with a steady grip. There's a pause as Juba looks at me. Aliya nudges me with her elbow.

"Oh, right, I'm Taj," I say.

"Pleasure to meet you both," Juba replies warmly. She looks at our makeshift campsite. "You all have traveled a great distance. The village isn't far from here. I'll guide you, and we will be there by late morning." She puts her arm around Arzu. "I see you've gotten better at making friends. But worse at staying out of trouble."

Arzu lets out a chuckle that turns into a blood-rich cough. She falls to one knee, and Aliya rushes over to her.

"I'm fine," Arzu murmurs. "I'm fine." Juba helps her up, and the two of them begin walking ahead of us while Aliya and I trail after. I have so many questions, but I'm still struggling to process what's happened. In the center of the whirlwind in my brain is the knowledge that Arzu's still alive. I can worry about who saved her and how later. For now, I should just be happy that she seems to be healthier.

Aliya punches me in the arm so hard it almost throws me to the ground.

"What did I tell you?" she hisses at me.

"Ow! What was that for?" I say, rubbing my arm. "Whose ruby did I crush to deserve that?"

"What did I tell you about butting in when you're told not to?"

I shrug, but I can only use one shoulder. "It all worked out, didn't it?"

Aliya shoots me a look almost as fierce as those sin-wolves. Then she stomps off after Arzu and Juba.

I feel good, useful. Then I remember the sharp pain in my right arm. If we have to fight any more inisisa on the way, she's going to regret that sucker punch.

CHAPTER 12

THE SUN HANGS high in the sky. As we crest a hill onto open desert plain, the first thing we see is a ring of silver-haired men and women. Their hair comes down to their shoulders in thick, knotted braids, and they all wear sand-colored robes with red threaded through. They're completely still, like statues. They wear necklaces, bracelets, and anklets with smooth stones in them that stir in the breeze. The ridge they stand on reminds me of the ridges that circle the dahia back in Kos, the ones that make those neighborhoods and their slums look like chunks of goat meat at the bottom of a bowl of stew.

Juba appears beside me. "I'm not sure how much Arzu has told you of our land, but what you in Kos call the arashi are as common as lightning and thunder here. They cannot be done away with, so we are always outrunning them." She points to the men and women we approach. "Sentinels. Sometimes, when we get old, we can sense oncoming storms in our bones. One village elder, his left knee aches when rain is near." She chuckles. "For some of us, it is the same with the arashi. We can smell when they are near. And we can run." Juba's own bracelets make music as she walks.

During the Fall of Kos, the arashi had descended from the sky with such suddenness that at first, everyone had frozen. None of us could move. Something we had thought existed only in old tales or to scare children into behaving fell out of that huge hole in the sky and floated over the Palace, nearly blocking out the moon and stars. Each monster hung over a single dahia, hovering, then spat their fire and lightning in bursts of destruction, setting the city ablaze. These Sentinels might have saved the people of Kos. I shake myself out of my reverie. "That's pretty solid," I tell Juba. She raises an eyebrow at me, and I realize my mistake. "In Kos, 'solid' is like . . . tough. Like a tough stone. It's a good thing."

"Yes," Juba says, smiling in a way I can tell means she still doesn't get it. "It is good."

The Sentinels don't move, even as we pass the village's perimeter. No expressions flicker across their faces. They just stare, blank-eyed, into the distance, each in a different direction. I want to make a feint, but I don't know if they can do what Juba did when she fought off the sin-wolves. Better not to invite a beating or a knife to my throat.

As we descend the bowl's rim, I stumble and have to bend down to keep my balance. Arzu and Aliya are slow to come down as well, but for Juba, it's like the ground itself is rising to make steps for her. It's clear she's made this journey many, many times.

"Hey," I say to her as we get to more even ground. "How'd you do that?"

"Do what?" she asks as the entirety of the small village comes into view.

"Fight off the sin-wolves like that. It was like you were completely made out of light."

"Oh." She smiles and looks at her hands. Sin-spots cover the backs and trace lines across her palms. "These old things?" She chuckles. "It is just how we learn to fight." She says it so casually, like she hasn't just defeated half a dozen murderous sin-wolves. As though Arzu, whom she apparently knows really well, weren't about to kick death's door down like a Palace guard looking for aki in the Forum. "We are a simple people, but rich in here." She taps her chest and continues down the slope.

"Does everyone in your tribe fight like that?" I ask. I can't get her moves out of my head.

"Everyone fights," Juba tells me. "Some because they have to. Some because they want to." As we walk, she turns to me and squints, almost like she's trying to figure out what makes me move. "It is dangerous to fight merely because one wants to." She doesn't elaborate, so I'm left to spend the rest of the walk wondering whether or not she's already decided I'm trouble.

Eventually, we make it to the bottom, where we're surrounded by the quiet bustle of the desert village. It suddenly looks so much bigger. I see buildings I didn't see before, maybe because their color blended into the surrounding rock walls and sand dunes. I don't know what I was expecting. But this place looks less like a temporary campsite for wanderers and more like a town that's been here for many moons. Throughout the camp, small jungle cats amble around while hyenas play-fight. A child in the street tosses a ball into the air, and a small fox leaps to catch it. They remind me of the wild animals that would wander the alleyways of Kos. The animals that adults tell you never to touch but that we aki used to feed anyway. They were as wild and abandoned as we were. These animals are different. Under their skin, lightning pulses.

In the shade of one building's overhang, an older tribesman sits on a wooden box with a bunch of little kids in a semicircle around him. Numbers and letters have been scribbled into the ground, and the children pore over them. Proofs! Like the ones Aliya carved into the dirt. "Those are proofs!" I shout before I can contain myself.

Juba smiles as we continue walking. "Ah, I see you are familiar with one of our languages. It is like—what do you call it in Kos—religious studies?"

"Religion?"

"The word of Olurun. These . . ." She searches for the word, then snaps her fingers. Her bangles chime. "Algorithms! And equations are his teachings." I look over to Aliya, and a slow smile forms on her face as she watches the circle of children all with their heads bent toward their teacher.

Women outside of an adobe dwelling sit in a perfect circle, each with a child in front of her. Chatter hums in the air around them as they joke and laugh. Their fingers work deftly, braiding the hair of the children, who wriggle and squirm, trying and failing to sit still. Occasionally one breaks loose and swings at another, giggling. Animals wander around them. One of the children scruffs the neck of a tiny jungle cat.

Juba smiles at them. We walk by a stretch of tents with laundry hung on clotheslines among them. The wooden beams propping up the structures are adorned with intricate carvings of faces and animals. Then there are rows of small adobe dwellings. Each has a different brightly colored mask hanging from the front door. The masks are engraved with beasts carved into the wood. A long-tailed bird on one cheek. A wolf running along a jaw. We walk by a carpenter with a row of staffs laid out on a table in front of him, perfectly straight, and carved into them are what I realize are animals too—dark and whispy, like inisisa. So small, so detailed. Torches line the streets, unlit now in the bright afternoon, but even the poles holding them up have entire stories etched into them. Aliya reaches out and traces one of the carvings with her finger.

"Where are we going?" I ask Juba.

She smiles at her village, like she's happy to be showing it off to me. "Before you are settled, I must take you to meet the Elders."

A troop of women approach. Brightly colored robes that bare their shoulders hug their chests and waists, coming down to their ankles. Small sticks hold their braids up in complex, perfectly symmetrical patterns.

"Ayaba," says the first woman. She puts her hand to her heart. Juba steps forward, and the two gently press their foreheads together, wide, warm smiles on their faces. Their sin-spots glow when they touch. Juba does this with each of the women, then steps back and gestures toward us.

"Please, these travelers are weary." She looks to Aliya and Arzu. "Bring them to the sick tent, where they can be cared for. "This one—"

I slide my hand out in greeting. "Taj," I say.

But before I can say any more, the first woman places her hand on the back of my neck and pulls my forehead to hers. "Welcome." The others come forward and perform the same gesture. I look down at my arms and my hands. I'm glowing too. All of my sin-spots pulse with lightning, except for the black band on my forearm—the mark of the armored sin-beast.

The women reach out and take Aliya and Arzu by the hands, guiding them toward the healer's tent.

By the time they're gone, my sin-spots have returned to normal.

Eventually, we arrive at a large circular dwelling made out of adobe with a straw ceiling. The front door is guarded by men with braids running down their backs. As we step inside, my eyes have to adjust to the darkness. I see older men and women, all with sin-spots on their skin. Arms and legs, fingers, and even their toes are covered with markings. Some have sin-spots etched into the sides of their faces, circling their eyes. They look fresh. Or permanent. Like mine. But how can they live for this long with so much sin in them?

Juba gestures for me to take a seat on a cushion in the part of the circle closest to the door. Then she walks to a throne that sits on top of a raised platform at the far end of the room. She nods at one of the tastahlik, who rises and hands me a bowl with some nuts in it.

All around us hang masks. Like wooden people staring down at us. Just like the ones I saw earlier.

"Taj," Juba says, and I wonder how she's able to speak so softly yet so loudly at the same time. Her voice fills the entire chamber. "Will you break kola nut with us?"

What do I say? Is there a special phrase or sentence?

She smiles again, noting the confusion in my eyes. "A simple yes or no will do."

"Oh, yes, then." I take one. Everyone else already has one. At the same time, everyone bites into their kola nuts.

I almost spit mine out, it's so bitter. But I manage to hold it in. Uhlah! This is just going to have to be one of those things people do that I'll have no hope of ever understanding.

"We must begin by thanking you. For bringing us back our Arzu."

"Wait, I didn't bring her back." I think of Osimiri and how intent Arzu was on getting back here anyway. "She had already booked passage on a ship to head here from Kos. I didn't do anything, really. I can't take credit."

"That is not what we mean." They all look my way, and Juba's smile vanishes. She's as serious I've ever seen her, and I can't tell if it's because I've done something wrong, broken some long-standing tradition or something. "We mean her Healing. You participated in her Healing, and for that, we express our eternal gratitude. May you remain blessed and Balanced for the remainder of your life."

"Th-thank you," I manage to get out. "I . . . I just did what I could to save her life." I look around nervously. I don't know any of the decorum or anything, so I figure, what's the harm in just charging forward with my question? "May I ask, how do you know Arzu?" I wait. "I worked—well, served, really—in the Palace in Kos. I was aki for the royal family. Arzu, at the time, was a servant too. She was my sicario. She told me then that she had been born in the Palace but that her mother had emigrated to Kos from here. Has she ever been back here?"

Juba shakes her head. "This is her first time home. But my family and I have visited Kos many times. We have long maintained good relations with the Kaya family. As a child, I lived for a time in the Palace, even. I knew Kolade's father and mother. Karima and Arzu were inseparable, but for Arzu and her mother, I believe it was a blessing to have contact with their homeland." She smiles at memories I can't even fathom. The Kolade and Karima she speaks of, they're like people from a whole other life—so different from how they are now. "I am familiar with your odd traditions. It saddens me to hear what has befallen your city. Not long ago, word reached us that a new queen rules your city. For some time now, we have seen refugees like yourselves pass by in the caravans. A few live among us now, but most don't stay for long." She looks at her arms, at the animals running up and down them and over her hands. "I believe we frighten them."

I realize then that Juba thinks we're just regular refugees. She has no idea who I am—that I'm the reason there are refugees in the first place. I open my mouth to say something—to tell them the truth—but then I think better of it. If they know who I am, it won't be long before they know Karima is after me. They'll run me out of town. And then where would I hide? What would happen to Aliya and Arzu?

"We pray that your city finds Balance once again."

"Me too," I whisper.

A moment of quiet descends on the room. Then Juba's voice breaks through the silence. "While I imagine some of our traditions and customs are strange to you, Taj of Kos, I think you will find that we share with Kosians quite a few things."

A plate arrives in front of me, and already my mouth is watering.

I've never been so grateful for a plate of moin-moin in my entire life.

"And now we eat."

It's night by the time I leave the Elders' hut. It has been so long since I've eaten that much that I'm practically dizzy with it. During the meal, Juba told stories of holiday feasts when her uncles and the other older men of the village, after massive meals, would lumber through the settlement like bears, loosen their belts, and find wooden stools on which to pass out. She and her friends would run around and play all kinds of pranks on them to see what they would sleep through—flicking their ears or making dyes and painting their faces or tickling their noses with birds' feathers. The answer was "nearly everything."

Outside, the village has quieted. Juba steps out and smiles at me.

"Shall we go for a walk?" she asks.

We wind through the village's center until we arrive at a four-floor mud-and-stone building. It sounds like a war is happening inside, all shouting and loud bangings and what I realize are curses, but Juba chuckles warmly.

"This is where you and Aliya will be staying." She points to the top floor. "The family has cleared space for you."

"Wait. This is all one family?" It sounds like two armies dueling in there.

"The village is small," she replies by way of explanation. "We have no choice but to keep our family close." She turns. "Walk with me." And we head toward what looks like the edge of the village.

I make my way up to the bowl's edge, tripping and scrabbling, while Juba walks with the same grace as before. Maybe, with time, I'll figure out the proper pathways. Right now, it's like climbing a very, very steep hill, and I'm slipping all over the place, trying to find footholds and handholds. But eventually, I make it to the top and dust myself off.

To our left and right are the Sentinels. The arashi-watchers. Their eyes are white like the aki, like the tastahlik, but they don't have any sin-spots. Maybe that's why they're able to grow so old. Who can live a long life doing what we do? That doesn't explain the Elders, though.

"I come here sometimes as well," she tells me. "The air is different up here. And it reminds us of the vastness of the world beyond our own." She looks to me. "Even our Onija are lulled into peaceful contemplation when they set foot here."

"Onija?"

"Fighters." She turns her gaze out over the expanse. "The women who welcomed you when you first arrived in our village, they are Larada. Our Healers. We are born with a remarkable gift. What you in Kos call Balance. It is the same for us. We pull blemish from the soul and wear it on our own when no one else can. We round the Circle. Our custom dictates that we tastahlik are to be either Onija or Larada. I believe Olurun made us to be Larada. Others in my village believe otherwise." She looks at her hands, clenches one into a fist, then unclenches it. "I would prefer us all to be Larada—Healers."

Quiet hangs in the air around us.

"Can I ask you something?" I pause. "You and Arzu . . ."

Juba lets out a soft chuckle, a smirk twisting her lips. She bows her head, like she's calling up memories, like she's jumping into a lake and fishing them out with her own hands. "I've known Arzu since we were children," Juba says at last. "Being the chief's daughter came with certain perks. And certain drawbacks. I used to hate our visits to all these foreign parts of the Kingdom of Odo. All these other cities with all these other rulers with whom we had to exchange gifts and keep up relations. Sometimes, when no real gift was appropriate, they would give me as their gift."

"What?"

She smiles at me wryly. "I was a hostage." She shrugs. "I was treated with the utmost respect, of course. But, yes, I was a hostage. If relations soured between my family and another's, I was to be the sacrifice. A way of repaying debts."

"How could your father do that to you?" I try to imagine Mama and Baba doing the same with me. I remember how Mama cried when she saw my eyes had changed and they realized I was aki. I remember how stone-faced Baba got when he realized what this meant for my future. It broke their hearts to have to give me up. Yet that's exactly what Juba's parents did to her.

"Another of our customs that I'm sure is very odd to you." She looks to me, scrutinizing me for my reaction, then focuses her gaze back on the night-black horizon. "I was often held a hostage of the Kaya family. They treated me wonderfully, and the food in Kos is almost without peer. It is perhaps why you will recognize some of it here."

"You stole our recipes?"

"Borrowed." She winks. "Anyway, that is where I met Arzu and her mother."

"And became friends?"

Juba seems lost in contemplation. "More than that."

"More?"

"For Arzu and her mother, my visits to the Palace were their only remaining connection to their homeland. I would bring news with me. News of births. News of weddings. News of deaths."

"I see."

"They made sure that the Palace knew all of our customs so that nothing the Kaya family did would offend me or my father. And, in return, Arzu would teach me of Kos." Juba looks to the sky, and her brow furrows like she is searching for memories or stories in the stars. "We would sneak out and spend whole days wandering the Palace grounds before guards would find us and scoop us up. We upset our handlers so much. She would show me the Forum, and she would show me Gemtown. One day, she showed me gemstones she had jewelers make for me. I would wear them in my ears, and whenever I would return home, the rest of the tribe would marvel at what I'd brought with me from Kos." Tears start to form in Juba's eyes.

"You were in love."

"Yes." She nods, and it is the saddest thing I've ever seen. Like watching her get her heart broken all over again. "Even as children, we knew we were meant for each other. There was no one else I wanted to spend time with. I would detest visiting other royal families. But I would look forward to every visit to Kos and to the Kayas. Every visit meant that I would get to see my Arzu once again."

"But what happened? You no longer wear the earstones she gave you."

Juba touches her earlobes. "No, I do not." Her hand falls to her side. "I am a Healer. And what we Healers do taxes us immensely. It is a severe drain on the body. As you know, few people who Eat sins last into old age." She looks at her hands. "Long ago, it was decreed that tastahlik were forbidden from forming attachments of the nature that Arzu and I wanted. We could never marry. Never form a family. All tastahlik are made to live this way. When my eyes turned, it was the end of me and Arzu. My father died soon after, and the visits to Kos ended. Because I was his only heir, I was obligated to remain behind and send emissaries in my stead."

"So this was your first time seeing Arzu since . . . since you were both kids?"

She nods, mournful. "Yes. Yes, it was."

We stand on the ridge for a long time, neither of us speaking, then Juba turns to leave. "I wish you a peaceful night, Taj of Kos."

"Taj of Kos?" I laugh. Makes me think of the little titles the younger aki who looked up to me used to give me back when we lived in the shanties of Kos. Lightbringer. Sky-Fist. Like I was some sort of hero. It always annoyed me—or, at least, I would pretend it did. Secretly, it made me feel pretty good. Legendary, even. Now it feels like a lie. "Just Taj is fine."

"Taj, then."

She turns to leave, but one of the Sentinels stirs. Then they all turn and face the same direction. East. I follow their gaze. There's movement in the darkness. What looks like a single writhing mass turns out to be people. A lot of them. More refugees.

My heart leaps into my throat.

They're from Kos. I don't know how I know it, but I feel the certainty in my heart just as much as I feel the ground beneath my feet. They're from Kos.

CHAPTER 13

THE REFUGEES STUMBLE into a run when they see the lights of the village. By now, the tastahlik have gathered to greet them, and some of them rush out to meet them in the desert. But the first of the refugees stops where they are. I can see even from where I stand on the ridge the fear and horror in their eyes.

"Aki!" someone shouts, then everything turns to chaos. A woman carrying a child in a wrap at her chest runs off into the darkness, leading a mass of others where we cannot see. Some of the younger children at the front pull out stones and slings and knives from their packs. They jump to the front of the group to protect the others. Some of the refugees collapse where they stand, weeping. That's when I realize what is happening.

They've just fled Kos. Where the aki serve as Karima's soldiers. Maybe some survived Bo's rampages. Every time they have seen sin-spots, it has meant death and destruction.

Before I know what I'm doing, I break away from the tas-tahlik and wave my arms. "We are not aki!" I shout. It sounds strange to say it. It's true, but I have been aki all my life. Spit on because of it, stepped over because of it, used by Mages because of it. I pray that none of these Kosians recognize me for who I really am—or who I once was. "We are not aki!" I shout again.

Three of the young refugees charge toward me, their weapons raised high. Their clothes are tatters on their ashen skin. I skid to a stop. "No, no! We are here to help you. We have water! We have food!"

"It is a trick!" someone shouts from the crowd. "They are Queen Karima's soldiers."

A little girl with makeshift knives carved out of stone in each hand charges to the front of the group, ready to cut whoever comes closer. Her shoulders shiver with anger.

Suddenly, Juba is at my side. "We do not serve Karima." Her voice booms into the night. It does not sound like it's coming from her throat. It sounds like it's coming from the sky itself. Like thunder. "We do not serve Karima," Juba repeats. "We are not aki. We are tastahlik. We are healers." She unsheathes her sword and lays it at her feet. The kids charging toward me stop. Juba takes a single step forward. Then Aliya joins her, and Arzu. They look healthy and rested and determined. They both carry baskets of puff puff and bread. Someone from the village arrives with a massive jug of water in his arms. Juba leads them forward, and they meet the children, the other refugees cowering behind.

I cannot hear what Juba says to the children, but they speak for a long time. Quietly. Then one of the boys slips his knife back

into his torn shoes and dips his hands into the jug of water, cups
it in his palms, and brings it to his mouth to drink. At first, he
is shy about it, unsure. It leaks down his arms. But then he gulps
it down and falls to his knees. The two girls with him each grab
a piece of puff puff and turn it over into their hands before biting into it. They smile.

When the other refugees see the children walk past Juba and
Aliya and Arzu and toward the rest of us, they begin to make
their way. They walk slowly, haltingly. But then I see them stop
worrying. Some of them start to run. Many of them weep with
thanks. Those who collapse are pulled up by others and carried
in their arms or on their backs. We hurry to the front of the
group and lead them toward the village.

In the chaos of arriving here and meeting these new people
and being welcomed, I hadn't been thinking about Kos. Guilt
spreads through my chest. I hadn't been thinking about Mama
and Baba, the Aunties, the aki who were once as siblings to me.
If they're somewhere in this crowd, I don't know that I'd even
have the courage to show them my face.

One of the women—a Larada—with braids tied and twisted in
a zigzag pattern behind her head, leads some of us to a nearby
stream. As soon as I crest the hill, I can see the line of villagers filling pots. They dip them into the water, then, when they
are full, they make the return climb up the hill to where the
refugees are camping. I've been given a jug of my own, and so
has Aliya. The air is chilly now, so it no longer looks strange for
me to wear this sand-colored cloak that covers the skin of my

arms and legs. I thought I'd never be ashamed of my sin-spots again, but then I remember the looks on the faces of those first refugees who saw me, and my cheeks burn. My mind flashes to what they must've gone through back in Kos. What others are still going through. Mama, Baba, the Aunties . . . None of them were among the new arrivals.

"I'm sure they are safe," Aliya says next to me, and I know she's talking about my parents.

I try to smile like I believe her, but we both know that I do not. We arrive at the river and walk into it so that our robes float around us. All around us, people talk in whispers. The more I listen to the stories the refugees tell—of the arashi that hover over the city, of the way Karima indiscriminately demolishes the dahia with dynamite and rearranges the very streets of Kos, of the way aki patrol the Forum with armored inisisa—the more difficult it is not to worry. It feels as though I have left them behind—abandoned them.

Villagers glance at me and Aliya when they think we're not looking. I see the suspicion in their eyes. We're not familiar merchants in caravans they're used to seeing. We're something different. We're strangers. And we've brought our problems with us.

Aliya silently finishes filling her pot, and I wonder what she's thinking about. With the pot on her shoulder, she walks ahead, and I follow. She slows down like she's adjusting her balance. Her body sways a little. Her left arm goes slack, and without warning, she collapses, her water pot shattering on the rocks at her feet, spilling water everywhere.

"Aliya!" I rush to her, dropping my own pot as she scrabbles in the dirt, trying to recover the water. Her left arm no longer works. She falls onto her back, and I try to bring her head into my lap as her body seizes. "Aliya, are you OK?"

She shakes so violently that several times I worry she'll bloody my nose. But I hold her as tightly to me as possible. Beads of sweat dot her upper lip. Her eyes bulge. A film glazes over them.

Her shaking grows more violent, then I notice it. The wetness in the ground around us moves. Then, slowly, streams of water, like string, rise from the dirt. They form fingers that arc like sins ready to be Eaten. My mouth hangs open at the sight.

Aliya stills in my lap. The thin columns of water collapse. I look around, but no one else seems to have noticed it. Was this real? Did I just imagine it?

When I look down, Aliya's eyes return to normal.

This time, when she shakes, I know it's from fear and not from whatever had overtaken her. I want to ask what happened, where she went to when she was possessed, but I know the best thing for me to do is to hold her like this and let her believe—let her know—that whatever difficulty she must walk through, I am here to walk through it with her.

CHAPTER 14

AFTER HER EPISODE at the river, I'd wanted to get help for Aliya, but she insisted on walking on her own. "It was a fainting spell—I'm just dehydrated," she said.

Inside the building, we walk up the winding stone stairs that lead up to the little attic door in the ceiling. Aliya climbs through first, and I follow.

The dwelling Aliya and I occupy is never quiet. There's always a party going on underneath us: singing, glasses clinking together, bowls landing on wooden tables, kids giggling. The happy noises are pleasant, and we're grateful Juba was able to arrange for us to stay here, but our quarters do feel a little cramped—more like an attic than anything else.

A single family lives in this building, but the family's large enough to occupy three whole floors. It seems like there's one floor for every generation. I can't imagine what it must be like to have everybody you're related to practically living on top of you.

They've given Aliya a desk here, and parchment and half-rolled books litter it. The discards form a graveyard of sorts at the feet of her chair. But now she lies in bed, resting. Her breathing starts to slow, and I can tell she's fallen asleep.

I sit on the floor looking through the pieces of parchment. It's all equations and proofs and all sorts of lahala. It boggles my mind how she's been able to make such a mess in so short a time. I hear Aliya stir in her sleep and turn around. Her eyes are still closed, and her hair falls in strands over her face. Her cheeks are flushed a light ruby red. My heart trip-hammers in my chest, and my throat tightens.

The way my stomach dropped when I thought she was hurt terrifies me. Back in Kos, Eating sins for a living, watching others die from the work, I learned that caring about what happened to others always led to heartbreak. And, anyway, warming my heart for Aliya? It would complicate everything. Besides, with what she's going through, Aliya needs a friend right now. Not a heart-mate.

Aliya's eyes flutter open, and I look away quickly, pretending to be busy cleaning up the papers.

"You're awake," I say, my back turned to her.

"Barely," she says.

She props herself up in her bed and rests her cheek in the palm of one hand and looks at me, her head cocked to the side like a bird.

"Do you remember that boar from the forest?" she asks sleepily. When I don't respond, she continues: "When you called forth your own sin and the inisisa came out, it came out as a wild boar. You put your hand to its head, and its shadows melted away, and it became a beast made of light."

"Yes, I remember." In all honesty, I only have flashes from that time in the forest. I remember running away from Kos, leaving it behind. I remember my lungs getting ready to burst. I remember vomiting my sin onto the forest floor, and I remember the intense mix of pain and guilt and sadness that I felt when the sin came bubbling up in me. Then bits and pieces of the animal. But I must have passed out right after. "A little bit."

"Well." She slowly gets out of bed and stumbles. I rush to her side, but she waves me away. Dark spots, like copper ramzi, dot her pillow. She takes a staff from the wall. Minutely detailed carvings of sin-beasts run up and down its length. "It looked very interesting when I first saw it in the village. The carpenter gave it to me as a gift. Who knew it would be so useful?" She uses it to get to her desk, then shuffles some curled papers around. She pulls one sheet out from under a stack of parchment slips, rolls it into a cylinder, then hands it to me. "Read that."

It's been so long since I've had a chance to spin a book—to watch the words become images before my eyes. I take it, put it to my eye, and begin to let it slide apart. At first, it's just a jumble of lines and curves. Black ink on brown parchment. Then, all of a sudden, I freeze. It can't be. For a long time, I'm staring at the thing my eye takes in. "But . . . how?" My memory of the boar returns. I can see it now, all of it. "That's . . . you drew the boar."

She pulls the book from my hands and spreads the parchment out on her desk. It's numbers. All numbers and letters.

"You wrote a proof . . . of the boar."

She turns over her shoulder, still holding down the parchment at its corners, and nods, smiling.

I rush over to her stack. "And these?"

"More inisisa."

I roll one up at random and put it to my eye. A series of bats. Then another. A dragon. I look up and see Aliya wiping blood from her nose.

"I'm fine," she says, voice muffled by her sleeve.

She holds the cloth to her nose and tilts her head back. I must look as concerned as I feel because she waves her hand at me and says, "Taj, it's nothing. The air here is too dry, and I haven't been drinking enough water." The cloth bunched on her nose reddens. "It'll stop soon."

Soon enough, it does.

Of all the emotions I expect to feel now, I'm not counting on anger. It surprises me to find my fists balled at my sides. "The river."

She sighs, and her shoulders slump. "The inisisa have been coming to me in visions ever since we left Kos. And they wear their colors like in the Before."

"You mean like how the Scribes draw them on the Wall around Kos?"

"Precisely."

"Is this what happened during your . . . when you collapsed by the river?"

She nods. "It's what I see. I see the inisisa as proofs. As equations. And I see . . ." She trails off.

I'm about to ask about that trick with the water when we hear a crash from downstairs, and a young child starts wailing while an older one shouts at him to stop being so dramatic.

After a moment, Aliya and I chuckle. More voices have joined the kids, and now everyone's shouting.

"Sounds a lot like home," I murmur.

"They would have a difficult time in the Great House of Ideas."

I move to sit in her chair. "No shouting, eh?"

"No, Taj. No shouting."

"And if a lizard runs over your foot, you are telling me you would be able to keep from shouting?" I point at her and close one eye, like my finger is an arrow.

"Plenty of lizards have crossed my foot without me screaming," she says.

"I don't believe you," I tell her, smirking.

The noise downstairs gets louder, but I can tell it's just a family being a family. It's what I dream of families sounding like. Noisy and loving. Sometimes mad at one another, sometimes playful.

"Hey," I tell her at last. "Let's get some fresh air."

Morning is almost here.

The refugees, for the most part, set up camp outside the village. It's starting to become clear that they still don't care much for us. Some of them try to give the gemstones sewn into their clothes for Healing or food, but the villagers always refuse to accept any sort of payment.

Aliya stops to look at them. I walk to her side, and together, we stare in silence. "They look like they're already preparing to move on," Aliya says. "They have no intention of going back to Kos."

Who would want to go back? I want to ask Aliya, suddenly annoyed. When she speaks of the refugees and their movements, I feel a pang of guilt. Like she is saying, *Taj, you're weak to give up on your home so easily.* And it would be easy to tell her about what it was like to be aki in that place. It would be easy to use that as my weapon against her. To make her think that life as aki was nothing but horror and embarrassment and, eventually, a painful death. But there was friendship in it. There was love in it. There was Bo and the others, the Aunties, the aki at the camp—the family we made for ourselves.

To avoid having to keep looking at the refugees in their makeshift camp, I wander the other way, into the empty desert, slowing eventually to let Aliya catch up.

"I know you like it here, Taj," she says, quiet but insistent. "You don't have to tell me for me to see it."

She's starting to sound like a housefly trying to find my ear. My fists clench at my sides.

"Sure, we can vanish here. Make new lives. But eventually we have to—"

"Go back," I say under my breath.

"Yes. We have to go back."

I turn around. "What is there for us, Aliya? Everyone, everything I've ever loved is gone. It's time we admit it."

"It's not about us, Taj."

Something catches in my throat. I can feel the anger bubbling up too fast to stop. "I can't save anyone," I hiss. I turn on my heel and storm away.

"Taj!" Aliya calls out after me. But I don't have time for her lahala anymore.

I stop at the sick tent, not entirely sure why.

The beds are spaced out wide enough for nurses to attend to the sick. Juba stands in a circle with some of the Larada. When she sees me enter, she smiles and beckons me to a young man shivering on his pallet. Nurses hover over the boy. Sweat pours from him. He wears nothing but a cloth tied over his waist. His ribs poke against his blue skin.

Arzu stands against a far wall of the tent, arms folded across her chest. Her blond hair comes down in braids over her shoulders, like some of the other tribespeople. The vest she wears and the striped pants that hug her legs hold so many colors it dizzies me to look at. A loose headscarf covers the scar I know winds along her neck. But she stands alone, observing, and I note that from where she stands, she can see all entrances and exits, just like she used to do back at the palace.

Juba and the nurses whisper to each other. From time to time, Juba looks up and chances a glance in Arzu's direction, and something secret and silent passes between them, and they both try not to smile afterward as they return to whatever they were doing before. So that's what Arzu's been up to. She has made herself Juba's sicario. Juba's keeper. Her bodyguard, her shadow. Heh, clever.

Behind me, a woman who looks like she must be the boy's mother clutches the gemstones sewn into her sleeves so tightly in her fingers that her knuckles grow white.

After consultation with the nurses, Juba moves toward the boy. It's more like she's gliding over the ground than walking. She drops to one knee and looks the boy over. Then she runs a hand over the boy's forehead. It comes back slick.

Juba moves to the head of the bed and comes down to both knees, then presses her forehead to the boy's. She murmurs words that sound like the prayer I heard earlier. Her voice starts out soft—barely a whisper—but then grows louder and louder. Suddenly, the boy seizes. Juba breaks away. All at once, several other Healers and nurses are at her side.

"A bowl," Juba says suddenly, and one of the nurses rushes off and returns a moment later with a calabash bowl. "Now sit him up." The others slowly gather the boy into a sitting position. The nurse with the bowl slips it beneath the boy's chin. Another nurse stands behind the boy, hands pressed against his back.

The boy gags, then chokes. A nurse whispers to him, "It's OK, it's OK, it's OK," over and over.

The boy's shoulders heave, then it all comes out. Black ink spills into the bowl. The boy dry-heaves a few times before collapsing into the waiting arms of another nurse. The nurse with the bowl brings it outside, and Juba follows her. I watch, frozen, as the boy's mother rushes over and throws herself onto her son.

People hurry back and forth, making sure the boy is comfortable on his pallet. When I see that the boy has at least stopped shaking, I head outside. I follow the sound of Juba's voice. She and the nurse are behind the tent. The sin, in the form of a lynx, leaps from the bowl, and I rush over to help. Juba holds up her hand, silently telling me to stop. I pause just as the beast sits quietly and regally before her and the nurse.

Juba takes one step toward it, and it doesn't move at all, then she puts her hand to its forehead. The darkness rolls off its shoulders, its legs, its back. It glows beneath its fur.

The lynx comes up on all fours and cocks its head at her quizzically before turning around and leaping into the streets. I run out to see where it goes, and I watch it run and run and run, glowing more with each step until it's nothing but light, and then nothing at all.

Juba appears behind me. "Sometimes we keep them around. The children enjoy having pets. Most times we free them. More boring than how it is done in Kos, I imagine." She smirks. So that explains all the animals in this village. I walk with her back into the tent and see that the boy is sitting up on his own now, and his mother is whispering hurriedly to him. Then she reaches down, takes off one of her slippers, and whacks him over the head with it. She's shouting now at the poor, cowering boy. He tries to dodge his mother's strikes, but she's too fast, and before long, he darts out of the tent with her chasing after him.

Juba laughs to herself, and I see a few of the nurses chuckling as well.

"Sometimes," she says, turning to me, "it is not sickness that keeps a child from sinning, but the bottom of his mother's slipper."

At this, the tent fills with laughter.

Aliya hovers in the entrance to the tent. I catch her smiling just as the beaded curtain swings closed.

CHAPTER 15

OUTSIDE, ALIYA IS nowhere to be found.

I start to head in the direction of our dwelling when I hear it. The kind of loud, excited yelling I haven't heard since we left Osimiri.

It's easy to follow, and when I get to it, a crowd of people blocks my view. All I can see are the backs of people's heads, but I think I recognize some of the refugees. Their skin is no longer as sallow and gray as it was when they first got here, but their faces, even the children's, have that haunted look in them. Even while they cheer and shout, scattered throughout the crowd, they don't look fully alive. I weave my way through just as the noise reaches a roar. Some of the tribesmen and tribeswomen in the crowd notice my sin-spots, and they make a path for me. It feels weird. In Kos, people got out of the way because they didn't want to be touched by disgusting, marked aki. Then, when I served in the Palace, people cleared a way for me because they didn't want the Kayas' wrath to fall like a hammer right on their heads. But now people make way for me and smile. A few even pat me on the shoulder. They sway when they do it. And for a brief second, Zainab's face appears in my mind, one of the last aki I buried with my own hands.

Zainab had sniffed crushed stones to quiet the shouting in her head, to help fight down all the guilt she'd accumulated from Eating so many sins. It had numbed her. Made her dizzy sometimes. But it made the pain bearable.

Is that what these people are doing? There's a sickly sweet smell in the air. Sort of like refuse left in alleyways to boil in the sun before monsoon season.

Somewhere nearby, people are beating a fast rhythm on drums. The shouting gets louder. A cheer erupts timed with the beats, then quiets, and it's just drumming again.

Eventually, I get to the front of the crowd and can see that a circle has formed. In the center is a small tastahlik dressed in leathers similar to what Arzu used to wear when she too served in the Palace. He stands with his feet wide apart, arms outstretched so that from fingertip to fingertip, he's one straight line. In one hand is a longstaff with a blade fixed to one end.

The people are cheering. The tastahlik boy has a cut on his cheek, but he's smiling. Across from him is a sin-bear so large that when it stands on its hind legs, it towers over the tallest member of the crowd.

All at once, tastahlik and inisisa move toward each other. The bear slams its forepaws down and charges. The tastahlik twirls. His staff whistles through the air, and the blade slices right through the bear's arms and legs. But the beast whirls around a moment later, legs re-formed. It lunges forward, and the tastahlik can't spin out of the way fast enough. When he does roll away, the front of his shirt hangs from him like rags. He puts his free hand to his stomach, and his palm comes back red and shiny. The crowd's noise has vanished.

The boy tries to get to his feet, using his staff to pull himself up, but falls down to one knee. The bear rears up, then rushes forward. No one else in the crowd looks like tastahlik. They drink from flasks and sway left and right. A few let out gasps, a few more cheer, but nobody's going to do anything. Are they . . . *enjoying* this?

Before I can stop myself, I break from the crowd and put my hands out in front of me, then close my eyes and try to focus.

Everyone is silent.

When I open my eyes again, all heads are turned my way. There's confusion on some faces and, weirdly enough, anger on others. What in all of Infinity could they possibly be mad at? I'm trying to help.

My concentration is broken, and the sin-bear breaks away from my hold. It dashes my way. Its jaws are wide open. Shadowy saliva drips from its fangs. Before it can leap at me and swallow me whole, a spear comes flying through the air and cuts straight through the nape of the inisisa's neck, sticking itself in the hard ground. The sin-bear crouches there for a moment, impaled, then collapses and dissolves into a swirl of sin-mist.

The wounded tastahlik is standing now, holding his hand

to his stomach, and he looks at me like I just spit in his egusi soup. He's so focused on me, he barely even blinks as he opens his mouth and lets the dissolved sin swim down his throat. He gulps it like he just drank from the inside of a coconut.

Murmurs ripple through the crowd. I have no idea what people are saying, but I know they're disappointed. Slowly, people begin to disperse. Not a single person steps in to thank me.

The tastahlik stomps my way, then angrily pulls his staff from the ground.

"You don't look like you're about to say thank you," I mutter.

The tastahlik glares at me. His stomach's practically ripped open, and this boy has the audacity to glare at me? I have half a mind to crack his stone right here and now. But I calm myself. Take a few breaths. Aliya would be proud of me. Arzu too. Maybe. "You should visit one of the, uh, one of the Healers; that looks deep," I say.

For a few seconds, I wonder if the tastahlik is mute, because he says absolutely nothing before turning and stomping off.

"You're welcome!" I shout after him.

"Hey!" I follow the boy back to the village, elbowing my way through the crowd. He's heading to a part of town I haven't been to before. The houses are few and far between, and there aren't any torches for light. The whole neighborhood is shrouded in shadows. Only thin beams of sunlight cut across streets and alleys.

We keep walking, and things get quieter. There's a steady hum of conversation, but it's sort of in a different language or dialect, so the accent chews up any words I might know. Still, I recognize the sound of it. For a moment, I'm transported back to Kos. It's the sound of pickpockets and kids with knives in hand, waiting for their targets. It's the sound of homeless, newly turned aki, desperately plotting how to steal their next meal. It's the sound of newsboys comparing routes through the city, how to get from one dahia to the next as fast as possible, which alleys are good and which ones aren't, where to watch out for Palace guards. It's the sound of the part of the city that lives in shadows. To me, it's the sound of a city breathing. It's the sound of home. I don't know what the kids lounging by the wall of that empty building are saying, but I understand them completely.

There are maybe eight of them, if I'm guessing correctly at how many are cloaked by the shadows. The boy I followed is gone. These others all wear similar jackets, like a uniform. Some striped, some solid colors. Some of them wear bangles all up and down one wrist, while a few of the others are covered in nothing but sin-spots. Their pants billow, cinched at the ankles, and some of them have one pant leg bunched up their calves. Not all of them, and I wonder if it's a rank thing, like how high it is means you're the boss or something, but I don't see any order to it. All of them eye me but don't move a muscle. I can tell they are picking me apart in their heads. They're trying to figure me out—to see if I could be one of them. These must be the Onija that Juba warned me about. The ones who fight because they want to. I can see it in the cocky way they carry themselves. Anyone who fights inisisa for fun must contain a certain level of arrogance.

They dress so differently from the aki back home, but I know their look. I know why they're sizing me up like this. I know because I used to do it all the time to new aki. They'd come to us on their own, having been on the streets for a few weeks or maybe longer, foraging for food all by themselves, and I'd size them up to see if they had what it took to do our kind of work. Or Auntie Nawal or Auntie Sania would bring new orphans from the marayu and put them in our care when they'd outgrown the orphanage. And I'd do the same. Take their measure. I'd make sure they saw me do it too, because that was part of the test.

Hyenas growl from the shadows. Only after I hear them do I see their eyes glinting in the darkness. That same lightning pulses beneath their skin that I've seen in the other animals roaming the village.

I make sure to stand straight. The tallest Onija breaks away from the wall and chats with a few of the others. He moves like he's made of rubber, swaying and occasionally pawing at the dirt with the toes of his flats. And he's always grinning. I squint and realize I recognize him. He was at the fight where the small tastahlik almost got his stone cracked by that sin-bear.

One of them fishes a flask out from a belt at their waist and spins the top open. Instantly, I can tell where that smell came from earlier. It's whatever lahala they're drinking. I almost vomit. I want to block the stench with my hands, but I manage to keep my reaction to a flinch. Can't let them think I can't handle this sort of thing. It sends fire up my nose just being near it, but I'm not going to crack. They'll have to try harder than that.

"Eh, who is this olodo?"

I squint into the darkness, and out steps that tastahlik I saw fight in the street. He's still wearing the same torn shirt.

Dried blood spots it. And beneath the tears, white bandages are wrapped around his torso and chest. He's got a flask in his hand, and as he walks forward, he takes a couple of huge gulps.

"Eh-eh, what are you doing here?" He walks up, and because he's so short, he has to crane his neck to see me.

I make sure not to move at all.

He looks me up and down as he walks in a circle around me. "Abeo, who brought him here?" He raises an eyebrow at the tall one, the one who moves like wheat avoiding the scythe. The short one takes his place against the wall where he stood before. That stench from earlier almost overpowers me. The boy sways with it, moving like water in a glass. I start to get dizzy.

Abeo slings his arm around my neck. "Do not worry. This one"—he slaps me on the chest hard—"this one is strong. You saw how he beat that beast for you, Wale."

Wale glowers at Abeo, then at me. "Strong? He is not even able to stand the smell of stagga-juice. I bet he still only drinks his mother's milk."

I slip out of Abeo's grip, and before I know it, I have Wale pinned against the wall. His flask hangs limp in his hands. My face is so close, his hot breath wafts over me. My hands twist his shirt. I nearly lift him off his feet. "How about I make you eat that flask?"

Wale grins. Everyone is silent.

Then someone yanks me back, and I'm slammed against the wall and Wale is behind me, my arm twisted so high up my back I yelp.

How did he . . .

Anger rips through me. I flick my wrist and break out of his grasp, spin around and try to hit him with my elbow, but he catches it, and somehow I'm upside down in the air. I land hard on my back, staring up at the sky.

The crowd erupts in a cheer, and some of the older, taller tastahlik gather around Wale. One of them shoves a flask in his hands, and he takes three long gulps that look like they'll go on forever. Stagga-juice runs like a river down the side of his mouth, but he barely blinks. He finishes drinking and coughs, and I half imagine him breathing fire. The others roar and clap him on the back.

"I think that is a new record," says one of the female tastahlik, upside down from where I lie.

A hand appears in front of me. I look up and find myself staring into Abeo's face.

I grab his hand, and part of me tenses in the event that this is all some trick that's gonna land me on my backside yet again, but he pulls me all the way up, then starts patting the dust off my clothes.

"Not bad," Abeo murmurs, sounding very unimpressed. "I think that makes you two even."

Pain wraps around my torso. "What do you mean?"

"You interrupted his show."

"His show?"

Abeo steps back and looks over his handiwork like he never heard my question. Then he nods, satisfied. I've apparently been cleaned up enough.

The others peel off the wall and start slinking away in the same direction.

"Where are they going?" I ask him. It still hurts to say words.

"We're going to eat. Watching you two took a lot of energy out of us." He nudges me in the ribs with his elbow, almost sending me to my knees. Then he jogs off.

"Wait!"

He turns, running in place.

"What does 'olodo' mean?"

Abeo grins from cheek to cheek. "Olodo is 'one who owns zeroes.'" At the confusion on my face, he says, "One who only knows how to lose."

CHAPTER 16

MANY OF THE refugees have been moved out to rest in the camp on the outskirts of the village. But a few remain. My ribs are paining me, but I know it's best right now to walk off the fight—if I can even call it that. Which is how I wind up at the sick tent.

The little girl who was out in front of that crowd of refugees when they first got here, weapon in her hands, ready to cut me down, has the whole place to herself.

I sit down by her bed and watch her chest rise and fall with every breath. Sweat sheens her forehead. They've dressed her in a white gown made of light, coarse material to keep her cool.

She looks so small and sickly on that bed, and I wonder at all the things she's done to get here. What did she survive to make the journey? What did she have to fight? Or kill? I remember being a street child in Kos, having to lie and steal and fight until

Mages found me and put me to service Eating sins for a living. Where are her parents?

I know this feeling. It's the guilt—my own guilt—for not wanting to go back.

I remember Juba's words about tastahlik and Larada and how we're meant to pull blemish from souls, and I close my eyes and try to still my heart. My breathing slows. I put my hands to my chest and feel sin bubbling up my throat.

I open my mouth, and the inky sin jets out onto the ground. It takes the form of a small, sharp-taloned eagle. Sitting on my knees, I can see eye to eye with it. It flaps its wings a few times to hop back, then does a quick circuit in the air before landing in front of me again. We stare at each other. I can see the sin inside the inisisa. My selfishness. It moves in the rippling shadows of its feathers.

To Eat it would be nothing. But that's not what I need to do.

I close my eyes and empty my mind of thought. "I'm sorry," I whisper. My hand goes out to the eagle and touches its forehead, like I saw Juba do with the boy's sin.

Slowly at first, then with greater speed, its shadows peel away. As though it's being bathed in light.

When its true colors are revealed, its skin glows. Its feathers are on fire. I feel lighter.

A voice rings in my body, but it doesn't feel like a voice. I know someone—something—is speaking to me. It is touching my heart, poking and prodding and caressing it.

The Unnamed . . .

This is forgiveness. It is sin and guilt melting away.

"You did it," someone murmurs behind me.

I turn to see Aliya propped up on her staff, tired, her eyes barely managing to stay open. But she's looking at the eagle, returning its gaze.

My heart hammers in my chest. I gather myself, gulp a few heavy breaths, then try to go back to that place. I put my hand to the eagle's forehead and close my eyes.

I can feel it growing warmer. Warmer. Like light is pulsing beneath its skin. And I know it's only a matter of time before it turns into a flash of light like the inisisa that Juba cleansed. I try to hold my focus. I press my palm a little harder into its feathers.

I open my eyes to chance a glance, and the eagle still stands there in all its color, staring at me through my fingers.

It hops back, out of my grasp, and I nearly fall forward. I catch myself just in time; then, with a few flaps of its wings, the eagle darts out over my shoulder and past Aliya through the tent flap and out into the village sky.

I let out a breath. It's still there. It didn't turn to light. I didn't cleanse it.

I wanted to be a Healer. Juba always says the word "Larada" with such pride. I wanted to be part of that. That has to be why this hurts so much.

I am on my knees, staring at my hands, when Aliya kneels next to me. She's stiff getting to the floor, but eventually she settles and puts her staff to the side. She closes her eyes and leans her head on my shoulder.

"Taj?" she asks softly.

I steel myself, afraid she'll talk about Kos again. About duty and Balance and going back to fix things.

"Can I show you something?"

I nod.

She starts shaking and takes her head from my shoulder. I watch as she grips her trembling arm and closes her eyes and wills calmness into her body.

"Aliya," I say softly.

Scratches and marks cover her arms. When she sees me staring, she wraps them around herself, hiding them in the sleeves of her robe. "Come for a walk with me."

I smile. "I can do that."

The path begins at the edge of the village and winds through a low, sloping plain. Here, the rim of the bowl isn't so steep. It almost feels like I'm walking on a straight, level path, but eventually I turn around and see the village tiny and quiet beneath us. Aliya leads the way, making slow but steady progress with her cane. After a while, grass replaces the dirt. I look around. I've never seen this before. The line between desert and greenery is so stark that when we reach it, I step back and forth over it a couple of times to make sure it's real. But as I continue, the green deepens and spreads out in all directions.

Up ahead, not far away, is a small shack. It looks like it was made from stuff that doesn't come from this land. The buildings in the village are largely mud and stone with some wood, while the structure before me is some melded combination of wood and brick. It's a simple house with a shingled roof and a path leading up to it lined with flowers. They sprout in bunches, carefully arranged clumps of gold and light purple and red. Everything about this house and the land it sits on feels impossible.

We get to the entrance, and just as Aliya reaches for the doorknob, I put my hand on hers.

"Whose house is this?" I ask her. "What are we doing here?"

"Trust me." Aliya pushes open the front door, and I follow her in.

The place is sparsely furnished. A chair or two made out of wood, a desk, and that's about it. Books form a pyramid against one wall. On the desk is a stack of parchment; some of the papers have fallen to the floor. I don't have a daga with me, or any weapon, really. But I try to keep as much of the room in my line of sight as possible. My ribs still throb from the way Wale cracked me.

Aliya leads me through the living room to a smaller room, what looks like a study, then hunches over a desk, digging through cabinets.

"Aliya. What are you doing? This is someone's stuff."

"Exactly!" she says, turning to me. She points to the books rolled and stacked on top of one another on shelves that line the room. Then she gestures at the books on the floor, a few of them unrolled, the text disjointed and nonsensical. "These are someone's things. And they were here recently!" She grabs one of the books from the desk and thrusts it toward me. "Look. Equations."

I put the thing to my eye and twist it. The same gibberish that Aliya's always talking about. Algorithms and proofs. Numbers and letters, all lahala to me.

"This is the work of a Mage. A kanselo."

Suddenly, I understand what Aliya's getting at. "We don't know that it is. Juba says they do equations and all of that other stuff here too. It's one of their languages." I look around at the mess she's made. "Have you been here before?" She doesn't answer. "Have you been taking things from here?"

"At first, I only found this place because I needed to practice walking. My . . . my illness has made it hard sometimes. While you were off doing whatever it is you were doing, I found this place and saw these advanced equations, and so I brought them back to our room."

"Aliya, you're stealing from our hosts."

"Whoever this Mage is, they do not belong to this tribe!" She shouts loudly enough that it shuts me up. "They're from Kos. Taj . . . Arzu's father was a Mage."

"And you think this is his place? All the way out here? Where no one can find him?"

"Where no one can bother him."

"Sounds a lot like you." I snort.

I look around at the room. So many pieces point to Aliya being right. "We can't tell Arzu about this . . . not yet."

"Why not?"

In my mind's eye, I see Arzu's face when she looks at Juba and the way her face glows even more brightly when Juba looks back. I see how happy and content Arzu is to be here. To be home. Why would I disturb that lake? I struggle to figure out a way to tell Aliya what it's like to hope for something, to wish for it with all your heart, then to realize the dream will never become reality. What has she ever lost? "Let's just figure out what this is first." I turn toward the desk and reach for the parchment. Hurt shoots through my ribs, and I nearly double over. That fight took more out of me than I thought. Aliya shoots me a questioning look. And now it's my turn to say, "I'm fine," and wave her away in completely unconvincing fashion. "Let's just not steal anything this time."

We get outside and close the door behind us, and I sense Abeo before I see him. I turn, and he peels himself from the shadows in front of the building. Hands in his pants pockets, he sways back and forth like he's been drinking stagga.

"Eh! Taj, you did not tell me you had a heart-mate. Chai!" He circles us, leering at Aliya, and I want to crack him across the jaw for it. He must have been listening. How else could he have learned my name? "Come on, gal. Tell me your name."

Aliya stares at him, then glances at me.

Abeo snorts a laugh. "They don't let me be a part of the welcoming committee, and for the life of me, I do not know why."

"Abeo, this is Aliya. Friend. Not heart-mate," I say.

"Pleasure to meet you," Aliya says, but I can tell by her eyes that she's lying.

"The pleasure is mine! Anyway, I should be going." He turns and heads back down to the village. "Taj!" he calls over his shoulder. "When your *friend* gives you permission, come eat with us."

Aliya waits until he's out of earshot before nudging me. In the ribs. "Taj, who was that?"

"Abeo. He's . . ." I struggle for breath. "He's Onija." I straighten, then shuffle forward. Aliya opens her mouth to say something, but I cut her off. "I'm heading back. Are you going to stay here awhile?"

"Yes," she says, "just a little longer."

"OK. Be careful."

As I head back into the village, I wonder if Abeo ever tried to be a Healer. If he ever had a moment when he tried to cleanse an inisisa, turn it into a beast made of light, and opened his eyes to see the thing, his failure, staring right back at him. I wonder if he has inside him the same anger I realize I'm always carrying around. Anger I can't seem to let go of. I wonder if the fighting, the battles—or "shows," as they call them—help with that. It'd sure be nice to find something I had permission to hit.

When I look behind me, I don't see Aliya. Part of me worries for her. In her condition, she can't defend herself. But another part of me is relieved. Without her around to remind me of the past, of Kos, I don't feel frustration crawling like a swarm of ants under my skin. I don't feel guilt.

So I don't feel bad trailing behind Abeo, following him to where the fighters hang out.

CHAPTER 17

BY THE TIME I find my way to where little Wale stretched me out, the sun is on its way down. It's quiet here. A few animals slink through alleyways, but no one seems to live here anymore. After a little bit of wandering, I hear chatter. And laughter.

In this part of the village, there are more shadows. The place where everyone has gathered has a beaded curtain, and I can't see what's inside until I walk through. It takes my eyes some time to adjust. I hear them before I see them, and then there they are, lounging in a far corner of the room on cushions with plates of fruit and bowls of chin-chin spread out among them. They have that same pretend-laziness about them, their feet up on cushions stacked high or spread out along the floor. I see Wale there, laughing with some of the others at a story someone's telling.

Abeo notices me. "Eh! Boys, I think he sniffed his way here."

One of the others, with some gray braids threaded through otherwise black hair, barks out a laugh. "Abeo, is his nose still working after having to breathe Wale's air? Or did it get broken in the fight?"

"My nose is working just fine," I tell them.

They pause for a second, then burst out laughing, and Abeo beckons for me to join them. When I find a space, he hands me a bowl of diced melon. "You'll begin with soft food," he says. "Wale hit you pretty hard." He looks at the Onija with gray mixed into his black hair. "Ignore Lanre. He never learned proper manners."

I have to take my time sitting down. My ribs are still on fire. I let out a sigh when I settle, then take a few melon slices from the bowl and pop them into my mouth. The juiciness provides such relief that, out of instinct, I close my eyes. It feels like what I imagine eating that first date after a day of fasting must feel like.

"Ah-ah!" shouts Abeo. "Are you making love to the melon or what?"

The others holler, rolling on their backs or their sides.

"My side is paining me-oh!" cries one of the tastahlik, tears in her eyes from laughter.

"Easy, Folami!" Lanre shouts. "Before you knock over our dishes!"

I suddenly feel a pang of homesickness. A wave of of guilt washes over me, and I swallow hard, forcing the lump in my throat away.

I sit back and pick up more melon pieces, then grab some chin-chin from other bowls as I listen to them talk about the

village and about life and joke about every old thing. Their bra-
vado, their cockiness, the way they always seem ready to strike,
even as they lounge and make themselves comfortable . . .

It's like sitting in a circle full of other Tajs.

This is not what I expected when Juba first told me of the
tastahlik and how they had to separate themselves from family.
Or when she seemed to warn me away from the Onija like they
were the wrong kind of sin-eaters.

"You look confused," Abeo says.

"I just . . ." I shake my head. "When Juba told me about you,
about the Onija, well, this isn't what I pictured."

Abeo looks around and laughs. "What do you mean?"

"I don't know. I thought you would be maybe different.
More serious, I guess."

Abeo arches an eyebrow at me. "There are some tastahlik
here and in other tribes out west like that. They frown all the
time, and sometimes they even live apart from their communi-
ties. When their tribes migrate, they remain in their own separate
caravan. But not all tastahlik are like that. For some of us, we
like to have fun. Life is too short. And when you can do what
we do, it gets even shorter."

"And so you fight inisisa for fun?" The idea sounds even
more absurd when I say it out loud.

"We control them too, so it never gets out of hand." He
shrugs. "In the end, we get to decide when and how it ends.
But it gets boring if you're just walking around, calling sins and
Eating sins and calling sins and Eating sins." He smiles so wide
it splits his face. "Anything can be a sport if you let it."

It sounds ridiculous, but I can already feel myself getting tugged toward it. I'm intrigued. "And you use dagas?"

"We use all sorts of things." He pushes himself to his feet. "Here, come with me. I'll show you."

The others watch as Abeo leads me down a corridor at the back of the room, then down a flight of stone stairs.

"Careful. Even in the day, there are no lights down here. But eventually, you'll walk up and down these steps so many times, you will do it with your eyes closed."

Our footsteps get louder and louder the deeper we go, then I hear the creak of a door opening.

We're in complete darkness. I can't even tell shapes apart. "Where are we?"

"The weapons room." Abeo stands by the door. "Go on. Your eyes will adjust. This is where we keep everything."

I walk in and can hear metal and stone rattling softly together. Almost as though blown by a wind. The door shuts behind me.

I shuffle forward. The rattling sounds again.

But how? There's no wind.

"Abeo?" I hiss. "Abeo?" Then, louder, "Abeo!" I rush to where I remember the door to be and feel around for a handle or a knob. Anything! But nothing. Just solid wood. I slam against it as I hear a long growl from behind me. "Abeo! Open the door!" Nothing. "This is not funny!"

The growl gets louder.

By the Unnamed, he's trapped me here with a sin-beast.

CHAPTER 18

THE INISISA GROWLS behind me. I whirl around and curse the darkness. I have no way of telling what it is or how big. How many arms it has, how many claws on each hand, whether or not it has a tail. I don't even know how big the room is. Its growl gets louder, then it pauses, and I can hear it sniffing. Slowly, I edge along the wall with the door, so maybe I can tell just how wide it is. The floor is cold underneath my feet. My hands touch something cold and smooth running along the walls—metal. It makes a rattling, shimmering sound as I brush by it. Then I hear wood bounce against the stones as well, and I think of Wale's staff and remember that this is the weapons room.

A rush of wind signals the beast's attack, and I dive to the floor. I feel the bottom of the sin-beast glide over me as I roll forward. It bangs into the door, and I come to my feet, backing up quickly so that I can see how far the room extends the other way.

The sin-beast turns. I hear scraping along the stone floor. Claws? A tail? Then clicking as it steps forward. Definitely claws.

It lunges, and I jump to the side. The impact from the wall jars me. Metal edges prick me under my shirt. I fumble about to try to get something off the walls and meet only chains. Before I can pull a weapon loose, something swings for me, and I get my arm up just in time to shield my face from what I guess is the beast's paw. It hurls me across the room. I land with a thud. When I try to get to my feet, pain knifes through my stomach, and I collapse. I never properly healed from the fight with Wale.

My eyes start to adjust slightly, and I see the shape of something swing for me—another paw. I duck just in time, then try to scramble out of the way and brush by one of the thing's legs. It swipes at me again, catching me right in my back and slamming me into the wall. Sharp edges dig into my skin. I hang for a second before tearing myself away. I can't see it, but I can feel blood trickling down the front of my shirt. I'm not fast enough to beat this thing. I grab at the wall again, trying to pull something loose, and then I feel the whole of the sin-beast ram into me. It throws me off my feet, and when I land on the ground, it lands on top of me. In my hands is a tangle of chains. Both forepaws are crushing my chest, and I struggle for breath. The thing's tail flails from wall to wall, banging against the weapons and sending some clattering to the floor. Its face leans in, gets closer and closer to mine. I still can't breathe. My head feels like it's about to explode. I'm starting to get dizzy. My arms refuse to move.

It's going to eat me.

Just as its jaws are about to snap on my neck, I raise an arm to catch it and scream in pain. It burns where I've been bit. Tears leak down my face. It shakes its head with my arm clasped in its teeth. My arm's starting to go numb. With all my strength I lift one leg and kick the beast hard in the chest. It stumbles back, and I break free. I clutch the chains in both hands and throw them over its head so that they loop a couple of times, then I squeeze with all my might. I try to inch my fingers up. My heart pounds. I'm losing energy.

Blood leaks from my mouth, and my arm is wet and shiny with it. I can't reach the beast's face to try to control it, so I hold the chains fast and pull, even as the inisisa leans on me and presses down on its paws. Circles of light, like coins, pop up in front of my eyes.

But I pull and pull and pull until I hear a snap, then the whole animal goes limp and falls on me.

I can't move. I have my breath back, but I can't move.

For a while, I'm completely still. I'm covered in sweat and blood. The inisisa dissolves into a puddle that pools at my sides. I close my eyes and await the sin, and, compared to the fight, Eating is like drinking milk and eating chin-chin.

I try to roll to my side, because I know I won't be able to get up all at once. I come to one knee, and I'm huffing so loud I can hear the wheezing in my chest. Pretty sure at least a few important things are broken.

I don't care that I'm near to death. I'm going to find enough energy in me to kill Abeo twice.

Light spills into the room. I didn't even hear the door creak open.

There's someone standing the doorway, holding a lamp.

I drag myself across the ground and don't even realize I'm still holding the chains until I hear them scraping against the floor. There's a strange sound coming through, muffled, which makes me wonder if maybe something in my ear is damaged. I get closer. My vision is blurring.

I see a single figure standing in the doorway. Tall, hands moving together. It's Abeo. And that ruby-licker is clapping.

I'm wrapped in so many bandages when I wake up that it's a wonder I can move at all. I'm happy to be alive, but everything hurts, and I just want to close my eyes again. I remember everything clearly: the fight, the fear, the way my body moved anyway, all instinct and with no thought, and then pride swells in my chest at the memory of me snapping the thing's neck. Looking back, even though my mind was empty of all conscious thought, emotions rioted inside me. As I lie here, it's like I'm also looking down on myself from the ceiling, and I can see through my own chest, my own skin and bones, to watch feelings swirl around in me: heart-racing fear, anger at the inisisa, fury at Abeo, satisfaction at winning, and residual guilt at the sin I had to consume after the fight. I know the guilt isn't mine; it belongs to whoever spawned that sin. But it hasn't gotten easier to stuff down.

I glance out of the corner of my eye, and Juba is sitting at my bedside. I look just past her to see Arzu, arms folded, standing near the entrance. She's glowering at me. Juba's expression is a bit kinder. But there's still steel in it.

"The Onija did this to you," Juba says, looking me over.

She's not wrong. Abeo did trap me in a room with a murderous sin-beast he said he could control, and he did let it almost kill me. But I want to tell her about sitting with the Onija and eating melons and chin-chin and how we laughed and joked and how, for the first time since I got here, I felt like I'd found my people. But I realize, just as I'm about to say those things, that they would only anger her. So, I turn my gaze up at the ceiling. Masks hang from it. Masks with inisisa carved into the wood. Masks painted with stripes of color, blue and red. Masks no one ever seems to wear.

"They have disgraced our tribe."

I look over, and she is trembling with fury. I don't know what to say.

"Treating a guest, a refugee, like this when he is only seeking shelter."

"It was supposed to be a game," I tell her.

"You nearly died!" Arzu shouts. She breaks away from the wall but still stands half a dozen paces from the bed. "It took several Larada to attend to you. Taj, how could you?"

She's prepared to say more, but Juba raises a hand to stop her. Her fury has turned cold. Juba stands to her full height. A part of me worries that I will be the one punished for this. But, instead, she says, "It is decided then. I've let this pass for far too long. Fighting is to be banned. There will be no more Onija. In this tribe, you are either Larada or nothing."

I have broken something here. I just wanted to find someplace where I felt I belonged, and now I feel I've done something that can't be fixed.

Juba turns to Arzu. "The Elders will hold an emergency council tomorrow where I will make the announcement." She spares me one last look. "I will not let this happen again." She waits at the entrance, then turns to face me again. "Your friend, the scholar. She is precious to you. Sometimes, when we lose something dear, we are fortunate enough to get it back." She looks to Arzu, who looks back wordlessly. Thankful. "But sometimes that is not Olurun's will. And sometimes when we lose something precious, when we are halved, we are never restored." She faces me fully. "Your friend is ill, and I do not know if it is an illness one survives. Concern yourself with that, not this . . . lahala, as you call it." Then she's off, her robe flowing behind her. Arzu glares at me one last time before following her out.

CHAPTER 19

I BARELY SLEEP in the hours that follow, the pain is so intense. But eventually, I am able to move my arms and get my legs to work. Getting out of bed, I nearly fall on my face but catch myself at the last minute on a stool. A few heavy breaths later and I'm upright. If I breathe just right, the pain becomes bearable. Soft breathing allows me to make it all the way to the tent's entrance. I need to find Aliya.

A few animals stir in the early part of the day. The sun's not yet high enough to chase them into the shadows. But no one's out yet. My footsteps are the only sound I hear. Then, in an alley between two abandoned huts, I see movement. Two people.

Something glints in the darkness. Coins.

I press up against a wall so that if I crane my neck around the corner, I can spy them.

"That was a big one." That voice—Abeo. "What did you do to give me such a big beast, eh? Steal from your mother? Hit your sister?" He chuckles. More coins jingle. "What will you buy when the next caravan comes?"

"I don't remember." It's a child's voice. I can hear the smallness in it.

"Well, then. Don't spend it all at once." Then another chuckle from Abeo. I peek out from behind the wall and see Abeo whisper something else in the child's ear. I get out of the way just as the child darts out of the alleyway and races past me. Ash dots his ragged shirt. He runs barefoot into the maze of huts and is gone.

I watch him run.

The kid is no taller than Omar was when I first found him. Alone at the top of a ridge, no flats for his feet, face covered in snot, his shirt little more than rags as he watched us bury an aki. He became our little brother so quickly. I remember his Daga Day, when we gifted him with his own proper weapon and stood in a circle and cheered for him while Sade carried him on her shoulders.

I'm pulled out of my thoughts when a heavy hand falls on my shoulder.

"Eh-heh, so the warrior awakens." Abeo's grinning his traditional face-splitting grin.

I shake off his hand and take a step back. "You tried to have me killed," I tell him, trying to maintain enough calm to sound deadly. "I ought to slice your throat right here for that."

Abeo looks me over, gaze staying a bit longer on my bandaged forearm. It looks like he winces, but that could just be my eyes tricking me. If I tried to fight him now, he could easily kill me. And he knows this. "Well, we had to see. You can fight one of us, but how well can you fight a sin-beast?" He leans toward me. "We have a tournament coming soon. And I have addressed my committee. They would like to see you fight for us."

My body's screaming at me. Between Wale and the ini-sisa, I don't know how much more it can take. And lately it seems like all I'm doing is fighting. Wait, does he know that Juba will soon meet with the Elders? Instinct moves me to warn him, but I keep my mouth shut. This is tribe business. Not *my* business.

"You do not have to decide now. But there will be many pretty girls from the refugee camp watching." But he's stand-ing there with his hands on his hips like he's waiting for a yes or a no at this very moment. When I don't give him one, Abeo smirks, then stretches his back so that it cracks loudly, and lets out a yawn. "You miss it, don't you? The fighting. The Eating."

I look down, refusing to answer.

"You know what you are." He leans in close and whispers his words in my ear. "Even as they try to make you into something you are not." He snickers. "I know what we are. Juba thinks we are one way, but really we are the other way." Then he walks off.

I stand there for a while longer, wishing he were wrong. The village starts to stir awake. I look back down the alley. The shadows have stilled. But I swear I can hear something in there growling at me. The urge rises in me to fight it. But I tamp it down. This was the sin-lust the Aunties used to tell me about when I was a little aki in the marayu. You fight until you know nothing more than fighting, then you start to seek it out until it consumes you.

My thoughts are such a jumble in my head that I don't even notice Aliya until she's practically on top of me.

"Taj! Taj!" She waves her staff at me. Her skin has paled, become almost see-through.

"Aliya, what's happening to y—"

"Taj! Come! Come now!" She grabs my arm and yanks me along, plowing forward with her staff. Her limp has gotten worse, but she doesn't slow down.

"Where are we going?" I manage to say behind gritted teeth. I realize now that it's too soon for me to be running.

"To the house! There's something I have to show you." Her words trip over themselves coming out of her mouth.

"Aliya, slow down. Please."

She stops and stares straight through me. "Taj, this is important."

And I don't know why, but the way that she says it is enough to shut me up all the way to the house on the hill.

"Taj, I think I know what all this is." She's standing in the study amid a graveyard of unrolled books. She gestures around. "It all makes sense now. It's Iragide. The art of binding."

"Aliya," I say, keeping my voice gentle. "When is the last time you slept?"

She looks at me like I've just asked her if she's a lizard. "Taj, don't you understand? This is a Mage's work. Whoever was here, that was what they were doing. Taj, it's the secret!"

"Aliya, the secret to what?"

"To saving Kos!"

For a moment, I'm silent. Anger and sorrow battle inside me. Every time I see her, she looks less and less well.

"Taj! Whoever this is is looking for the Ratio!"

That makes me pause. The Ratio. The same piece of knowledge Karima is searching for. The key to controlling everything. But . . . what is it doing here? Questions buzz inside my head. I stalk past her.

"Taj! Wait! He's still alive!"

I stop at the door. "What?" I turn, and she's standing there with a new look in her eyes. Pleading.

"Arzu's father. He's still alive. And he's planning something." She reaches out to me. "This isn't an abandoned home," she says quietly. "Somebody didn't just leave all these books here." She picks some of them up from the floor. "Some of these are old, but some of them are new. The ink is fresh."

"If they were a Mage, why wouldn't they just study this... Iragide in the Great House of Ideas? Back in Kos?" I can't believe I'm even entertaining this lahala, but there's an earnestness in Aliya's gaze that I can't break away from. And even though I can't understand what's happening to her, what sickness is taking over her, I know her better than anyone else here. She trusts me.

"Because it's forbidden. Remember? It was the power the Seventh Prophet could wield. Before he became too powerful. Taj, if someone else was learning how to do what Ka Chike could do . . ." Her eyes widen, and as soon as the thought crosses her mind, it hits me. Whoever learned how to do what Ka Chike could do . . . they'd rule Kos.

"He would be in very big trouble."

The voice comes from behind me. I whirl around. In steps a man so large he towers over us. He has a silver beard folded into a long, single braid. Like the other Mages, his eyes have no color. They are like the shedded skin of a snake. He holds a longstaff tight in his hands like a weapon.

I turn to Aliya, and joy glows on her face. Then I turn back to the man whose frame fills the entire doorway. A small smile curls on his lips.

"So, you are the one everyone's been making such a fuss over." His voice is soft, barely audible. He sticks his hand out, palm up. When was the last time anyone greeted me that way? "My name is Zaki."

I slide my palm over his. "Taj," I say slowly.

"To you and yours, Taj."

"To you and yours, Mage."

He takes his hand away and lets out a sigh. Then his eyebrows crease in a frown. "Now, clean this mess before I pafuka your heads!"

After Zaki makes sure every inch of his home is spotless, he bangs around in the kitchen, splashing spices and fresh herbs from his garden into a boiling pot. Aliya and I wait in the living room. We each have rugs to sit on, and I know a good meal awaits us. I can smell it. In fact, the house is so small that I'm sure half the village can smell it.

Zaki returns with bowls of steaming egusi soup and a plate piled high with fufu. "I am not used to cooking for more than myself, so please forgive me if I've misjudged the portions. I fear I may have cooked too much."

The entire time, Aliya cannot take her eyes off him. Like she's still not sure he's really there. I half expect her to reach out and try to touch the hem of his robe.

Zaki closes his eyes and murmurs a quick blessing over the food before scooping out his first ball of fufu. I follow suit, minus the prayer.

"There's no such thing as too much fufu and egusi," I say, testing the waters. I'm not sure where I stand with this man. His face remains stoic, and it's unclear what he thinks of me. I have no idea what he thinks of Kos or how much he knows of what's been happening. So, of course, I have to joke.

There's an uncomfortable beat of silence before Zaki bellows with laughter. Aliya smiles while she tries to wipe bits of fufu from her mouth with her wrist.

I make a ball of fufu in my palm, scoop up some soup, then stuff the ball in my mouth. It's delicious. "So," I say after the slick ball of fufu slides down my throat, "are you Arzu's father?"

Aliya elbows me so hard I almost choke on my food. I look at her as though to say, *Why waste time?* She'll thank me later.

Half a minute passes before Zaki smiles. "Yes, I am." He takes another long pause, looking down at his staff. "I met her mother one day in the Forum. She had found work as a merchant, and I do not know why or how, but the very first time I saw her, I was struck by her. No, not struck. I was decapitated." He smiles. "She was the most beautiful person I'd seen in my entire life. And so different from me. She came from outside of Kos. It was like the world I'd spent my life studying in the Ulo Amamihe, the Great House of Ideas, had come to life before me. To be nearer to her, I arranged for her to work in the Palace. A servant's position was the best I could get her without arousing too much suspicion. Arzu was born just under a year later."

I frown at him. "She doesn't know you're here, does she?"

He shakes his head. "I'd been in communication with Mages in Kos after my expulsion, and I'd heard of a young, gifted Mage who could solve proofs far beyond her years." He looks at Aliya, who beams. "We'd been plotting rebellion for years, but our intention was to overthrow King Kolade and his chief Mage, Izu. Then I learned of what Karima had done, and that threw our plans into ruin."

"So, what is all this, then?" I ask, gesturing at the books and the parchment now neatly arranged on desks and shelves around his house. I know I sound like an interrogator, but a part of me can't quite square with the fact that this man hasn't yet greeted his daughter, who believes him dead. I try to imagine what it would be like if I saw Mama and Baba again. If I knew for certain that they had survived Queen Karima's reign, that they were still alive in the prison she has made of Kos, I would want to know.

"Iragide," Zaki says at last. "The secret to control. It is how you control the inisisa. It is how you can mold them into new weapons." He looks to Aliya. "And it is how Karima controls the arashi."

"What?" I drop the ball of fufu I'd just scooped onto the floor.

Zaki nods. "That's right. She can control the arashi. They hover over the dahia, shrouding the entire city in permanent darkness. She has not yet learned how to send them far. She cannot reach us here. But the algebraists and Mages are hard at work trying to figure out how."

"How do you know all of this?"

"The rebels have informed me of these things."

"And is that what you've been doing all this time?" I turn to Aliya. "What *you've* been trying to figure out? With all that scribbling?"

This time, it's Aliya's turn to speak. "Solving for the Ratio is the key. It is what connects the living to Infinity. It is also what binds us together. So far, our understanding has been incomplete, but the Ratio unlocks the ability to control."

"It's just a number," I scoff.

Zaki points at me. "It is written in the world around us. In fact, it is written on your very skin."

Startled, I scan my arms and the backs of my hands, feel my neck. "My sin-spots?"

Zaki squints. "Did you think they appeared at random? There is order to how they are written onto your body."

I remember what Aliya said to me that first time we'd met at Zoe's. She'd been the first person to look at me not as something to step over but as something to gaze at in wonder. She said she'd seen poems on my arms. Equations.

"Like these?" Aliya says, her voice small. She rolls up the sleeves of her robes. The bruises on her arms have faded, revealing what I realize are letters and numbers. I almost choke. Aliya has the look in her eyes of someone who's grown used to carrying pain in silence.

"Who did that to you?" I ask. My voice is faint.

"The Unnamed," she says with a smile, letting her sleeves fall back down over her arms.

Hurt grips my heart. I can't bear to watch this happen to her. Whatever it is, it's surely killing her. All this talk of the Ratio and saving Kos and the rebellion and Iragide. I can't take it anymore.

I jump to my feet.

Aliya scrambles up. "Taj, where are you going?"

"Out," I say. And before she can say another word, I hurry outside. It's dark. We've been at Zaki's for hours. But in the distance, on the other side of the village, I see lights. Torchlight. And I hear the hazy hum of music. Someone is drumming. Others are cheering. There's a fight going on.

As fast as my legs will carry me, I run in that direction.

CHAPTER 20

SPECTATORS RING THE open-air pit on the outskirts of the village. The refugee camp lies in the distance, starting to turn into its own little town. People here shout out numbers, and pouches of coins trade hands. So much noise in the crowd. And everywhere I walk, the smell of stagga-juice makes me want to retch. Aliya finds me here, over the lip of the ridge surrounding the village. I worry Aliya's going to bring up Zaki or the Ratio or Kos, but she remains silent and simply stands close to me and watches the pit. She doesn't even look like she's casting judgment on the Onija who must be getting ready to fight. But she doesn't look like she's all right with all of this either. Even I feel uneasy. Eating is not supposed to be like this, I know, but still, I can't shake the sense of excitement in my belly.

Standing not far from us, surrounded by a group of tastahlik, is Abeo. He doesn't look my way, but I know he sees me. And it looks like it makes him happy. He has this intensity in his eyes, even when he's laughing or smiling, like he is the type of man whose brain is always turned on.

I recognize one of the girls—Folami—from that day with the Onija. She breaks away from the group, holding her jointed staff in one fist.

"Eh-heh!" Abeo cries out. "A true champion steps forward." He lounges on a small boulder. "How many for you tonight?"

She raises four fingers, and several in the crowd gasp.

I catch her smile over her shoulder before she jumps into the pit, landing softly on her feet.

There's no expression on her face. When she comes to her full height in the pit, she doesn't even glance up at the crowd. I can tell from the way she stands that her body is loose. There's no tension in her. Maybe her mind is already empty.

No emotion registers on her face, even as three inisisa—a sin-bear, a lynx, and a wolf—leap over the edge of the pit and land with a thud, raising a massive cloud of dust. As they spread out to circle her, she jumps into her fighting stance, feet spread apart, both hands gripping her staff. A griffin hovers overhead, flapping its wings, preparing to make its descent.

We all wait. No one claps any rhythm. We're all too rapt. How can anyone fight four inisisa at once?

The sin-bear in front of her charges first. She flips her staff so that one end digs into the dirt. Using it as leverage, she leaps into the air, sailing right over the bear. She lands on her feet and swings her staff around so that the blades whistle through the air. She catches the handle with her free hand and glides to a stop. We all let out a gasp. Now all the beasts are in front of her.

The griffin swoops down at the same time that the sin-wolf to her left runs forward, and she steps to the side like she's dancing, swinging one blade to catch the wolf in the nape of its neck, then swinging up with the other arm and cutting straight through the griffin's jaw. It flaps furiously, trying to fly to safety, but collapses. As it writhes at her feet, she brings her blade down on its neck, killing it.

The lynx leaps at her back, and she spins, the free end of her jointed staff slicing straight through the thing's flank mid-flight. It falls in two halves far away from her. It didn't stand a chance.

Then, standing tall, she turns to face the bear. They stand at opposite ends of the pit and eye each other in silence. Then the bear sets off, and Folami runs straight toward it. She flips her blade over her so that it sticks in the ground again, and that's when I notice the hook on the front of her blade, like half a hilt. She hops onto it, then springs forward, the blade flipping over her again. With her hand to the blade's back, she meets the bear, the blade digging into its shoulder. Using her momentum, she pushes the blade even farther with her hand. It tears the sin-beast apart, and the beast separates into two wispy shadows of blackness. Folami walks to it slowly and stands over the larger half of the bear, which squirms in the dirt. With one swipe, she severs its head from its body, and a cheer goes up from the crowd, louder than anything I think I've ever heard. I can feel it in my bones.

I stare at Folami in shock and awe and wonderment. She's barely broken a sweat. She doesn't even breathe heavily. And she just killed four inisisa in less than fifteen minutes.

The inisisa dissolve and gather in a single pool at her feet, then the ink springs into the air, and she opens her mouth. The thick combination of sins jumps down her throat, and I watch, waiting for pain to flicker across her face at having to consume so many sins at once. But . . . nothing.

I turn and see Abeo on his boulder. He's holding his dagas and smiling. He leans back and begins tying them to his feet so that the blades stick out past his toes. Then he hops off the boulder.

"Wale!" Abeo calls out.

Wale scurries forward with his staff behind him.

"Wale, tie my hands behind my back." He grins at the crowd, chest puffed up. Then he sees me and winks. "That's right. I'm going to fight these inisisa with my hands tied behind my back."

He backflips over the edge of the pit and lands in a crouch. Several sin-hyenas break away from the group of Onija and jump down to join him.

At first, they charge, and he bats them away with his bladed feet. Kicks one across the mouth, then another. All the while, his arms remain behind his back.

One rushes forward, he kicks up, and while it hangs in the air, he spins and slices it once, twice, three times before landing on the ground. The hyena falls apart in the air and dissolves before it even touches the dirt.

People start throwing their stagga-juice flasks in the air and clapping. Abeo grins for the crowd and does a little dance on the ground, spraying dust everywhere. Some of the girls in the tribe giggle at him, and he winks back.

One of the hyenas tries to take Abeo from behind, but he flicks one foot out, hooks the hyena by the jaw, and flings it into the remaining hyena. Then, he runs forward, leaps into the air, and smashes his feet onto the tangle of sin-hyenas, twisting so that the blades cut into their necks.

The hyenas begin to dissolve, then one of them rears, knocking Abeo back. It growls at him, then turns back and scrabbles up the wall.

The crowd parts in a rush, and the sin-beast makes a straight line for me. I reach for my daga out of instinct, but there's nothing there. This thing is fast enough that if I ran, it would chase me down almost instantly.

"Aliya," I hiss. "Get ready to run into the crowd. I'll distract it."

I square up, ready to fight, when suddenly something dashes in front of me, kicking up dust.

When the dust clears, Juba stands with her back to me, in a fighting stance, her staff piercing the hyena's jaw.

They're frozen like that for a moment, Juba and the hyena, before Juba flicks her staff back and forth, and the sin-hyena's head comes apart. She Eats the sin, no problem. By the time it's done, Abeo has climbed back up the edge of the pit.

"You smell too good for the inisisa to pass up," Abeo bellows, but I hear the nervousness in it. "If you can stink a little more, then maybe they won't be drawn to you." The others join him in laughter, but I keep my eyes on him.

He goes to stand with the crowd of Onija, and the air around them has shifted. They hold their weapons more tightly. Their stances have widened.

Juba now stands at her full height next to me. I look back over my shoulder, and I see the Larada arrayed behind me. Stern faces, arms bared. Tensed.

I find myself leaning onto the balls of my feet, fists ready. *Just tell me who to hit.* Someone puts a hand to my arm. It's Aliya. Even now, she's strong enough to hold me back with just a touch.

"This ends tonight," Juba growls.

"Ayaba," Abeo croons, smiling, "my queen, what law have we broken?"

"This practice cannot be permitted to continue!" Juba shouts, and it comes out as a roar. Out of nowhere, cleansed inisisa appear before her. A row of hyenas and forest cats and lizards as large as some of the children and spiders as tall as she is. I realize with a start that these are some of the animals I've seen roaming the camp. The cleansed sins. They stand in a menacing row, protecting her. When the beasts crowd her, her sin-spots begin to glow. Soon, all the other Larada shine too, so that it looks like a wall of light has risen at Juba's back. Arzu stands at Juba's side, her knives at the ready.

Abeo falters.

"It shall be hereby decreed that all tastahlik must submit themselves as Larada and must train to become such. Eating sin is not a game. Sin-beasts are not playthings." Her voice carries over the entire land. I'm sure even those in the faraway refugee camp can hear it. As she speaks, the clouds swirl above her head.

"Taj." Aliya's voice is weak at my ear. "Taj."

I turn to face her, and all color has drained from her face. She leans on me, and I struggle under her weight. "Aliya, what's wrong?"

"Taj," she murmurs. Her eyes droop closed, then shoot open again, like she is trying to keep from falling asleep. She gulps. "Taj, it's . . ."

Thunder crackles overhead.

The crowd stirs. All is silent. The villagers feel it too. Something in the air has changed. Suddenly, Aliya seizes. Her neck snaps itself straight, her gaze fixed on the sky, arms bent stiff at her sides. She convulses and collapses to the ground, limbs thrashing, hurling sand everywhere.

Before I know what I'm doing, I'm on my knees, holding Aliya in my arms. Her eyes are fixed on the stars in the sky like she's trying to see straight through them. Suddenly, she goes still.

"Aliya." I shake her. "Aliya, say something." My heart's like a lizard in my chest, bouncing all over the place. Her eyes glaze over. She looks like she's Crossing. "Somebody! Somebody, help! Please!"

She says something in a language I don't understand. It comes out with the rest of a massive breath she's been holding in her chest.

"Aliya, what are you saying?"

More babbling, like what Mages say when they call forth a sin.

Older tastahlik run at us from the desert expanse. The Sentinels.

Behind us, in the distance, the village stirs awake. People leave their homes to see what is going on. They crane their necks toward the rim of the bowl. The streets are full. All eyes on the sky.

I'm shaking Aliya so hard I worry I'll break something precious in her, but I want it all to stop. More words spill out of her mouth. Thunder booms nearby. What is happening?

Clouds form and swirl in the sky above the village. They grow thicker, rumbling with thunder and lightning, and I hear it. Faint whispers. Like inyo in a Baptized dahia. I feel them swimming around me. The left-behind sin-heavy souls of the dead. Lightning forks down onto the refugee camp, striking a roof, setting it on fire. A hole opens up in the sky.

Aliya stares straight at it.

Another *BOOM*. Then a sound that brings back all my memories of the Fall of Kos. A shriek so loud and piercing that I fall forward into the sand, still holding Aliya.

Slowly, the arashi descends from the sky.

The Sentinels shout at us. Their voices are faint at first, then louder as they near. "Run!" they shout.

The villagers are screaming. Fire falls from the sky in waves, and before long, I can see nothing but flames where the camp used to be. Everyone moves at once. I pick Aliya up in my arms, and several Sentinels surround us, hurrying us back to the village.

"To the village!" Arzu shouts over the thunder.

A group of us runs, but not all the Sentinels can keep up, and a column of dirt erupts in an explosion behind us. Falling from the sky are the remains of the Sentinel who stood there. Blasts of lightning burst open the ground, heading straight for us.

Behind us, in the distance, the earth opens up beneath the refugee camp, swallowing groups of people until their screams are just whispers in the thunder.

"Keep going!" screams another tastahlik.

Juba is frozen, staring at the sky. Arzu is up ahead, leading a group of villagers to safety. Now Juba is alone.

"Ayaba!" It's Folami. Her jointed staff in a scabbard behind her back, she grips Juba's shoulders. A moment ago, she'd been ready to fight Juba. "Ayaba! Please. Let's go." Juba breaks out of her trance.

The four of us run toward the village. I glance up and swallow a scream. Black wings hover overhead. They seem to stretch out forever. Jagged lightning streaks the clouds, illuminating the rest of the flying beast. Revealing a sleek, ribbed torso and giant legs with talons that can pluck an entire house off the ground. It hangs there in the air, flapping its wings, its face twisted in a snarl. Then it lets out another shriek.

The sound topples us, and we scramble to our feet, Aliya still in my arms.

"Taj . . ." I can barely hear Aliya as I run with her in my arms. "She sent . . ." Aliya gulps for air, then quiets. "She sent the arashi. Karima. She sent the arashi. She knows . . ."

Then she goes limp in my arms.

My heart lurches in my chest. I have to keep moving, keep focused. I tighten my grip on Aliya. Energy leaks out of me like my chest has been punctured. People cry and scream and run all around us.

The earth shakes beneath us. The arashi is getting closer.

Wind whips around me. I turn and see a robed figure whirling so that something wet forms a circle on the ground around him. Blood. He jams his staff into the ground and murmurs a string of words. Above him, holes open in the sky, and water descends in giant, twirling columns.

Zaki. He's calling water from the sky. He's making a storm. Iragide.

The columns surround the arashi, then close in on it.

I can't stop staring.

Rough hands haul me to my feet.

"Wake up! Are you mad?" the young woman shouts as I stumble to keep up with her, Aliya completely still in my arms.

"I . . ."

"Come! Follow Zephi!" She snatches Aliya from me and flings her over her shoulder. "Come!"

"Who is Zephi?"

"Me! Idiot!" And she takes off.

Thunder and fire rage behind us.

We leave Zaki behind.

CHAPTER 21

BY THE TIME we get close to the village, the fire in the desert burns even larger than I imagined. It is everywhere. Even as far away as we are now, we can't escape its wrath.

"Come!" Zephi shouts, pointing toward the sky. "Big-big!" and I know she means the arashi screaming and vomiting fire down on us. We run, dodging collapsing huts and falling roofs until we get to the back of the building where Aliya and I have been staying.

Wind howls around us, almost screaming. The inyo swirl in a whirlwind above our heads. The air is thick with them. Over the tops of some buildings, I can see fire stretched out in a long line along the ridge. Stones and dirt fly up as the lightning pelts the ground. If I keep my eyes open for too long, dust blinds me.

Zephi sweeps a patch of dirt aside to reveal a metal door in the ground. She kicks on it twice with her heel—*doom, doom*. It swings open, and I see a whole gaggle of faces lit up inside. A half dozen hands reach out all at once, and we send down Aliya's body, then climb in ourselves. Zephi is the last one in, and she closes the door tight.

I look behind me and see a whole family spread out across the large cellar. There are cushions down here and mats, and in a far corner, a woman nurses a baby, gently rocking him in her arms. Three kids fight over a ball at the woman's feet. I think I even see someone smoking from a shisha pipe.

Nobody here seems all that worried that a mythical demon is circling their home and raining death and destruction down on their heads. The stone walls shake with each blast from up above. I notice that the hideout is reinforced in some places by splintering beams of wood, which doesn't inspire a lot of confidence.

Zephi lays Aliya on a pallet. A little girl brings over a bowl of water. For these kids, this is normal. Arzu once told me that arashi attacks are common in this land.

I look around. The adults appear calm, but when I look closer, I can tell that for some of them it's forced. They are scared, but they're trying to be brave for their children. Arashi attacks *are* common here, but Juba said that the Sentinels could detect them far enough in advance that the villagers could travel to somewhere safe. Why couldn't they raise the alarm beforehand this time? I glance toward Aliya. My mind flashes back to what she whispered in the desert. About Karima sending the arashi. I try to shake the thought away.

There's another boom overhead. I startle and look up.

"You know of our *storms*?" Zephi asks me, crouched at Aliya's side. As she makes her comfortable with blankets and pillows, I notice she doesn't have any sin-spots.

I nod. "An arashi destroyed my home."

She raises her eyebrows. "So that's something we have in common, then." She sticks her hand out, palm up. "To you and yours, visitor."

I slide my hand over hers, palm down. "To you and yours, Zephi."

"Yes. Finally. A proper introduction." She sighs, satisfied. "Come. Break kola nut with us."

Oh, no, not those again.

After the meal, Zephi sits with me as we both watch over Aliya. She's woken up a few times, sipped some water at my insistence, and then gone back to sleep. At one point, Zephi gets up to play keep-away with a bunch of the younger kids before coming back to join me in my watch over Aliya. The thunder outside has largely stopped, but I've never seen the end of an arashi attack. I wouldn't even know what that looks like. I just thought they kept going until there was nothing left, no more sin to swallow or no more sinners to drain. If we keep on living, do they just keep circling? Looking for us, for sins? I glance at Zephi, whose gaze has fallen over Aliya. With one hand, she straightens the blanket wrapped around my friend. I want to ask Zephi about the Sentinels and how they could have missed this one, but Aliya's words ring in my ear again: *Karima. She sent the arashi. She's found us.*

"So, your friend is ill." Zephi makes it sound like a question and a statement at the same time.

"Yes." I don't want to reveal too much. If I start talking about equations and the Seventh Prophet and how it looks like Aliya's going mad before my very eyes, I have no idea how she'll react. How anyone in the tribe will react. "I don't think she's drinking enough water."

Zephi snorts out a laugh, then pulls it back. "I'm sorry, but I do not think that is what's wrong with your friend." She strokes Aliya's blanket. "So, you were at the fights?"

I nod. "We were."

Zephi tuts. "Your friend is a scholar, no?" She squints at me.

"Um, yes. She, uh, she studies algebra."

"Ah, so your friend is knowing algebra?"

I smirk. "And she's very good at it." I puff my chest out, proud to brag on Aliya's behalf. "You could say she's fluent in that language."

"If you continue talking like this, we will have our Elders test her, and she will be very upset that you praised her abilities so much." While she speaks, she twists a rag in a calabash bowl of water and squeezes out the excess, then pats Aliya's head. "She will be upset, and we will tell her, 'Oh, your friend said you could do this, and he said you were so good at that.' And we will then ask her, 'So, is your friend a liar?'" She leans back on her knees and looks at Aliya's resting form, content with her handiwork. "And what do you think she'll say?"

"Heh. I think she'll gladly accept your test." I'm trying to play along, but I keep looking over at Aliya, willing her to wake up. Willing her to be OK. Zephi can tell. Her hand lands on mine, covering the tattoo of a bird in flight.

After a moment, I pull away. "Don't worry," I say, gathering myself. "As soon as she wakes up, ask her any question about algebra. She will write a whole entire proof for you." I stand up because I feel I need to and accidentally bump up against a shelf, sending a bowl crashing to the floor. Because I have the worst luck in the world, that's when everybody gets quiet. Suddenly, I'm the only one making noise.

Wait.

I'm the only one making noise.

A moment later, we all look skyward. Nothing. No booming. No pebbles falling from the cellar's ceiling. No screeching. No howling wind. Nothing.

A few of us look around nervously, then Zephi and I lock eyes. Without saying a word, we both know what we need to do. So, we make our way over to the ladder entrance, and both of us climb up, perched right beneath the metal doors to the cellar for a few tense seconds. It takes us some seconds to gather our courage, then Zephi puts her shoulder to the door.

"You're not tastahlik," I whisper before she pushes.

She looks at me. "No, Olurun has given me a simpler diet." She snorts, then pushes. The door groans.

Sand falls like a curtain through the opening, but Zephi pushes through. I see that others have the same idea. More and more people are creeping up from their cellars. Some of them have to dig themselves out of new piles of sand, and a few of them hold large palm tree branches to sweep sand out of windows and through doorways. Some of the older tribespeople are stunned into silence. At first, I think it's the same sort of sad silence people in Kos feel when they come out of their homes after their dahia has been Baptized and find their neighborhood destroyed. But this is different. There's shock. Wonder. Like they've been spared.

Zaki. I run through the streets, and before I know it, I'm back at the rim of the village. Already, others have gathered to survey the damage. Bodies litter the land. Those who weren't able to make it back in time. Those who were swallowed by the attack and spat back out. Inyo cloud the air around us, howling softly in our ears. Zephi stands with me, then begins walking among the dead, scanning faces, kneeling to listen for breathing.

Someone calls out in the distance. A voice ringing clear. Then shouts and signals being sung. Then a rush of footsteps. Are the Sentinels warning of another arashi attack?

I look to the sky to try to see if the telltale swirling clouds are forming, the ones that will spit out those monsters that set fire to whole cities. But the clouds are the same.

People from the tribe rush past us into the night, and Zephi and I stand, following them with our eyes.

Then several of them emerge, carrying something heavy.

Zaki is with them. His staff can barely hold him up. The villagers returning hold a blanket between them. A body. They dash by us in a blur, but it's not fast enough for me not to notice the tattoos running up and down the exposed arms and legs. Arms and legs covered in blood. All of the person's clothes are soaked through with blood. Shock numbs me, knocks all thought from my head, and before I know it, I've shaken off Zephi's hand and am hurrying after the tribespeople, following them to the large tent where they've brought the body.

They lay it on a raised bed, and several of them, men and women, move around the body with the practiced quickness of people who have done this many times before and know exactly what to do. Soon, enough of the blood is washed from the body and the face that I recognize it.

His face is thinner, more drawn. And his nappy hair has grown out thick. His fingers are longer and more gnarled. And his arms are now sinewy with muscle. But I recognize him. He looks like a ghost, and maybe that's what he is. He was supposed to have died back in Kos, defending the city alongside me against the army of inisisa Queen Karima and the Mage Izu had unleashed upon us. But he's here.

"Tolu," I whisper, hoping the aki I once lived with and grew up with and Ate sins with as a young orphan in Kos can hear me.

He does not move.

CHAPTER 22

ONCE THEY'VE CLEANED all the mess away from his face and body, he looks more like the Tolu I remember, but he's still like a ghost to me. It's like he crawled out of the desert. I don't know how long it'll take me to adjust to the fact that he's alive. If he doesn't survive whatever it is that happened to him out there, I won't have to.

But occasionally, I hear whispers of the tribesfolk outside the tent. They wonder about these people who have all of a sudden started coming to their homeland and changing their lives. And they wonder whether or not this new, young sin-eater is from Kos as well.

They know that I know him. Anyone who walks into the room or spends any time breathing the same air as us can tell that there is something between us, something that links us, and that perhaps it has to do with more than the fact that we both wear sin-spots.

I'm happy to see him again, overjoyed that he's still alive, but a part of me is in mourning. Dispirited. No matter how far I run, what happened before somehow always runs me down.

I want to start over here and learn to be a true tastahlik. Maybe even Larada. I want to learn how to fight, but I also want to help cure sinners among the tribe. I want to be revered. I want to migrate and wander and discover lands I've never seen before. I want to feel what I felt when sailing off from Osimiri. That sense of adventure, of movement. I want to feel as though I'm running toward something instead of running away. I burn with shame at the thought of leaving Kos the way it is. But . . . but I can't go back. The thought of making things worse is even more painful.

I have no idea what's brought Tolu here, how he survived the Fall of Kos, nor how he escaped past the city wall. And I'm so stunned when his eyes finally flutter open that I can't even bring myself to ask him.

Color has begun to return to his face and limbs. One bandaged arm rests on his stomach while the other remains at his side. Bandages have been wrapped around his head, and his shirt lies torn in half to expose the cloth that the Healers strapped to his chest and stomach. His legs are similarly covered, and for several seconds, he rhythmically blinks his eyes, cracks his knuckles, and flexes his toes.

I can only guess at all the questions he wants to ask, and I watch his eyes dart back and forth as he puts pieces together.

Then he squints and turns to look at me. He doesn't gasp, and his eyes don't shoot wide open at the sight of me. There's a new softness in them—like he thinks he's in a dream.

"We all believed you'd survived," he says at last, more a breath than a sentence.

"Hey, don't talk," I say, moving my stool closer to him. I don't want him to raise his voice, in part because I don't want anyone outside to overhear us. I also don't want him to use more energy than absolutely necessary. "Rest." I take one of his bandaged hands in mine. "We can talk about everything later. Now that you're awake, we can maybe start feeding you properly. They have some of our food here. Moin-moin, and I'm sure if I dig around, I can get us some fufu."

Tolu tries to smile through his cracked lips, but it turns into a grimace. "I don't have much time."

"What do you mean?"

"He's coming." Tolu's grip tightens. "He's near."

"Who's coming?" Even before I ask, I know exactly what he means.

"Bo," Tolu says. His head sinks back into his pillow, taking my heart with it. "Bo is coming. You must run."

I feel like everyone's been telling me to run, one way or another. I know I have to or, rather, will have to. But I hate it nonetheless.

"Anywhere. Just run." He's running out of breath. "Stay alive."

For what? I want to ask him. *Who am I supposed to stay alive for?* There's nothing waiting for me in Kos but an army of murderous inisisa wearing armor and a queen I thought I loved who is setting the whole Kingdom of Odo on fire to rip my head from my shoulders. My best friend is slaughtering entire villages trying to fulfill that very queen's greatest wish. Where would I run to? What use am I to anyone?

A tear runs down the side of Tolu's face.

"What is it?" I ask him, even though I know it will hurt to hear the answer.

"So many have died under Karima."

I want to push him, find out everything I can, but he doesn't have the strength, so I let him go at his own pace.

"After your escape, Karima, she crushed the rebellion. Turned us against each other. Those who could escaped through the tunnels." He swallows. "She made Bo the commander of her army of inisisa. Sin-beasts, they roam the streets of Kos. There is no more Eating. Only more and more inisisa that the Mages are forced to call forth from the sinners in Kos." He chuckles, then chokes on it. Once he finishes coughing, he continues. "There is no more sickness," he says with a bitter grin. "No one need worry they will perish from living with a sin. She claims she is purifying the city and that she will do the same for the entire kingdom." He looks straight at me. "She is spreading her rule. Expanding. She has already taken the mines in the north. Before long, she will have swallowed everything west of Kos." He winces at new pain that runs through him. "She can even command the arashi." He waves a weak hand in the air. "They circle the dahia. Like patrols. Every citizen of Kos, every Forum-dweller, lives in fear of the shadows above. The skies above Kos have been dark for a long time."

Aliya was right. The arashi that attacked the village was sent here.

I had imagined Kos as a ruined city, but to hear my fears spoken out loud crushes my heart all over again.

"Taj," he says, smiling so much now that he's showing his teeth. "Taj, Taj, Taj." He raises his hand. I lean in close, and he moves to touch my face. He probably thought he'd never get the chance to see me again after I escaped from Kos. Maybe he's just trying to confirm to himself that I am indeed real, that I'm not a dream. That whatever his mission was, he accomplished it.

I lean back and look at him. I can't bear to see how sickly he looks now. No more muscle, just skin and bone at this point. Like he's been deflated. "If it's a sin killing you, let me call it forth."

He chuckles. More like a gasp than anything else. "Any sin you could call from me would kill me with the effort. Do not bother, brother. It is enough to know that you are still alive." He rests his hand back on his stomach. Tolu looks at me out of the corner of his eye and smirks. "The trouble people have gone to in order to keep you alive . . ."

There's no need to remind me.

"But remember this: Right hand or left, we are all of the same body." He coughs, and blood appears on his mouth. He weakly raises a hand to wipe it, but before he can get to it, I tear off a piece of my tattered shirt and dab at his lips. "That is supposed to be Bo's job."

"He always was the caretaker," I say, managing a small smile.

"But we knew you cared. Even when you would pretend not to, you were fooling no one." Tears pool in his eyes. "We knew it was you who planned everyone's Daga Day. We knew it was you who made it so that Omar could witness his sister's Jeweling ceremony." A tear leaks down the side of his face. "We saw how you mourned Ifeoma when she Crossed during the Fall of Kos. And we heard stories of the army of renegade aki you raised in the forest to help defeat Izu."

I shake my head. "That was Aliya's doing. I . . .." Even as I try to shrug off responsibility, I can't.

"Arzu is here," he whispers.

"What? How do you know?"

"A message. Sent back to the rebels. We have friends . . . among the refugees. We have all been at work. It's not over, Taj." He speaks like he no longer hears me. "It's not over. You must come back. And you must forgive her for what she has done. Forgive her. And come back. It's not over."

Questions swirl in my mind around Arzu, around what it is Tolu says she has done. Whether it has anything to do with the scar on her neck. But I know he doesn't have much time left. I want to tell him that it is over. That Karima has won. I want to tell him that all I want is peace for myself, even if that means a life on the run. Even if it means being a wanderer, moving from new land to new land. Even if it means never laying my head on the same patch of sand or grass or stone to rest. I've already left everything I've ever loved behind. All I want is peace, but instead I tell him, "No, Tolu. It's not over." I hold his hand and thread my fingers through his. "You did well. You reached me. We will save Kos. All of us. Together." I'm lying to him; the sin grows in me. "There are aki here. An army of them." My voice is down to a whisper. Tolu's eyes slowly close. "And they fight like nothing I've ever seen before. I saw one of them kill four inisisa in less than the time it takes to bake good jollof. And with them at our side and Aliya and the others waiting for us back in the city, we will . . ." I trail off. His hand has gone limp in mine. "Tolu?"

I know he's gone, but I shake him anyway. Gently. "Tolu?" Then again, "Tolu?"

My lips quiver. My hands shake. I try to sniff back the sobs, but they come anyway, and I bury my face in his blanket.

I don't know how long I spend weeping into Tolu's blankets, but eventually nurses arrive, wrap up his body in many-colored blankets, and carry him away.

They vanish through the tent's flap. It is several long minutes before I can find the strength to rise to my feet. When I stand, something on the bed catches my eye. Where Tolu's hand had been, there's now a stone. It might have glowed blue on a necklace around his throat or green in an anklet. He might have worn it in his ear. But here he must have kept it sewn somewhere in his clothes. Now it's a dull, ashen piece of crystal. I scoop it up and hold it so tightly in my fist that I can feel blood seeping through my fingers.

When I leave the tent, I wander in a daze. The fires have all been put out. But everywhere, groups of people are carrying bodies. Some of the bundles are smaller than others. One woman walks past me solemnly, a bundle held closely to her chest. Tear streaks mark her cheeks. But she wears the same expression on her face as so many others. A coldness, as though their faces are carved out of stone. Why don't they cry? Why don't they *let* themselves cry?

I search for familiar faces—Zaki, Arzu, Aliya, anyone—but stop when I hear hushed tones.

On a crate in an alley sits Juba with her face in her hands, her shoulders heaving with sorrow. Arzu kneels before her. I'm witnessing something I shouldn't be seeing. Something intimate and precious and secret passing between them. I feel like a spy.

"I have failed my people," Juba sobs. "We have always moved. Always migrated. But I saw the river." She looks into Arzu's face. "I saw the river. I saw the water. I saw a home for us. And it had been so long since the last storm. And . . ."

Arzu puts her hand to Juba's face and shushes her.

"Arzu, what have I done?"

"Ayaba," Arzu says in a voice so low I almost don't hear it, "you do not control the arashi. You cannot govern the weather."

That hits me so hard and so suddenly in my chest that I nearly fall back. Juba can't control the arashi. But, apparently, Karima can. And she sent this one after me. The reason for all this fire, all this death, is me.

Juba's posture straightens. Something in her face hardens. "Leave me," she whispers.

"Juba . . ." It comes out of Arzu as a whimper.

"Leave me, sicario." Juba rises from the wooden crate. "Go make yourself useful." She has that coldness in her face now, the stoic look of her people. "They will need many hands to bury our dead. I must serve *my* people."

Arzu grows so still it is as though she has turned into stone. I can't see the tears that pool in her eyes, but I can see the way her shoulders shake as Juba turns to leave.

I hurry away before either of them notices me.

I've come out of my grief-haze enough to feel the desire to be helpful. Villagers, those carrying bodies and those carrying tools, all head to the rim of the village where the arashi attacked. Arzu walks beside me but says nothing. Her face is expressionless. We are both just part of the crowd heading to the mass graveyard. Someone hands us thick wooden trowels for digging.

When we get to the rim, I see many already at work. Some dig graves while others smooth out the clothes on the dead. Inyo darken the sky above us and the air around us. Their howls rise, then subside, then rise again. Through it all, people work.

Arzu and I head in the same direction. She finds her way to a tall, wide-shouldered man having trouble with his trowel. He falls to one knee, trying to hold himself up with his staff. Zaki. Arzu rushes to his side and kneels next to him. Shadows swirl around his black robe.

"Rest," she tells him. "I will dig while you gather your strength."

I find an empty plot nearby and get down on my knees and begin digging. I know I shouldn't be listening, but I can't help myself. Will he reveal who he is?

"I don't know what you did," Arzu says, like she's trying to make conversation, "but I thank you. For your part in saving the village."

Zaki coughs. I hear the blood in it. "Just a little forbidden magic is all that was."

Arzu digs. "You are from Kos. Your accent."

Zaki picks his trowel off the ground and resumes digging, and the two of them are so close together they look like they know each other. But they are just two people joined in intimate labor. Sharing tragedy. After Baptisms in the dahia, Kosians would look at one another as though they knew one another. Absolute strangers would help or comfort one another, would pick through the rubble of the homes of people they'd never met before. They shared a tragedy. They were bound by it.

"Yes," Zaki says after a long pause. "I once lived in Kos." He stares at the ground and smiles. "I was a Mage, in fact. A lawmaker. What we call kanselo." In between his words is the sound of wood scooping up dirt. "But I loved to study. I secretly hoped to gain a place in the Ulo Amamihe. The Great House of Ideas. Unfotunately, what I loved to study was dangerous. Dangerous enough to have me cast out of Kos, never to return." He looks up at her. "And you? I hear Kos in your voice too."

Arzu touches her neck, as though she has just now remembered what happened to her. "It's in the past." She bunches her scarf up around her throat, and the scar is gone. "We must move forward." I inch my way closer to them to hear better. They dig in silence for a quarter of an hour before Arzu speaks again. "I escaped. I left by choice. I was part of a rebellion. I don't know how long since you've last been to Kos, but now a queen rules who cares nothing for her subjects. I was part of a group who wanted to save the city. Our city." She looks at the grave she's been digging the whole time. "But I was captured and made her servant. Again. This time, my task was to choose captured rebels for public executions." Her hand shakes. "I wanted to fight back. I would rather have died than do this thing. I even tried once to . . . to end it. A rope around my neck, but I couldn't go through with it. My friends, they told me it was best for the rebellion if I went along. If I let Karima believe she could trust me. I was to be their agent in the Palace. I was forced to select many of my friends for death." She grips her shaking wrist with her free hand, holds it close to her chest.

Zaki tosses his trowel to the ground and hugs his daughter. He silently strokes her hair.

A few moments later, she pushes away and starts digging again. More violently than before. "I escaped," she says, her words punctuated by her trowel turning the soil. "Mages who were part of our rebellion made me a special palm wine. It simulated death. I was to appear as though I had murdered myself out of guilt. It did not take much to imagine such a fate. The aki who were tasked with burying me brought me outside the city Wall, and that is where I woke up. I did not know if I could trust them, but they let me go." She digs and tosses dirt over her shoulder. "I left and, later, waited for others. I did not know if I could face them. After what I'd done."

You must forgive her for what she has done, Tolu had said before dying. Tears sting my eyes without warning. I blink them away, but more come. When I look up, all I see around me is death. I feel so lost.

I need to be far from here. As far from here as possible. I drop my trowel and walk away from the camp. I don't know how I carry myself there, but when I stop walking, Zaki's house stares at me from the top of its hill. A place of peace and quiet. Where no one will see me. Where no one will try to tell me what to do. Where no one will remind me of who or what I abandoned.

When I open the door and see Aliya lying on a table, eyes closed, wet cloth on her forehead, I want to laugh at the absurdity of it all. Of all the people I could run to who wouldn't speak to me of Kos . . .

But something has willed me here. So I decide to stop fighting it. And I take a seat next to my sick friend. And I take her hand in mine.

It's the warmest thing I've touched all day.

CHAPTER 23

ALIYA LIES ON a pallet placed on two desks moved together. She's been given a white robe, lighter than the heavy dust-colored robes she's taken to wearing here. I move slowly. I don't even want to disturb the air around her in case it does something to harm her.

Zaki must have brought her here after he defended the village. Before he joined the others in burying their dead.

Aliya is not sweating as much as she was just before the arashi attack, and her breathing has slowed. It sounds normal again, though I'm not a nurse or Healer, so I have no way of knowing. And, really, at this point I'm too scared to go and ask for one. If I leave and Aliya wakes up and doesn't know where she is or what happened, who's going to explain it to her? So, I stick around and try to remember how the nurses moved when they were working on a patient. I get up and put my fingers to the skin under Aliya's jaw and take her pulse. Then I put my ear to her mouth, and I listen for her breath. It's almost like when I woke up after nearly drowning in the river and Aliya was sucking the water from my lungs and breathing breath back into me. I know I look foolish, but it feels good to be doing something.

"If there's anything I can do to help," I say to her, stupidly, because she probably can't hear me, "just, you know, say so or, well, you can't say anything, so I guess just knock on the wooden desk or something."

I think of how drained she looks when she comes out of these episodes. It has happened a few times now, and every time, it gets worse. It takes her longer to come back to normal. She always seems to leave a piece of herself behind. Somehow, Tolu's stone has found its way into my hands, and I fiddle with it, turn it over in my hands, watch it glint in the candlelight.

I look up from the dulled gemstone in my hands. "Do you remember that time at Zoe's when we first met? You had a bunch of dates on your table, and you kept rearranging them in rows, and I walked over and snatched one off your table and popped it in my mouth. And you said you were using it, and I think I said something like 'If you were using it, you would eat it' or something foolish like that." I laugh at the memory, and I think I see a smile cross Aliya's face too. But it's probably just a trick of the light. "You held my hand and my arms, and you looked at the sin-spots on them, and for the first time, it was like someone wasn't repulsed by them. They didn't shock you or put you off or make you want to spit at me. You called them equations. You called them poems." It feels good to talk like this—to remember how it used to be.

"Back then, I was too proud to admit it or let you see it, but it's something I go back to a lot in my head. That moment. You had this . . . this look of joy on your face, like you couldn't believe it. And the idea that these ugly sin-spots could bring someone joy? That was . . . it's still tough for me to believe it happened." It occurs to me that the appropriate thing to do, if these were normal circumstances, would be to give Aliya a stone, a family jewel or something like a heart-stone. Something to show her what she means to me. But I have nothing on me. Of course. I'm about to get up to get her another blanket when I see her stir. She blinks her eyes open.

"I remember that day," she says at last. I feel tears prick the backs of my eyes at the sound of her voice. "That day at Zoe's. It was supposed to be a break from my studies. I was to meet other students, but they never arrived." She smiles.

Heat rises in my cheeks. "You brought your study materials anyway."

She chuckles. "Oh, the dates. Yes, I was a dutiful student. It was how I was raised." She flexes her fingers absently into fists, like she's testing them for feeling. "I was so rude," she says at last.

"Rude?"

She turns my way, slowly. "The way I grabbed your arm as soon as I saw your markings."

"Oh. My sin-spots." I roll my sleeves back and look at them. A lion on my forearm, the tail of a dragon curling down one shoulder, snakes ringing my biceps, a griffin whose wings are wrapped around my wrist, and on it goes until only a little dark flesh shows through.

"I was so entranced. I couldn't believe it." She swallows. "They were beautiful."

Now my entire body warms. "I'm going to get you some water," I say suddenly, because I need to start moving or else she'll see how much I'm shaking or how heated my face feels.

"Taj," she murmurs, and grabs my wrist.

"Yes?"

For a long time, she's silent. Then a hand falls onto my shoulder. I start and knock over the stool, turning to see Zaki standing over me. He no longer leans on his cane. Behind him, in the doorway, is Arzu. She steps tentatively over the threshold and into the living room, where our journeys have brought us. I hide Tolu's stone in my belt.

"Arzu," Aliya whispers.

"My friend." Tears pool in Arzu's eyes, and she rushes to Aliya's side, pressing her forehead to Aliya's. Something private is passing between the two of them. I remember how it was for us when we left Osimiri, and it was Arzu who was sick and Aliya who cared for her. And I imagine something important happened between them when they first decided to keep that secret, the truth of what Arzu had done in Kos. *Forgive her*, Tolu told me.

I head out the front door to breathe fresh air and clear the fog in my head. So much has happened so quickly. My mind is a mess of images, all whirling about like a dozen dogs chasing their tails.

Zaki closes the door behind him and joins me. We both look out onto the village. Juba's tribe wades through the rubble and sand piles and burnt bits of houses. From up on this hill, I can't hear a single sound they make.

"Your friend is touched," Zaki says finally.

I grit my teeth. I have no patience for riddles or circle-talk right now. "What does that mean?"

"It means that she, more evidently than the rest of us, is a vessel for the Unnamed. She sees the world in its truest form. The equations she speaks of, and the proofs she performs on her parchment—she is describing the world as the Unnamed sees it and has designed it. All of it. It is being written onto the very skin of her body." Zaki waits for me to absorb that. Her equations. My sin-spots. Are they the same? "She is learning how to do things we have not been able to do for hundreds of years. Pretty soon, she will have discovered how to turn coal itself into diamonds." Zaki turns to me. "She is learning the world in order to remake it."

"Like what you did with the water."

Zaki nods. "Like what I did with the water."

I turn to face him. "What was that? Will Aliya be able to do that?"

Zaki steps closer to me. "If she remains strong enough to survive this trial, she will be able to do so much more. I am a tiny lizard compared to the power within her." He settles his shoulders. "I did not believe it when I first heard word of an apprentice who could write proofs with extraordinary skill back at the Palace. I had been settled here for quite some time after my escape when news drifted on the caravans that there existed a novice Mage so skilled at algebra that her elders could hardly follow her. She had been an unremarkable student in the dahia, not even making it to the Palace competitions as a child, but when she was brought in to work for the Palace, she showed unparalleled skill." He shakes his head. "As a Mage, you hear such stories all the time. People trying to bring glory to the dahia where they are from or trying to proclaim that they have the best students and, therefore, they must be the best teachers. But then this young Mage vanished."

"Is that what you heard?"

"Eventually, I learned from my agents of the rebellion in Kos. I learned of what had befallen the city. And I knew the time had finally come." He frowns. "We had missed our chance before. We had been too slow. But we will not make the same mistake again."

I look back at the door, and suddenly my body feels so heavy. Everything is pulling me back to Kos, even as I want to stay here. I'm not ready to go back. "I don't think I'll ever be ready to go back." I don't realize I've whispered that out loud until I see the look on Zaki's face. Concerned, but patient. Like a parent who knows he must watch his child suffer his way into a lesson.

"Come," says the exiled Mage. And he walks to a bed of flowers running along the pathway to his front door. When we arrive, he tucks his staff under his arm and pulls two trowels out from his robe.

I turn mine over in my hand. "Oga, what is this now?"

"We will just turn the earth a little. This is far from the most difficult thing this garden has asked of me."

I kneel beside him, and together we dig into a patch of moist soil. It gives easily.

"I enjoy this," he says. His voice is quiet but strong. Whatever strength he lost battling the arashi, he seems to have gotten it back. "I find it demands things of me that no other activity does."

"Like what?"

"Attention. Patience." He pauses. "Kindness." He turns the earth with his trowel, then puts it to the side and pulls out of one sleeve a tiny metal contraption that looks like two knives joined at their middles. With one deft motion, he snips off a branch of a tree so tiny I can fit it in my two hands held together. "It is the same with the tastahlik here. What they do." He frowns. "Not the fighters. The Onija? That is the opposite of patience, what they do."

The tastahlik Juba was prepared to cast out of the village. They are probably burying their dead. Maybe some of them have become inyo, their sin-heavy spirits moaning over the ground on which they once stood. I have not seen Abeo since just before the attack. I don't know how to feel at the idea of him maybe being dead. I suppose I should finally feel safe. No longer under his watchful eye. But I feel guilty for feeling safe. I did not wish for him to be dead.

Zaki examines the tree he has just pruned. "The Larada. Now, what they do requires much more patience and strength. It is easy to fight. It is difficult to forgive.

"In the north," he continues, "they have machines that assist in the healing of ailments. These are things that can issue a diagnosis; they can tell you what is wrong without the aid of a medicine man. But I have found in my studies—and others have corroborated these findings—that the very act of speaking to an actual person is an element of the healing process." All the while, he's snipping flowers or pouring water out of a small vial into the ground around the plants. "It is the same with the tastahlik. Turning the act of Eating into a spectacle means the purpose of the Eating and, thus, the purpose of the sin-eater are both lost. It ceases to be about the Healing. And it becomes instead another act of violence. The person whose sin you have Eaten—you have taken their sin from them and the guilt that accompanies it, but you have not truly freed them of it."

"But what else is left?"

Zaki finishes with one plant, wipes his brow, then rises slowly. Like a true old man, he takes his time stretching his back. Then he exhales. "What is left, my son, is for the sinner to forgive himself." He puts an arm over my shoulder and turns me toward the house. "You have Eaten many, many sins. I see it. But the people whose sins you Ate, do you believe they forgave themselves?"

In my head, I see the colossal bedrooms of the wealthy. Preachers, kanselo, algebraists. The Kayas. I think of the Mages who called forth the sin, then ushered everyone out of the way while I risked my life. I think of how it felt for those first sins to rush down my throat, choking me. I remember crying from the pain, unable to scream because their horribleness was becoming mine.

"They don't feel anything," I spit. "Never mind forgiveness."

Zaki gives me that sad-but-patient-parent look again. "You are running—"

"Oga, do not be giving me that look when you cannot even tell your own daughter who her father is. Who is running?" I know I'm not angry at him. I'm angry at everything, but he is unlucky enough to be standing in front of me right now. "You talk to me of forgiveness. You stand here and lecture me about how the sinner must forgive themselves, but you abandoned her!" I'm shouting now, and I don't care. "You abandoned your daughter!"

I lunge for him, ready to crush his nose, but I stop myself just in time. Zaki hasn't moved an inch.

"I know you are angry," he says, taking a step toward me.

"Stop." I point a finger at him. "Stop! Don't touch me."

But he advances. "But what happened was not your fault," he says. He puts his hands on my shoulders and pulls me to him.

"Stop it!" I hold my head in my hands, but I don't pull away. I close my eyes and see the arashi flying over the refugee camp, and I see fire raining from the sky, and I see the field of dead bodies outside of the camp, and I see Arzu picking out rebel aki and Mages, selecting them for execution, and, at last, I see Tolu, broken and beaten and bloody, and I see his face just as he died. "Stop!" My voice has softened. Sobs choke me.

Zaki holds me to his chest. Tightly. My arms fall to my sides, and I bury my face in his robe and weep. For the aki I left behind in the forest. For the aki I left behind in Kos. For the refugees searching for lost family members in the camp outside the Wall. For the refugees who died, swallowed up by the earth during the arashi attack. For Tolu. For Baba. For Mama. And I weep and weep and weep.

When I finally wipe the tears and snot from my face, I look over Zaki's shoulder and see Arzu and Aliya standing a few paces back. The shouting must have brought them out. They stand completely still. Arzu's face has lost its color.

She heard.

She steps forward. One step. Two steps. Each one a stiff shuffle. Then she reaches a hand out. "You're my . . . baba?" she whispers so quietly I almost don't hear it.

Zaki has turned to her, and I can no longer see his face. For a long time, the two stare at each other. Then Zaki steps forward and wraps Arzu in an embrace. Only the very top of her blond head peeks up from over his shoulder. Aliya heads toward me, stumbling, trying to get her staff out in front of her in time.

"Taj," she says, and there's a warning in her voice. "Taj, look!"

I turn away from Zaki and Arzu.

Fire, nothing but fire.

The clouds in the sky above don't move. None of us hears arashi, but fire rages.

"Stay here," I shout over my shoulder. Before I can stop myself, I hurry back toward the village.

Several huts are in flames. Aki ride through the town on horseback. Inisisa run alongside them. Almost like they are following orders.

I swallow the bile that rises in my throat and run even faster.

He found us.

Bo.

CHAPTER 24

THERE ARE INISISA everywhere.

Wolves the color of shadows chase children through the streets while nurses try to protect tribespeople from the blood-covered aki who ride by on horses. Fire flanks the main thoroughfare, and huts crumble in on themselves. I rush into one of them to see if there's anyone inside. Just as I'm about to leave, I see a young girl cowering in a corner, screaming as a wooden beam falls from the ceiling. I dash over and swing her onto my back. We escape the hut just as its entire roof caves in.

I have no idea where to take her, so I try to find my way to the sick tent. Surely that must be protected. Already the ground is littered with the Crossed. Inisisa gnaw at motionless bodies, and a few tribespeople lie in the streets bleeding and broken. I move as fast as I can to keep the girl from seeing these things. Before

I get to the sick tent, a voice calls out. One of the nurses from earlier rushes to me, and I slip the weeping child into her arms.

"The others, where are they?" I ask. But before she can answer, a horse gallops our way. I dive to the ground, taking the nurse and girl with me just in time to avoid the sword that would have taken our heads off. "Take her somewhere safe," I say, then push myself to my feet.

All around me are screams.

I look around, trying to think of what to do next.

It takes me some time to reorient myself. I turn in a slow circle. People writhe on the ground around me, some of them begging for help. In side streets, tastahlik battle with the various weapons they've been able to find, fending bears off with dagas, swinging and striking at griffins with staffs and beams of wood, slicing through lizards with their swords.

An inisisa darts toward me from my left. Without thinking, I scramble to a motionless body in the street where I see a curved sword. I spin and slice through the inisisa. It splits into two, and before it can re-form and chase me, I dart down the street toward an older man trying to fend off an attack from an aki on horseback. He's trying to fight the aki with a flaming beam of wood, but the fire inches toward his hands, and he has to drop it, leaving himself open to blows from the aki's whip. I run as fast as my legs will carry me. The aki raises his whip, and just as it comes down, I stick my arm out, catching the whip's end as it wraps around my wrist. I pull with all my might, and the aki comes tumbling out of his saddle. He hits the ground with a thud, and just as he comes up, I flip the sword in my hand and hit him square in the temple with its pommel.

The villager falls back to the ground and murmurs his thanks before pushing himself up. I swing into the horse's saddle. The beast bucks and nearly throws me off, but I clench my knees and whip the reins to set off down the street.

Inisisa nip at my horse's legs. We zig and zag, trying to avoid them, but they're gaining on us. A group of beasts—wolves and hounds—breaks out from the burning huts around us. They're cleansed. Juba's. The beasts run alongside me and take down the inisisa trying to get us. The two groups of beasts tussle and writhe on the ground, biting and clawing and beating at one another. Shadows thrashing and struggling against glowing skin and fur. Snakes wrap around a bear's throat. A griffin swoops from the sky and claws at a lynx.

At the next intersection, five inisisa surround a bloodied Folami. Her torn shirt hangs from her body, and her ripped pants expose the sin-spots covering her legs. They all charge at once, and she swings her staff over her, cutting through all of them in one stroke. When they come apart, she falls to one knee. A bear rumbles straight at her from two huts down. I urge my horse forward at a gallop. Just as the bear reaches her, I swing my sword in an arc. It catches the bear's jaw and flips it over.

Falcons glide overhead, swooping down and snatching enemy aki from their horses. My horse leaps over one of the fallen and keeps going.

I see Lanre to my right, sabers in both his hands, dueling an aki who holds two dagas. They spin and swing and strike and parry. They kick up dirt with each move, but eventually Lanre gets a shot in that cuts open the aki's side. I ride by, glancing over my shoulder to watch Lanre deliver the killing blow.

A griffin dives down, and I don't see it until it's on top of me. I swing in my saddle, but its talons catch my arm, slicing through my sleeve. Just as I'm about to fall off, I cry out, and something hard and fast—a sin-bear—crashes into my horse, knocking me clear off. I feel nothing but air around me until I land on the ground hard enough to hear something snap. I don't have the breath in me to scream as pain burns through my chest and stomach. I can't find my sword.

The bear gets to me and rears up on its hind legs before something sticks it from behind. Its shadows fall away, and it morphs into a beast made of light, then bursts apart.

Juba stumbles forward, inky blackness dripping from her robe, and hauls me to my feet. Inisisa charge toward us, and she rushes forward. A lynx leaps at her, and she palms its forehead midair, and it explodes in a burst of light. In the same motion, she slams her palm down on a wolf, and the same happens to it. Two cobras slither toward her, then, when they rise, she grabs them by their heads and they turn to light, then shatter. A giant falcon dives straight for us. She leaps into the air, grabs its chest feathers, and slams it into the ground. It struggles, but before it can fly away, Juba grips its head and tears the falcon apart in a shower of sparks.

Beyond her, other Larada are doing the same. Just as inisisa reach them, the Healers stop them where they stand and, with a touch, burn away their shadows and turn them into stars that surge, then split apart.

The onslaught continues, more and more inisisa coming toward us, but Juba and the tastahlik form a semicircle around me, beating them back. They fight them off, and there's a lull. Our heavy breaths seem to be in sync with each other. It's all I hear—until it's not.

Metal screeching against metal.

Oh, no.

I push my way through the semicircle and look down both ends of the street. From our left, a group of armored inisisa storms. Aki sit astride them with bladed staffs and swords at the ready. Shock drains the color from Juba's face. The other tastahlik are frozen, their eyes wide.

"Iragide," I whisper, horror thick in my voice.

"That's blasphemy," murmurs Juba, terrified, next to me. "Olurun, preserve us."

I have no idea what to do. There are too many of them.

"Run!" I shout.

But the armored inisisa are too fast. They're already on top of us. The aki swing their staffs, taking down people and Juba's light-beasts like they're slicing through air. Tribespeople collapse all around me. I look over and see that Juba is wounded too. She has a hand to the deep cut on her shoulder. Her shoulders heave with each breath.

"We can't defeat them . . ." She sounds resigned when she says this. "My people . . ."

The armored inisisa turn around and rumble toward us to finish the job when I hear a battle cry. I look up. The Onija jump from the roofs of homes to land right on top of the aki riding their steel beasts. They plunge their dagas into them, tearing them to the ground. Folami leads them. She stands and raises her arms, and an army of inisisa bursts from the buildings around us. The fighters. These are their beasts. Our inisisa smash into the armored beasts, sending them flying through the air. In the attack, the two groups of inisisa meld until they turn into puddles of ink on the ground, the armor breaking off around them.

The tastahlik who saved us rush in our direction and begin attending to the wounded, putting pressure on their cuts and tearing pieces of cloth from their own bloodstained clothes to stanch the bleeding of their comrades.

"Arzu?" I ask Juba.

She shakes her head. She doesn't know where she is.

I have to find them. There's no way they stayed at Zaki's home. Not when there are people who need their help.

The weapons of dead aki and tastahlik litter the ground. I scoop up two dagas and set off at a run. Zephi chases after me.

"Come," she shouts as she nears me, "let us fight together."

She runs alongside me, her own dagas in hand.

We hurry past side streets, and I dart into every hut—or what's left of them—for any sign of Aliya or Arzu. Zephi stops when we get to the home we hid in during the arashi attack. Then she rushes inside. The house has been ransacked, and the rugs and cushions are stained with red, but there's nobody inside. I follow her closely up the stairs, and she bursts through the trapdoor leading to the attic. It's strange to be in this place when it's so eerily quiet. It's always so loud with the noise of family being family. Aliya had scattered parchment and rolled-up books all over the floor, scribbling equations and other mathematical lahala on them, writings I later discovered to be the secret behind inisisa. This was where she worked, and now it's completely empty. There's no blood here, no sign of damage. It doesn't look like anyone's hiding in here.

Zephi pushes against the ceiling, feeling around, then finds a loose set of tiles and pushes them free. She climbs through, and I follow her. We crawl out onto the sloped roof. Perched there, we scan the town. It hurts my heart to see so much of it burning. The fires look to be dying down, and much of the movement has stopped. There's not nearly as much chaos as there was a few moments ago.

Pockets of survivors stagger along, trying to avoid falling debris. The wounded try to find shelter. Then I see it. A single figure, hobbling forward on her cane, struggling with each step. Aliya. A horse gallops down a pathway not far from her.

Without thinking, I leap onto the roof of a nearby home and roll, then vault over the edge of the next. I fly through the air. When I land, pain sears through my side. Arm over my stomach, I shuffle forward, and that's when I see the face of the horse's rider.

I forget the pain. I want to call out to Aliya, to warn her about the oncoming attacker, but she won't be able to get out of the way in time. The horse is galloping toward her. I only have one chance at this, so my timing needs to be perfect.

I climb up to the edge of the roof with my dagas in hand and jump just as the horse passes beneath me.

I crash into the rider, and the two of us topple to the ground. The panicked horse runs off in the opposite direction.

I push myself to my feet and stagger forward. He gets up too, first on one knee, then standing tall on both feet.

He doesn't grin, but the scar that cuts across his face has turned his mouth into a permanent smirk.

Bo.

Zephi leaps from the nearest roof and lands at Bo's left. Then I see Arzu rounding a corner, stopping when she gets behind Bo.

He's surrounded.

Bo doesn't even bother looking around him to see who else is there. I'm the only one he sees. He's almost unrecognizable. His torn shirt shows a body almost completely covered in sin-spots. Tattoos have even taken over half of his face.

Feelings swarm in my chest. I want to ask him so many questions, and at the same time, I want to throttle him. I want to hold him close, and I want to beat him senseless.

My brother.

"Come home, brother," he tells me. His voice has changed. It sounds like stones scraping together. Like precious gems being crushed into powder. "I'm here for you and only you."

I bring my dagas up, ready. "I'm not going back."

"Bo!" Arzu calls out. "You're trapped. Surrender."

He doesn't even turn his head to acknowledge her.

"Bo, give up!" Aliya calls out from behind me.

He frowns and glances at Zephi, who twirls her dagas in her hands, ready to battle.

For several long seconds, we all stand there, poised for a fight.

Zephi rushes forward.

"Zephi," I cry. "Wait!"

Bo parries Zephi's strike and slices at her stomach, then steps aside while Zephi falls over, eyes wide in shock.

"Don't make me kill them too, Taj!" Bo shouts, his back to me.

Zephi takes a few stumbling steps, holding her side, and turns to charge again. Arzu rushes forward in the same instant. Bo's expression doesn't change as he fends them both off, dodging their blows, then kicking Zephi's legs out from beneath her. Just as he's about to drive his daga into Zephi's chest, Arzu leaps and wraps her legs around Bo's neck, twisting him to the ground. Bo rolls out of it and backflips toward me. He leaps into the air, and I jump away just as his daga comes down where my head had been.

"Bo, stop this," I hiss, but it's like he doesn't even hear me.

Anger surges in me, and I dash forward. But Bo presses a hand to his chest and spits out an inisisa that, in mid-flight, turns into an eagle. I dodge it just in time. Mouth still open, he vomits a snake and another pool of ink that grows into a many-tailed dragon.

He can call forth inisisa too. And so many almost at once. When did he learn how to do that?

The snake slithers toward Arzu. She jumps out of the way, but it's too fast. It springs from the ground and wraps around her arm, then slithers up to bite her shoulder. Crying out, she tosses it to the ground. Shadows spread like a bruise on her shoulder.

I roll under one of Bo's strikes and stab the snake in the back of its neck. The eagle turns around and swoops down on me, and the dragon roars into the sky. I raise my hands to block the eagle's charge, then see it heading straight for Aliya. I run to catch it. "Aliya!" I cry out, but one of the dragon's tails smashes into me, hurling me into a burning hut.

Thatch falls onto me, and I furiously pat at my clothes to get rid of the flames. Bo's knee crashes into my chin, sending me to the ground with him on top of me, grabbing at my neck. I hadn't even seen him coming.

Something moves behind him, and he drops me just as Zephi thrusts a sword forward. She must have taken the weapon from a fallen villager. Bo gets out of the way, but the sword cuts his shirt. I fall to the ground with my hands at my throat, struggling for breath.

As I writhe on the ground, the clink and clash of metal against stone fill the air. The hut burns around us.

The roof of the hut crackles over us. A large piece of thatch falls to the ground by the far wall.

Bo tenses, then lunges for Zephi. Zephi blocks the blow with her sword, but the strength of it sends tremors up her arms. Bo strikes again and again and again, new fury powering each move. His body is practically bursting with it.

One more strike, and Zephi's sword snaps in half. She dodges Bo's next blow, just barely, then the one after that, but Bo catches her again on the stomach, then on the wrist as she raises her arm to block the strike.

"No!" I shout as Bo brings Zephi to her knees, then, back turned to me, arcs his daga in a downward slice.

Zephi falls to the ground.

Bo turns.

Fury turns my entire world red. My hands ball into fists. My body prepares itself to tackle Bo and pummel him into Infinity, but just then fire crackles overhead.

I scramble to the hut's entrance just as more of the roof caves in. It collapses behind me, burying Bo with Zephi's body.

Arzu and Aliya run over to me, out of breath, but I see no sign of the inisisa.

Two of the Larada try to stand but can only rise to one knee, drained. Their power . . . it takes a piece from them. It's just like Eating, I realize with a start. You pay the tax with your body. Maybe they are not as marked on their skin as they are on their insides. One of the Larada coughs blood into the dirt, even though there is no wound on her body.

"Where is she?" Aliya asks me. "The one who fought Bo."

I come to my knees and shake my head. I'm trembling when I get to my feet and limp forward. Arzu sees the look in my eyes and bows her head.

"Come on," I murmur. "Let's go find the oth—"

I turn and can't believe what I'm seeing. Out of the burning wreckage emerge three sin-wolves. A bear rises to its full height. Underneath it kneels Bo. By the Unnamed . . . he called them forth and used them for shelter as the hut collapsed.

CHAPTER 25

THERE'S NO ENERGY left in me. Nothing. I try to feed off the anger I felt earlier, but my limbs won't obey me. I grit my teeth and face my enemy and try to summon the strength to fight the last of these inisisa off. They stalk toward us with Bo at the center of the group.

How did he get this powerful?

"Any ideas, Aliya?" I say loudly.

"Come home, Taj!" Bo shouts so loudly that I'm sure the entire village can hear him. "End this!" He steps through the wreckage of the hut, then stops and says, more quietly, "End this," and I hear the pleading in his voice, so soft and quick I almost miss it. He doesn't want to do this. He doesn't want to be this thing—this monster—Karima has made him into . . .

A cry from somewhere above us draws our attention. From the sky comes a tastahlik with a longstaff.

Wale.

I've never been so grateful to see someone who'd once beaten me up.

He comes down hard on Bo's head, then spins around to send him through the air and to the ground a dozen paces away. Without missing a beat, Wale swings his staff around, slicing through Bo's inisisa. All the beasts break down into boiling puddles, then shoot into the air and dive down into Wale's open mouth.

He wipes the lingering ink from the side of his lips, then assumes a fighting stance, longstaff behind his back.

Bo stands to his full height, then stretches his back and cracks his neck. He charges toward Wale faster than I've ever seen him move, and Wale lowers himself and spins his staff. Bo leaps over him and lands on the other side. Wale has his back turned and, just as Bo rushes forward, thrusts his staff out, catching Bo in the stomach, then Wale spins, smacking Bo twice across the face before sweeping his legs out from beneath him, pinning him to the ground with the wooden end.

It's done.

Wale saved us.

I fall to one knee, grateful and exhausted. I turn to say something to Aliya, but Bo grips Wale's staff, slips out from beneath it, then knocks it away, slicing at Wale's face with the daga in his hand.

Wale staggers away, bleeding, and raises his staff just as Bo strikes. He parries one blow, then the next, then spins his staff so that it whistles in the air before twirling away and swinging at Bo, who leans back, missing the blow. Bo straightens and launches himself forward. Wale leans back and twists in the air as Bo sails over him, straightens his staff, and catches it in his other hand, holding it close to his side. Bo skids to a stop, then they go at it again, Bo swinging and Wale on the defensive, spinning and twisting himself in the air, trying to put distance between him and Bo. But Bo remains close, practically on top of him, until Wale pops himself into the air just like he did before and comes down again, the bladed end of his staff slicing through the back of Bo's shirt.

Bo screams in pain, but he turns, dagas gripped tight, and charges again like he's never going to run out of energy. Blood runs freely from his wounds, leaving trails behind in the dirt.

He's slowing down, and it's easier for Wale to catch his strikes and knock them away, but they're still more powerful than anything I've ever seen from an aki.

Bo lunges forward. Wale ducks, then spins his staff upward, the bladed end slicing through Bo's right wrist. As Bo staggers forward, holding what's left of his arm, Wale comes from behind and stabs his staff through Bo's thigh, pinning him to the ground.

But with his free hand, Bo pulls a daga from his boot and flings it back at Wale, catching him right in the neck.

Stunned, Wale staggers backward, fingers reaching for the blade dug deep in his neck, but before he can touch it, he falls back.

Bo, mustering strength I can't even imagine, pulls Wale's staff from his leg. Blood gushes from the wound in his leg, then he twirls the staff with his good hand and turns to face me. How can he stand?

Before I can think, I've already rushed into him, and the impact throws us both off balance. I land on top of him. We both have our hands on the staff, and I push with all my might against his neck. I'm wordless with rage. Spittle spills from my mouth. I grit my teeth and push.

"Come. Back," Bo hisses with gritted teeth.

Tears come to my eyes, then something gives, and he kicks me away. I land on my back, and Bo stalks toward me. "I don't want to kill you." This he says in a voice small enough for only me to hear. "Please."

"Bo, what happened? What did she do to you?"

His eyes flicker. His face looks like his mind is battling against itself. Then it settles. "Karima has brought Balance to Kos. There is no more rich. No more poor. No more sickness." He raises the staff and cracks me across the face with it. Pain explodes in my head. I try to crawl away. But Bo limps after me. "I am protecting Kos."

I can't believe what I'm hearing. I can't believe that Bo believes it either.

"Taj, if you keep running, I will burn down all of Odo to find you."

Running. So much death and destruction because I've been running. That familiar guilt rises. Threatens to overwhelm me. When I turn, Bo stands over me, the bladed end of the staff pointed at my chest. Blood drips from it. His blood. Around us stands a pack of sin-lions. Snarling. He still has the strength to call them.

"How?" I ask, gesturing to them weakly. "How did you get these powers?"

"Karima has an army of algebraists and Mages." He looks at the hand holding the staff, his other arm. There is almost no clear skin on his body. "They have made me stronger. Their magic has unlocked these things in me. My body is no longer a prison. It is a weapon." He says these things like he's describing a gift. Something I could have if only I'd join him. Join Karima. The sin-lions draw closer.

I abandoned Kos.

No longer.

I grip sand and hurl it at Bo's eyes. He backs away, and I put my hands to my chest. My lungs tighten, my shoulders tense, and out of my mouth spills a river of ink that forms into a boar. The effort leaves me weak, but the boar charges Bo, who, caught off guard, can't raise his staff in time. The sin-lions all charge at once. I can't die. Not today.

As the boar rumbles toward Bo, I whirl around and see the first of his inisisa rushing toward me. Everything seems to slow down. My body moves on instinct. I put my hand out and feel the fur of the sin-lion's foreheard against the palm of my hand. Then warmth. Warmth that blooms into heat, then a burst of light. I stumble forward. Where the lion had been, there is now only a shower of sparks.

I did it. Just like Juba. Just like the rest of the Larada—the Healers.

Tiny stars hang in the air around me as I turn to face the others. The boar stands a pace or two away from Bo, snarling. I can't kill him. I can't leave him eaten.

The sin-lions all look my way until I see movement at the

other end of the street. It looks like a wall of light is heading toward us, blanketing everything in its path. Juba and the Larada. A robed figure walks in their midst. Zaki.

In that instant, a plan occurs to me. It's absolutely cracked. But if I'm right, it could end it all. It could bring Bo back.

The inisisa turn to the Larada as one once Bo sees them, and the lions charge, only to explode into fountains of light that spring into the air. The night sky glows when the beasts come apart.

Now the Larada are close enough to hear me.

"Zaki," I call out. "Call forth his sins! Quick, before he can move!"

Bo tries to rush me, but Zaki dashes forward and grips his head. No matter how much Bo struggles, he can't get out of his grasp. Other Larada hold him down. Veins bulge in his neck and forehead and arms.

Bo spasms. Ink shoots into the air like a burst from a fountain. One continuous jet arcs through the air while more sin leaks down the sides of his mouth and begins pooling beneath him.

Sin pours from his throat. It seems to go on forever. Bo gags, choking. Suffocating. The first wave finishes, and he trembles. The pool at his feet turns into a wolf. The Larada have not moved. Bo seizes up again, and another beast spills from his mouth, then another and another, each blast of black bile like an arrow coming out of his body. He continues spilling sins, and the pool beneath his feet widens and widens and widens, and the crowd moves back in horror as the inky sin begins to darken Zaki's robe, rising above his knees. There's so much sin that I wonder how Bo managed to even stay alive for this long. How much sin does he have on his heart?

I can hear the cries choked in his throat by the sin he continues to let out.

The crowd pushes back even farther until they're all behind me on one end and behind Aliya and Arzu on the other. All the while, the Larada murmur to themselves in their language of prayer, Juba at the front of the group.

Then it all stops.

Bo sags in their grip.

Out of the ink come inisisa. Bears and wolves and griffins with talons dug into the sandy ground and cobras and lynxes and hyenas and dragons. So many sins spread out around our little circle of Bo, me, Zaki, and the tastahlik holding Bo down. I look up, then behind me, then back at Zaki, who meets my gaze, then turns around and sees for himself. The inisisa fill the streets. An entire horde of them.

When I see all of those beasts, my heart aches for Bo. All that darkness inside of him. How could he live with that?

When I rise, the other Larada rise with me. Juba sees the look on my face and knows what I want to do. Then, without a word, the Larada and I form a line facing one group of inisisa.

Arzu joins Zaki, and the two of them stand watch over Bo's limp body.

I step forward with the rest of the Healers, and everyone else makes way for us. As we reach the first row of inisisa, we put our hands to their foreheads and watch as they begin to glow. Then, all at once, they are nothing but light that bursts, leaving behind sparks like fireflies that wink out of existence. The thrill of it all overwhelms the fatigue I know is creeping in, so I walk with Juba and the others as we turn the inisisa into beasts made of light.

We work until the sky goes pink with morning.

When we find ourselves at the edge of the village and there are no more inisisa, I collapse.

Something stirs along the rim above us. A frame silhouetted against the sunrise.

It moves, then I see it skidding down the side of the bowl, then it vanishes amid the half-burned huts and the destroyed homes. I'm too weak to move, and I see the same is true for Juba. None of the Larada has the strength to fight anymore.

Eventually, it draws nearer. I know even before seeing the figure's face who he is. The way he moves, the way he sways, like something never content with straight lines or rest.

Abeo. I realize I haven't seen him since before the arashi attack. In all the chaos since, I hadn't even noticed.

Several tastahlik emerge from the village and stalk toward us. Has he been waiting for all of this? Was this his plan? To take over when we were weakened?

I still have the impulse to fight, and I struggle to my feet before Abeo's fist crashes into my cheek, tossing me onto my back.

Everything hurts, but I can't move. Even as some of the enemy tastahlik bind me in chains and restrain Juba.

"Juba," Abeo begins.

"Address me as Ayaba!" she hisses, even though she can barely stand while in the grip of the two tastahlik flanking her. "I am your queen. Designated by Olurun to be your leader."

"You were designated by your blood," Abeo sneers. "You are only Ayaba because your father was Oba. When did you ever prove yourself worthy of your title?" He draws closer to Juba, and I want to hit him, but I can't get up from where I kneel. "We were once a fierce tribe. Wandering the lands and taking what we needed no matter the cost. We avoided the arashi because we would fight whoever held us in one place for too long. Then you became our Ayaba, and we found water, and we stayed. And we grew weak." He waves a hand at the death and destruction behind him. "So easily, we are broken." He looks to me. "You let a boy with a bounty on his head take residence with us. You endangered us all." His gaze returns to Juba. "No more." He gestures with an arm. "Take her away." Then he walks to me. "You, we will bury with your friend. You will go where the refugees died. And you will suffocate under the weight of their uncleansed souls until you die as well."

His back is the last thing I see before something hard hits me in the back of the head, and I fall into darkness.

CHAPTER 26

WHEN I WAKE up, my legs won't move. My head feels like someone is building a house inside it. I try to touch it, but pain burns through my shoulders and back. My arms are bound behind me, tied to a pole. All around me is darkness. The wind howls overhead, screaming. That's when I realize where we are. That's not regular wind. It's inyo. Uncleansed spirits. The air is thick with them. This is where the refugee camp used to be. Before the ground opened up beneath it and swallowed it whole. I'm probably surrounded by dead bodies.

Bo slumps in his chains. They've been wrapped tightly around the pole, so that his arms are trapped behind him. My eyes adjust to fully take in the sight of him. At the sound of my stirring, he looks up.

It might be a trick of the shadows, but his eyes look like they're glowing red. I can't take my gaze away from him, from how still he is, even though his entire body must be aching from having all of those sins removed. That could have been me. If I had stayed in Kos, Karima would have turned me into that. A soldier, a killer who would stop at nothing to fulfill her wishes.

The red glow in Bo's eyes flickers, then leaves. His eyes are normal again. And exhausted. A dirty, red-stained bandage wraps around his leg where Wale's staff had stabbed him.

"Bo," I whisper. "Bo."

He can barely support himself. I want to help him, to hold him upright, but with every move I make, my chains dig into my skin. "What did you do to me?" It comes out first as barely a whimper, then again, louder. Still a question. The anger in his voice has left him. The fury, the violence. He sounds lost.

I remember that first sin-lion I turned into light. Then I remember the army of inisisa that the Healers and I cleansed. I had been moving on instinct, getting my mind out of the way so that my heart could guide me. "Forgiveness," I whisper. The memory of Zaki's voice hums in my head. "Forgiveness."

"What do you mean?"

Even as I speak, I'm piecing it all together. But forgiveness is how I unlocked it. "I forgave."

I can see Bo's confused frown, even in the near darkness.

"I forgave myself. For abandoning Kos. For abandoning you. I . . . I wanted to save you."

For a long time, Bo is still. Then he sniffs away a sob. "I didn't deserve it. After everything I'd done for Karima, after all of that death. I didn't deserve it."

I jerk at my chains. I want to hold him. I want to tell him, *Yes, you did deserve it. You do deserve it.* "They tried to change you." My mind is only now catching up to me, so many questions, so many pieces falling into place. Zaki's words, Aliya's equations, Iragide. But there's still so much I don't understand. "What did they do to you?"

Bo looks to the sky, and we both watch the inyo blot out the sun. Then he looks to the ground, ashamed. "She made it easy." Bo sounds as though he is saying it to himself more than to me. "She made it easy to sin. To kill."

"She removed your guilt," I whisper.

This is how the Mages and algebraists did it. This is how they turned Bo into this hunter. My eyes widen at the idea of aki walking through Kos, now able to sin as much as possible without falling ill, now able to Eat as much sin as Karima commands them to without Crossing. Mages have removed their guilt.

Bo shakes his head. "But there are limits to their abilities. Still, I was able to carry an army of inisisa inside of me so that everywhere I went, I could call them forth and have them consume others. Then, when they were finished, I could Eat them again and have them live within my bones." He flinches at the memory of it.

My eyes widen at the power Karima has unlocked, at the consequences of it all, at the fact that she now has everything she needs to bring the entire kingdom to its knees. Then I remember how much it must hurt. Even with the guilt removed, it is still one of the most agonizing things in the world to Eat a sin. Yet that did not matter to Karima. Aki will always be nothing but tools for her. Weapons. She never saw me as a person, as a lover. Even back then, when I stood on the steps of the Palace and she tried to call me to her side while Kos burned all around us, tried to convince me that I was worthy of her, I was never to be her heart-mate. I would always be a weapon to her.

Bo relaxes in his chains and sits down. "There is only one way my journey ends." The raised edges of his sin-spots cover almost his entire face. This has been his work. This is what Karima did to him. "Will they kill me?"

Thunder crackles overhead. Right after, rain patters on our heads.

"I don't know," I whisper. My hair slumps over my ears. Before long, our clothes hang on us, drenched rags. I sneeze. And I can't even move my arms to wipe my face.

Soon, muddy water soaks into my flats. Bo hasn't moved at all. Even as the water rises past his knees.

"Bo," I call out. "Bo!" Is he asleep? "Bo!"

I look up. Rain pelts me in the eye. It's not stopping. It's not even slowing down.

"Bo!" I start to struggle against the chains binding me.

A peaceful look comes across Bo's face. Like he's grateful for what's happening.

"Bo!" Now the water is up past our waists. We need to get out of here. Water falls in sheets over the ridge of the crater. Something's going on. The crater is filling up too fast.

Bo is on his feet now, looking around nervously. Water rises above our chests.

My wrists and shoulders are on fire. Energy leeches out of me like blood from an open wound. This isn't normal. None of this is normal.

It's up to our chins now.

"Help!" I cry out. No one can hear me over the storm. "Help! Somebody!"

Bo sputters on muddy water.

Something bumps against me. I squint and see an arm, then a torso. A dead body. "Chai!" I shriek. Then more and more of them. The dead refugees. The water opened their graves. Pretty soon, Bo and I will be among them. "Bo!" I shout, tears streaming down my face. "Bo! Bo, stay with me."

He's swaying. He can barely stand upright. Water fills his nose.

"Bo!" I pull and pull and pull. Water starts to lift me off my feet. "Bo!" My feet catch on the wood of my pole. Pain, like fire, gallops through my shoulders, but I catch debris below my feet. And, balancing against the pole, I shimmy my way up. The water rises with me, chasing me. Just a little more. A little more. My arm is about to pop out of its socket. I have to close my eyes against the water that has swallowed us. Higher. Higher. Then, freedom! I reach the top of the pole and slip my arms over. My chains unfurl around me, but my manacles stay locked tight around my wrists. Still, I can move.

I break free and dunk myself underwater, then swim to Bo and take his chains in my hands.

They're solid. There's no key. I fumble around and stop when I get to the stump where his hand had been. It all comes back to me: the massacre, the fight. I shake myself out of my stupor. My lungs are about to explode. I make for the surface and gulp in air. I can't free him.

But I can keep his head above water for now.

Floating, I grip his face and tilt it upward to keep the water out. He chokes, then spits water out.

I bring my face close to his. "Bo," I say. "Bo, look at me." His eyes are wide—afraid—but there it is: He sees me. He sees who I once was to him. All of a sudden, we're two brothers again, running around Kos, tackling each other in the streets, trying to flirt with girls from other towns at Zoe's. Let this be how I remember him.

Peace seeps into me.

I hug him close, careful to keep his head above water for a little longer. Karima couldn't break us.

Thunder crackles, then booms overhead. I hear voices. Whispers. The sound of more inyo.

Then a loud splash.

Something heavy smashes into me, breaking Bo and me apart. I feel myself pass through a series of hands until I hit the wall of the crater. My gaze darts back and forth until I notice a rope ladder next to me. What? I look up to see Arzu several rungs down with her arm outstretched. Rain continues to blanket us. I look back, and someone has Bo over their shoulder, paddling to another ladder at the other end of the crater.

"Taj!" Arzu shouts above me. "Take my hand!"

I take it, and she pulls me up. Halfway up the ladder, the storm stops. No more rain, no more thunder.

More hands pull me up over the edge of the crater, and I try to get to my knees, coughing, but can barely find the strength.

It feels like I've been coughing forever, but eventually I stop. Standing over me are Arzu and Aliya. Not far from where I lie, Zaki attends to Bo. He's not moving.

"Bo," I whisper, reaching out to him. A hand grips my shoulder.

"Taj." It's Arzu. "Can you stand?"

I fall onto my back and try to catch my breath. "What happened?"

Aliya looks to the sky. "We came to free you."

"But Abeo. The others. Juba. Where is she?"

When I sit upright, Arzu slaps my back, and more water spills out. "We have to get out of here first. The storm bought us some time, but we have to move quickly."

"The storm . . ." I stare at Aliya. "You did that?"

She works fast at removing my chains. I don't know how she does it, but she breaks apart my manacles. They fall away. "I had some help." She darts a grin at Zaki before hauling me to my feet.

The inyo move faster around us now that we are out of the sinkhole. Arzu pulls a scarf up over her mouth and nose. Aliya coughs against the dense, poisoned air.

"Hurry," Zaki says.

We stumble out of the darkness, and, with a suddenness that stops me in my tracks, the sun is out again. The day shines bright. Zaki's house is a speck on a hill in the distance.

"Abeo's tastahlik are busy guarding Juba and the Larada who weren't able to escape. There aren't enough of his people to send any to my dwelling," Zaki tells us. So, we hurry in that direction. Aliya holds me up. The sun warms my body. Her touch warms me even more.

"I saved him," I tell Aliya in a soft voice. "I brought Bo back."

CHAPTER 27

THEY BRING BO inside, but Aliya and I remain on the front steps of Zaki's home. Feeling has started to return to my body.

"Aliya, I'm ready."

Her robes, still dark from the rain, hang off her frame. When she goes to squeeze water out of them, she has to roll up her sleeves and reveal the markings winding up and down her arms. Letters and numbers cover her skin the way beasts cover mine. I feel like we've been joined by something magical, something bigger than ourselves. Something Unnamed.

"I'm ready to go back to Kos."

She pauses in the act of drying herself, eyes wide with disbelief. Then a smile breaks across her face. She hugs me, and I sink into her. It feels genuine, full. It is, I realize, what I've wanted for so long. Almost without even knowing it.

Then she breaks away. "We have some work to do first."

"Juba," I say, and she nods.

Inside the cabin, Zaki and the Healers congregate around the two desks that have been turned into a bed for Bo. His eyes flutter open, then close, but his breathing is normal. When he hears me come in, he sits up and swings his legs over the side of the table. He's not ready to stand just yet, but color has returned to his face.

In two leaps, I'm before him, and I hold the back of his neck, pressing my forehead to his. "Brother," I say. He doesn't resist my grip. "It is good to have you back."

"Until I'm strong enough to beat you in a wrestling match again," he says with a weak smile.

I chuckle. "Should I press my advantage now?"

I look up. Zaki is pulling scrolls from shelves. Aliya comes in from behind me to help him. The Larada whisper among themselves, a few of them still eyeing Bo with suspicion. "Where's Arzu?"

Zaki looks up and seems to notice for the first time that his daughter isn't in the room with us.

"She left to pray," one of the Larada says.

I find her out back, behind the house, sitting down with a small string of prayer stones in her clasped hands. She murmurs words I can't quite make out, then says, "May my head and my heart find Balance." She stands, then looks to the sky. "The sky is our ceiling, the earth our bed."

I wait until she's finished. "Hey."

When she sees me, she has an expression of bottomless sadness mixed with anger on her face.

I raise my hands in defense. She looks at me like I've offended her, barging in on her prayer. "Your temper won't boil your beans," I joke, hoping to get her to smile.

She lets out a half-hearted laugh and wipes the tears from her eyes.

"Today's royal decree will be tomorrow's suya wrap." *Keep calm*, I'm saying. *Nothing lasts forever.*

This time, her chuckle turns into a full-on laugh. "A chicken can run from Kos and still end up in a pot of soup." *You can't escape your destiny*, she is saying.

"Spoken like a child of the Forum!"

"Yes," she says with a soft chuckle. She wipes tear streaks from her cheeks and looks at the prayer stones in her hands. "When Juba would visit, we would sneak out of the Palace and wander the Forum, listening to the way the people of Kos spoke. The proverbs . . . Juba was drawn to them. We were children, so it was easy to learn." The way she speaks of Kos, I can tell she misses it. She grips her prayer stones, then slides them through her belt. "I heard you and Aliya speaking earlier. I'm coming back too."

A part of me is glad Arzu is saying this. But a part of me breaks. I think of the way she and Juba look at each other and how she is never far from Juba's side. The way they move around each other, it's like they're in this really simple dance. Like they know each other's rhythms. And the way Arzu wept when she saw Juba for the first time since they were children. They are in love.

Arzu casts her gaze in the direction of the village, where the girl she loves is no doubt being held in chains.

"It is strange. I only know this place from the tales my mother told me. She painted such a vivid picture in my mind, so different from Kos and the Palace. But I feel lost still."

My brows furrow. "Lost?"

"I am returned, yes, but I feel as though I do not belong here. This is my homeland, but . . . it is more my mother's than mine. I can barely speak the dialect here. I am torn between two places. I belong to neither. No one here knows me. And my mother was so skilled at removing her roots from the soil here that few people know or remember her. The tribes migrate so much, and some tribespeople settle elsewhere while others from different tribes join ours, and there has been so much mixing and matching and mingling that I don't think my mother would recognize this place were she here to see it." She looks at her folded hands in her lap. "The people she told me of were always moving. I pictured caravans and growing up being chased by arashi and tastahlik who were . . ." She trails off. "These people have stopped moving. They have found shelter, and they live at the bottom of a calabash bowl made of earth. Just like the dahia in Kos."

"Can't seem to get away from the city," I murmur, trying to make it a joke again. Kos is the city of my birth. The city where both of us were born, really. Only, it was always *my* homeland. Mama and Baba had no tales of faraway lands for me, no stories about people who were so much like me and so very different from the people I ran with in the streets of Kos. My family was

Marya and Auntie Sania and Auntie Nawal and the aki I shared a cramped room with. That was my tribe.

"I have no home here," Arzu says at last.

"You have Zaki," I say. "You have your baba." Which is more than I can say for myself.

Arzu nods. "There is the family you are born into and the family that you make. You. Aliya. The rebels. That too is my family. That is my home. Where you and Aliya go, so I will go also." She smiles and walks up to me, then puts a hand on my shoulder. "Let's go home?"

I put my hand on hers. "Let's go home."

CHAPTER 28

ALIYA HAS MOVED all the books from the study to the living room. Zaki stands over a pot in the kitchen, and the aroma of egusi soup thickens the air. The house smells like my first memories of living with Mama and Baba. On days when we were paid well enough, the rooms I and the other aki once shared in the shantytowns of Kos would smell like this too.

My thoughts go to that afternoon I spent with the Onija. Sitting in a loose, unbalanced circle, eating melon slices and chin-chin. Young and powerful and laughing. The sun shining through the beaded curtain of that room, splashing bars of light over our sin-spotted arms and legs. There's a part of me that still sees myself there. Joking with Folami and Abeo and the others about foolish, dirty merchants from faraway lands who eat with soiled metal forks instead of with their hands. Play-fighting with the younger sin-eaters, defending the village with the older ones. I thought I could be one of them.

I shake away the vision. They're the enemy now. And Abeo leads them.

Aliya pores over the books, and when Zaki has finished handing out bowls of soup to the Healers, he joins her. It's like the rest of us have vanished, and all the two of them have eyes for is their work. Unrolled books are scattered across the floor, and I have to step over them in order to join their inner circle. They have their books unrolled side by side, and I see that the ones before Aliya are nothing but shapes. Shapes next to shapes inside of more shapes. But it's a jumble. And Zaki holds down unrolled books that show disjointed equations, like the writing on Aliya's body.

"This is it," Aliya whispers, pointing. She points first at the shapes, then jabs a finger at an equation. "Quick! Parchment!" she shouts to no one in particular.

I scoop up some half-rolled books and spread one out on the table. Aliya pulls the stylus from behind her ear and begins scribbling. On one end of the parchment, she starts an equation, then she peers at the geometric shapes, then on the other end of her parchment, she begins writing script, right to left. Then she goes back and beneath the first equation, she writers another, then a matching line of script. One side looks like lines from poetry, the other side her usual lahala algorithms.

"What's she doing?" I ask Zaki.

But he's just staring at her in wonder. When the others notice Zaki's stillness, they too crowd around.

Aliya's writing grows more feverish. Sweat beads her forehead. And she doesn't make a sound. Now even Arzu has come to see. Aliya pushes the stylus down so hard it snaps, and we all jump back in one loud shout.

"I need another!"

Arzu and I scramble into the study, pulling open drawers and knocking books down from shelves.

"EH-EH!" Zaki shouts from the living room. "THERE IS NO NEED TO BE BANGING MY CUPBOARDS AND MAKING MY HOUSE ALL JAGGA-JAGGA!"

"Got it!" Arzu holds up a stylus, and we get it to Aliya as quickly as possible.

She resumes and scribbles some more. Then some more, until she's filled the entire page. Before she slides that one away, I hand her another, unrolling the book and spreading it out on its empty side. She keeps going, writing faster than I've ever seen anyone write.

She's writing a proof, I realize. But a proof of what?

I catch movement out of the corner of my eye, and a shape darts past the window. I rush to it and see nothing until something else, fast and black, rushes past. Then, cresting the hill, a line of black shapes. Inisisa.

"We have to get out of here," I say, backing away. I rush to the opposite window over the washing area in the kitchen and see more. "We don't have much time. He's here!"

"Olodo!" a voice sings from outside.

Abeo.

Darkness covers the windows, blocking out the light.

Uhlah! Everyone stops moving. Even the sound of Aliya's stylus moving against the parchment has died.

"Come, come!" the voice shouts. "Come and let me collect my bounty, na! I went through all this trouble leading your friend here to kill my enemies and make my job easier; now let me come collect my money."

Someone in the room gasps.

I turn to Bo.

"I did not wander here," Bo says as the realization dawns on him. "I followed a trail. A trail I believed was made by aki. I was chasing a man covered in sins." He pauses. I can feel the air change with his frown. "I thought he was you."

Abeo led Bo to us. To the village. Knowing what Bo would do. So that was his plan: lead Bo to the village so that, once the killing was finished, Abeo could overthrow Juba. Then, when the dust settled, have Bo killed and take my corpse to Karima.

Except that we escaped.

"Foolish olodo! You had the chance to run, and instead, like a rat escaping a flood, you trap yourself."

Nobody speaks.

"Fine, then. If you do not come out, I will execute Juba right here."

We hear the scraping sound of chains. Then silence.

We wait. Maybe he is prompting Juba to speak and let us know she is really there with him. I imagine Juba refusing to make a sound. I imagine her being willing to sacrifice herself to save us.

"We don't know that she's out there," I hiss. "It could be a trap."

"We are already trapped," one of the Healers whispers back.

"I'm not leaving her out there to die," Arzu says. Before any of us can stop her, she rushes for the door and swings it open, charging outside. Light blasts into the room, and a moment later, screams mingle in the air. We all dart out at once into the day.

CHAPTER 29

INISISA SURROUND US. At least a dozen. Boars and bears and wolves and lynxes and snakes as long as I am tall. Folami has Arzu on her knees, the bladed end of her jointed staff pointed at the back of her neck. Juba stands upright, but Abeo is behind her, her chains firmly in his grasp.

"Ah, you have finally met my stable." He waves his free arm at the legion of inisisa.

My hands long for a weapon.

"They have been itching for some air. You see, keeping inisisa in captivity, it only makes them angrier. One would say, less easy to control. They are just like the refugee children I call them from. Unruly, unpredictable. Then your arashi had to come and cut off my supply." One of the Healers starts to get into a fighting stance, and Abeo makes a show of tightening Juba's chains. She grunts against them. "Do you value the life of your Ayaba?

Your queen?" The Healer relents. "Now come to me, Taj." He spits out my name like it's venom or the remnants of a sin he has just Eaten.

Lanre pulls his sabers out from the scabbards crossing his back and comes forward.

I look around and realize I have no choice. Bo has one hand, and neither of us has any weapons. Arzu can't move. Just as I take a step, Aliya trips and stumbles, landing on the steps in front of me, between me and Lanre. She crawls on her hands and knees, searching.

"My spectacles!" she shouts. "My spectacles! Oh no!" She crawls in a wide circle. I stoop to help her, and she pauses only for a moment to murmur, "Back away, Taj. Just step back."

When I do, I see that everywhere she puts her hand, she leaves a trail of something dark. Blood. Just like Zaki during the arashi attack.

She stops. A circle of dried blood surrounds her where she kneels. She touches her head to the ground, pretending to cry, like she has finally given up looking for her lost spectacles.

"What is this lahala?" Abeo shouts, and the others snicker. "Is everyone from your city this clumsy?"

Aliya is still, but just below Abeo's laughter, I can hear her murmur. Then the ground begins to shake. A small rumble at first, which gets everyone to stop moving. Then stronger. So strong that everyone stumbles back. Lanre falls down. Abeo staggers back, tightening his grip on Juba. Then a gash opens up in the earth. The land Aliya and I stand on breaks away from the land the Onija stand on. Some of the sin-beasts nervously step from side to side. One of the inisisa doesn't notice how near it is to the crack and falls in. So does another.

The cut in the earth widens. Suddenly, Bo leaps from behind me and barrels into Lanre. When he flips away, he has one of Lanre's sabers in his good hand, and he charges straight for one of the inisisa—a wolf—jumping and spinning in the air to slice open the nape of its neck. The wolf collapses and instantly turns into a pool of sin that jets into Bo's waiting mouth.

With Folami distracted, Arzu kicks out, tripping her and tearing free of her ropes. The gap in the ground is still widening, but Arzu jumps across and barely makes it. I rush to pull her up just as a wall of water rises from the broken earth. I turn, and Zaki too stands in a ring of blood. Arzu and I catch each other's eye, and she hands me one of the dagas tucked into her belt.

Together, we run and burst through the wall of water to see chaos around us.

Bo swings his new saber at the inisisa that surround him, wounding one but having to dodge another's attack from behind. He slips and just barely avoids the bear that towers over him and slams its paws down where his head had been.

Daga in hand, Arzu turns and just barely catches Folami's strike with her block. She kicks Folami away, then gets into her fighting stance.

I see Abeo backing away. His remaining inisisa gather around him. They advance toward me as one. I try to return to that place I was in when Juba and the Healers and I rid the village of the sins Bo carried within him.

Just as the first snake leaps for me, I sidestep it and try to catch its forehead. It twists in my grasp and wraps around my arm. It rears back to bite my neck when a hand grips its neck, and it bursts apart in a shower of fireflies. One of the Larada smiles at me, then rushes at where Bo keeps three inisisa at bay.

Another Larada rushes past me and easily fends off the rest of the inisisa Abeo sent at me.

Next to me, Bo slices and sweeps and swings, and the inisisa trying to consume him fall apart. He Eats them with ease.

Lanre charges him from behind, but Bo flips the saber in his hand and swings behind him, knocking away Lanre's saber just in time. Then Bo spins and catches Lanre in his side. Lanre falls to his knees. Then his head hits the ground.

Arzu has Folami's arm twisted high up her back with her daga at the Onija's throat.

"Abeo!" I call out to him. "You're defeated. Let Juba go."

"Far from it," Abeo says. "Far from it. Your Ayaba is just one wrong breath away from my opening her throat. I would be careful were I you."

He's right. We've finished the rest of his army, but Juba still can't move, and she still has a daga to her throat. Before I can figure out how to get to her, a loud *boom* rings out behind me.

An explosion. Screaming. Fire.

Abeo screams out, clutching his face. "My eyes!" he shrieks. He scrambles away on his hands and knees, smoke rising from his clothes. I smell charred flesh.

Behind me, the wall made of water has fallen. Zaki stands at the edge of the broken earth. His shoulders slumping, he leans forward.

Teeth bared in an animal snarl, Abeo turns and prepares to rush me when Zaki waves his arm and Abeo bursts into flames again. Aliya does the same with her other arm, and more fire swallows up the enemy tastahlik. He screams. Again and again, he lights up until he falls to his knees, unable to move.

All of us watch Aliya and Zaki in shock and wonder. Aliya's eyes are wide and bright, shining with a rage I've never seen from her. Even Folami twists in Arzu's grip to watch my friend, the Mage. The Seventh Prophet.

Aliya can turn the very air around us into fire.

Abeo twitches on the ground. Aliya prepares to swipe more fire at him when Zaki grabs her wrist.

"Enough," he says.

After a moment, her eyes return to normal. Wherever she went when she pulled fire from the air, she is back. She blinks as though she is just now figuring out where she is.

Arzu pushes Folami into the circle formed by me, Bo, and her.

"Your chief is gone," Arzu spits. "Do you surrender?"

Folami looks at all of us, her face blank. And I can tell she's hiding a riot of emotions. Just like how the rest of the village does. They wear the mask to shield their most extreme feelings from the world. They save those only for themselves. Even as they walk about, seeming calm and peaceful, emotions war inside them.

Folami bows her head. "I surrender," she says at last.

Smoke hisses from Abeo's body. Arzu is far from delicate as she rifles through his pockets for a key, then she unlocks Juba's chains.

We did it.

Zaki holds Aliya upright. I wait for them bring the earth back together, but Aliya sags in his arms. She stands outside her circle of blood, and Zaki stands outside his. He kneels, then puts his hand to the earth. A thin, unsteady bridge of dirt and stone arcs into the air to link them to us. Slowly, Zaki carries Aliya across, trying to maintain balance. The bridge behind him begins to crumble, and he slips. He drops Aliya on the bridge, and she rolls toward us, but stops. Zaki runs on what remains of the bridge as it collapses around him, scoops Aliya in his arms, then, just as he clears the bridge's apex, tosses Aliya with both hands into the air.

I cushion her fall with my body, but when I get up, Zaki is nowhere to be found.

"No!" Arzu screams. She lies at the ground's edge, her arm outstretched. "Hold on!" She's slipping, being pulled forward. She has Zaki in her grasp. She holds on with both hands, but she's about to go over.

I dash forward and slide to a stop, grabbing onto Arzu's boots just as she's about to slip over.

"Hold on!" Arzu shouts. "Hold on." Her voice grows softer and softer. "Please, Baba, hold on. Baba, please. Please, hold on. Please." I can hear her weeping. "Baba, I'm sorry. I'm so sorry. Baba, please come back."

I can feel him pulling us over.

"Arzu, let me go." When Zaki speaks, it's in a voice so weak that I think only Arzu and I can hear it. "Let me go." A smile crosses his face. "I'm too weak. But I am happy."

"Happy?" Arzu asks through her sobs.

"Yes. The Unnamed returned my daughter to me, if only for a brief time. I will die Balanced. Al-Jabr, my child. The reunification of broken things." With one last burst of energy, he snaps his wrist toward himself, breaking out of Arzu's grasp and falling.

"BABA! BABA, NO!" She reaches for him, scrabbling, dragging me down. But I feel hands behind me, pulling me back.

"Arzu," I say, but the rest of it chokes in my throat.

"No," she whispers.

When we pull her up, she lies on the ground, weeping into her soiled hands.

Aliya's eyes drift open. As soon as I see her move, I'm at her side. I have her head in my lap when she speaks to me.

"I know it," she says. "I know the Ratio. I figured it out." Then she notices Arzu weeping. "What happened?"

"We lost Zaki."

Aliya's bottom lip trembles. Then the tears begin to fall.

CHAPTER 30

ALIYA SLOWLY PUSHES herself off me. One of the Healers arrives at her side with her staff, and Aliya nods in thanks, propping herself up. I rise with her. At the place where the ground has broken, Juba kneels beside Arzu. Arzu has stopped crying and now has that stonelike expression on her face. Juba holds out a hand to Arzu, who sits in the dirt, her cheeks stained with mud. The bangles on Juba's wrists are bent. Some of them barely hang on.

Arzu stares at the hand in a daze, like she cannot understand where it has come from. Then it is like someone snaps their fingers inside her mind, and she comes to her feet, brushes the dust from her leathers, tightens her belt. She walks over to where I sit and where Aliya stands, and she stoops and scoops up the daga I had dropped. Without a word, she slides it into a sheath on her belt.

Folami collapses on the ground in our midst, her head bowed

to the dirt. Her hands and head face Juba. The smoke from Abeo's ashen corpse wafts through the air between them.

The Healers amass around her, and together, they march as one until there is only the width of a finger between Folami's head and Juba's boot. Juba is silent for so long that Folami eventually raises her head.

"Ayaba," she mumbles. "Forgive me."

Juba clenches her fists at her sides. As blank as the expression on her face is, she trembles with rage. Her wrists, where they show through her bangles, are rimmed with red. But the moment passes.

"It is not my choice to make," Juba says at last. "The village will hold court and decide your fate. First, you will tell your people to stand down. You have lost."

"Ayaba, please do not cast us out. I will volunteer myself in place of the others."

Juba's hand moves as swift as lightning. Her fingers wrap around Folami's throat. And there's that anger again. It looks so familiar. People you care about, people you love, have been hurt. And here is the person who did it, or at least someone involved. And here is the chance to hurt them back. Deeply. Dearly. But that's not Balance—not the right kind of Balance.

My hand rests on Juba's shoulder.

She turns her head only halfway. A snarl twists her lips. "This is not your affair, Taj of Kos. Stay out of it."

My grip on her shoulder tightens. "Juba, you know this is wrong."

Her fingers squeeze Folami's neck, raising her off the ground.

"Juba."

I could stand aside. I could watch this tribe's conflicts play themselves out. I could let Juba restore order as she sees fit. This is not my affair. But I am tired of death. I can't bear any more guilt. "Juba, let her go."

"Juba!" The call comes from Arzu.

At this, Juba drops Folami to the ground. The Onija coughs violently. Larada gather around her. I back away from Juba so that nothing and no one stands between her and Arzu.

When I see them like that, I'm reminded of the very first time I saw them together, the very first time they'd seen each other since they were children. Juba had just slain half a dozen sin-wolves with ease. And she had just Eaten Arzu's massive sin, the sin that threatened to kill her. And when she finished, she saw Arzu across the distance, and I can only imagine what images ran through their minds in that moment. What questions, what prayers, what whispers, what shouting.

Is it the same now? The same riot of emotions held behind a mask?

Arzu walks with infinite slowness until she finally reaches Juba. Juba's mask breaks. She begins to breathe heavily, like she's waiting for something. Arzu cups Juba's cheek in her hand, and Juba leans into it.

"Stay with me," I hear Juba say. "Help me repair my tribe."

"But you are tastahlik, and I am not," Arzu replies. Her voice is like rock that has begun to crack. "It would be against the laws of the tribe for me to be with you. And if I cannot have you as my heart-mate, I will not stay."

Juba puts her hand to Arzu's and closes her eyes. "I would abolish the law for you, Arzu. All the laws in the world."

Arzu's mask cracks even more. "I cannot ask you to do that, Ayaba. Don't destroy your world just to have me."

For a long time, they are both silent. Then Juba lets out a sigh so heavy it deflates her. She steps back and straightens. "You're right. My people need me."

Juba tries to smile, but her bottom lip trembles. "And mine need me," Arzu says.

Juba reaches out and wraps her fingers around the back of Arzu's neck. Their foreheads touch. "The sky is our ceiling, the earth our bed," Juba whispers.

"The sky is our ceiling, the earth our bed," Arzu whispers back.

Juba pulls Arzu to her in an embrace. "You will always have my heart."

Arzu says nothing but wraps her arms tighter around Juba.

When Juba steps away this time, she turns her back to us. She looks to the Larada. "Bring the prisoner." It's all she says before she begins her march down the hill.

We watch them go until they vanish into the distance.

Then Arzu whirls around. "Should I fetch some pillows so you can all keep staring, or should we be going now? Kos isn't saving itself."

I burst into laughter, and Arzu is smiling, and the rest of us are laughing and smiling too. It's the first time I've seen her like this in so long. Free. Like she was with the lascars on the ship.

"Now, how do we get back to Kos?" I ask, scratching my head.

Before I get a response from anyone, Bo is on his knees, retching into the ground. Black bile spills from his mouth. His shoulders shudder with each convulsion. Then he finishes and wipes the remnants of sin from his mouth. Four pools of ink writhe in front of him, then sprout first wings, then a beak, then a head, until they turn into full-bodied griffins. Bo climbs to his feet. "I think this is the part where you do your thing, Taj."

I smirk.

I'm still unsure of myself, of my ability to cleanse, so I'm slow to get to the first griffin, but when I touch its forehead, I feel that old warmth in my palm. Its shadows peel away, and when its colors are made plain, lightning pulses beneath its skin. There's a moment of shock when I do it, and the large beast tilts its head at me. Like it's trying to figure me out. Then, reassurance. I can do this. I cleanse the other three, then climb atop the one in the middle.

The others hesitate, reaching out haltingly to touch the things.

"Come now!" I snap. "Oya, let's go!"

They climb atop their griffins and grip the feathers behind the neck just like I do. Arzu ties her blond hair back, away from her face.

My griffin darts into the sky. Then, after a moment, the rest follow.

Below us, Zaki's home sits, separated from the rest of the land by a giant knife scar cut into the earth. It grows smaller and smaller beneath us, then it disappears.

We hover in the air above the clouds. The wind whips my puffy hair back. I look to the others. Each of them. Arzu. Bo. Aliya.

Our griffins flap their wings, and we slice through the sky, charting a course for home.

CHAPTER 31

Bo is silent while he holds tight on to the feathers of the griffin's back. He is looking down, and for a second, I wonder if he remembers walking this path. Maybe this is the route he traveled too. Then I wonder if there are any villages left down there. Any that he and his inisisa missed. He has a mournful look on his face. He sees something that we don't. Maybe he's looking for inyo, those uncleansed spirits of the people he murdered. Either way, we're too high up to see them. I want to make a joke about it, try to get his mind off his past deeds, but it seems inappropriate, and I don't know that it would work.

"It'll be good to have some proper jollof rice again," I shout to him over the wind. Nobody smiles. Uhlah, what will it take to relieve the tension? We're all a little afraid of what's waiting for us in Kos. We don't know if there will be help waiting for us or if we're flying straight into the maws of arashi.

Aliya can break the earth and pull fire and water from thin air. And I can cleanse sins. We just might be able to save our city.

I have to admit, I do like this other feeling, though. It's rumbling inside me, and it's something I haven't felt in a very long time. It reminds me of when I first saw Osimiri, and all of its newness hit me at once. It's what I felt when Aliya and I were on that ship heading westward. It feels like adventure. I look over to Aliya again. "Hey! Aliya."

"What?"

"Are you ever going to do that proof?"

She blinks her surprise at me.

"Proof of what?" she asks.

"Me!" I crow. "I think there's enough sand in that desert down there for you to do it." I'm smiling so hard my cheeks hurt, and when she blushes, my heart leaps. "You better hurry up; we are going to hit water soon."

She grins. And it's like we're two kids stealing kiwis and running along the shoreline again.

Bo, to my right, hasn't said a word the entire flight. Occasionally, he glances at the place where his right hand used to be. He looks mutilated with his scar and his handless arm, and it's like his outsides and his insides are the same. These broken things. But I know him. I know him down to his smallest pieces. I know him inside and out. We can make him into something new. The same Bo, but repaired. Rebuilt. Like the village. Like Kos.

Iragide.

He's the Bo who fought off inisisa so that we could rescue Juba. He's the Bo who will help us save Kos.

He glances at me, and that carved-out-of-stone look on his face cracks a little, and I think I see a grin. Or, at least, a hint of it. If, by some miracle, Zoe's is still standing, I already have plans for our celebration.

Soon, water spreads beneath us.

Our griffins glide downward and surf along the waves, cutting a path just above the sea so that clear, glistening walls rise on both sides of us. As though to say, *We were here.* Sea creatures leap through the water and arc in the air, welcoming us back. Bo's knuckles are white. His face starts to get this green color to it, and I stifle a laugh. This is revenge for all the times he beat me at wrestling. I grin, but then I relent and bring the griffin back up into the sky.

The first small boats dot the horizon. We soar toward them. Fishermen, hands over their brows, gaze up at us. Same with the lascars ferrying people and cargo back and forth to the larger ships we near. Osimiri looks subdued from this height. Maybe Karima's rule has reached here as well. Shadows prowl the shoreline, and I can tell from all the way up here that they're inisisa. Their armor glints in the sunlight. We're almost there.

We coast along the shore, rising higher and higher so that we're only specks in the sky to the people underneath us. I angle us toward a deserted patch of shoreline. From here, I can see where the green field meets the forest. Part of me wonders what haunts the land in that tangle of trees. Are there still aki and

Mages in hiding? What will they say when they see me again? *If* they see me again. My heart drops at the thought that maybe all that's left of them is their inyo.

When we land, I touch my griffin's forehead. It flaps its wings into the air, heading straight up until it disappears in a burst of light. I touch the others, and they follow. The forest looms before us.

"I'm going to get Karima," I say. "This ends with her."

Aliya comes forward on her staff. "Are you mad? How will you get there? The city is crawling with armored inisisa. We have to find the rebels first. We have Mages and aki on our side."

"We don't know that," I shoot back. I'm itching. Itching to move. Itching to get done what needs doing. "If you want, *you* can find your resistance."

Aliya starts. "Taj, what's going on? This isn't like you."

I feel a pull. I can't explain it, but I feel drawn to Kos and everything inside it. What I need is right within the Wall. I need to get to it as quickly as possible. I can save Kos.

I can save Kos.

"I will go with him," Bo volunteers.

Arzu frowns at the both of us.

Bo smirks. "It always was my job to keep him out of trouble."

I snort. "And you were always horrible at it."

But Bo puts a hand out to calm Aliya. "We will pretend he is my prisoner. I will have brought him back alive, according to Karima's wishes. We will do our part, and while Karima is distracted, you should have time to find your group." Bo looks to me. "She will be too focused on us. In fact, she doesn't even know you're all alive."

Aliya doesn't like it. I can see it in her face. In the way she bounces from foot to foot and puts her knuckle to her chin. Then she raises her head. "Fine. Arzu and I will find the others."

"The tunnels," Arzu says.

"Right." Confidence returns to Aliya's voice. "The tunnels."

She and Arzu turn to head off into another part of the forest. Before they leave, Aliya looks over her shoulder. "Don't die, you foolish boy." She's smiling. Tears well in her eyes. She blinks once, and they're gone.

"We're going to need a guard if we want to make this believable," I say to Bo.

Bo nods and goes to press his hands to his chest to call forth an inisisa but stops, then he staggers back. He's tired.

"Let me," I say, then put my hands to my chest. I shut my eyes. It feels like it's been forever since I've called forth my own sins. I've almost forgotten the feeling, remembering only that it's supposed to hurt. Bo wraps his fingers around the back of my neck and pulls our foreheads together. I feel his warmth. I seize in his grip. Then I vomit my sins into a puddle on the grassy forest floor.

They grow into four wild boars, each as big as us. I'm dizzy from it all, but Bo holds me up. It is now even more difficult to imagine how Bo was able to survive having all those sins called out of his body. He's gotten so strong. He could definitely beat me in a wrestling match now.

When I regain enough strength to stand on my own, I organize the boars into a diamond around us.

"Are you really ready to do this?" I ask Bo, as though I'm not the one who needs the most convincing.

He nods, silent, and together we walk into the forest.

I can't help wondering about the underground tunnels. Maybe they're empty. Maybe they've been discovered by Karima and destroyed. Maybe they're filled with rebel Mages and refugee families. In my head, I see Zephi's family underground during the arashi attack, with the adults entertaining the children and doing everything in their power to distract them from the horror happening above. I see everyone living their lives and continuing to be a family even as their homes are being destroyed. Maybe it's the same here, with playgrounds being built alongside libraries, and maybe booksellers shop their wares underground next to jewelers selling smuggled gems. Maybe there's this whole entire city underneath the city, just as vibrant and colorful.

I'm lost in the daydream until I realize I can't breathe. All of a sudden, the air becomes so thick that I wheeze whenever I exhale. Though Bo doesn't show it, his body is tense with the effort of trying to breathe as well. Then it hits me. Inyo. The forest is so thick with uncleansed spirits that it pollutes the very air we inhale. It's like what used to happen in the dahia right after a Baptism. Like what happened after the arashi destroyed the refugee camp outside of Juba's village. How many died that it has become impossible to breathe in this stretch of forest?

Then, with the same suddenness, the air clears. We've gotten to the edge of the forest.

The Wall is so high I can't see the top of it, and it is completely clear of any markings. No graffiti, no sin-beasts painted by the Scribes. Nothing. Just an unbroken sheet of gray. I feel so small this close to it. Even while training aki what seems like a lifetime ago, when we were all in the forest outside the Wall, it never seemed this huge and evil. I've never looked at it as something I wanted to knock down.

Until now.

Somebody's galloping toward us. No. Many people. Coming around a bend in the wall are four people on horseback, all of them wearing Palace colors. Red and white, but with a new symbol emblazoned on the front of their robes. A flame.

They slow as they get near. Palace guards with a prelate at their head. They've probably been patrolling the Wall.

Bo breaks formation to stand at the head of our group. After a moment of hesitation, only the prelate comes forward. The guards are scared of him.

Once the prelate dismounts, I catch her glancing at Bo's severed wrist. There's no expression on Bo's face. He just stands aside and gestures to me.

The prelate squints at me, then stands back in poorly disguised shock. Then she looks to Bo, then back at me. I guess she still can't believe he did it. I don't know what Karima's been saying about me that has this prelate is so surprised and even fearful of me, but it takes quite a bit of effort to keep from smirking. My reputation precedes me.

Once she recovers herself, the prelate takes spooled leather from where it hangs at her waist and walks slowly toward us.

The guards have joined her by now. The prelate starts to bind my wrists.

"Well, it looks like no one was able to collect the bounty," one of the guards whispers to the other.

"Which means you owe me the ramzi you put up," one of the others replies. "A wager is a wager."

The first mutters beneath his breath.

Bo doesn't turn to face the prelate all the way but inclines his neck. "Nothing is to be done to him until our queen has seen him."

The prelate stops in mid-motion with my restraints.

"That is her commandment." His words come out as growls, as puliverized stones moving against themselves. "She will have the head of anyone who harms him before he has been brought before her. I will be holding that head."

The prelate's hands shake, and she fumbles with my restraints.

Bo has no expression on his face.

It's the last thing I see before someone slips a bag over my head and cracks me right in the back of my skull.

I'm unconscious before I even hit the ground.

They have my arms held high, wrists shackled together above my head. I'm dangling. The tips of my toes just barely touch the ground. And when they do, they meet a puddle.

Water drips from the ceiling. My shoulders are on fire. That's what woke me up. The pain is enough to snatch me right out of unconsciousness. I grunt and struggle feebly against my chains.

They've shackled my ankles too. A larger chain loops through the rings on my wrists and connects to a pulley in the wall. They're going to torture me.

There's got to be some way out of here. Then I hear footsteps. Not slow, not fast. Just stately, with purpose. Two aki stand outside my cell, glaring at me. They have cloth wrapped around their faces so that only their eyes are visible. That's the only way I can tell they are aki—their white eyes. The skin of their arms is unblemished. Not a sin-spot to be seen. Their inisisa are probably all a part of Karima's army.

I don't know how I expected this last part of my plan to go. I can even hear Aliya in my head nagging me for not thinking it through all the way. But I'm close. My body feels electrified with anticipation. Purpose.

I hear more footsteps, slower than the last pair. Like a methodical march. The corridor outside my cell fills with Palace guards and Mages. At first, they are all I see: guards with their weapons at the ready and Mages with their hands folded into the sleeves of their robes. Then the crowd parts, and out she steps.

Queen Karima.

She's even more beautiful than I remember. Her emerald dress shimmers in the torchlight from the corridor. I don't even know how it manages to sparkle like that. It must be magic. The skin of her face is smooth and dark. Touching it would probably be like touching the smoothest river-worn stone. It's so black it glows blue. She's the color of night, emerald gemstones beaded in threads through her dark hair. I forget to breathe.

The look she gives me crushes my heart. She looks almost sad to see me here, like she truly wishes things were different. I try to shake away the haze filling my brain. With a single word to her guards, she could have me killed on the spot.

"Leave us," she says softly to the guards. The Mages hang around for a little bit until she turns to them and says, almost kindly, "I am protected." What does she mean?

They give her a reassured look, then one of them leans forward and tells her, "We shall remain near. If you should need us."

"Ngozi, it is much appreciated. Now." She nods toward the end of the hall, and I see in that gesture the power she commands over them. It looks like a gentle nudging, but I can already tell it's the gesture of someone who has complete and utter control.

When we're alone, she walks forward and pushes open the door to my cell. I sputter, letting out a ragged breath. She's so close.

She closes the door behind her, and I hear the latch click. What is she doing?

Without a word, she slips a daga out of a sheath strapped around her calf and steps toward me. Out of instinct, I twist and turn. But she puts a hand to my chest, and it's enough to still me completely. My body chills at her touch.

"Please hold still," she breathes. I'm powerless to resist her.

She brings the daga to my chest, then, in halting, downward strokes, slices my shirt open so that it hangs from my upraised arms. Light glistens in her wide eyes when she sees my skin.

Drawing closer, she stares with even greater intensity, then her face softens. Slowly, she brings a finger to my chest and traces the outline of a sin-beast. Her fingers move to my neck, running along the spines of sin-snakes that circle the base of my neck. She's still holding her daga.

"Oh, Taj," she whispers. "How many nights have I dreamed about this?" Her eyes rove over me, taking in every sin-spot. Her hands move to my stomach, my waist. She feels the new scars beneath my sin-spots. "There are so many now," she murmurs. "You've Eaten so, so many sins." There's sorrow in her voice. "Oh, the places you've been to." She pushes away but keeps a hand at the small of my back, her arm wrapped around my waist, her other hand—her daga hand—still at my throat. "When this is all over, you must tell me about it."

"When it's all over?"

"Why, yes, Taj. Not only has Bo, my most loyal lieutenant, brought you back to me, but he has presented to me the most gifted Mage in the entire kingdom. Oh, I've known for quite some time that Aliya was special, like yourself. That you two were capable of untold wonders. We will study her closely. The way she sees the world, the markings on her body . . . Oh, Taj, her body is covered in them. Equations like we've never seen before. I'm sure they explain so much of the mysteries of this land. I can only imagine what insights they'll unlock." Excitement makes her face glow. "It's like poetry, Taj. Oh, you should see it!" Her face hardens for a moment. "Did you think they would be able to just sneak into my city? Crawl like worms through the shadows?" Then serenity washes over her again.

She moves her daga so that the blade presses against my throat. "While I am overjoyed at our reunion, you took some very valuable things from me. It has cost me quite a lot to bring you back. And no one escapes punishment for their sins." Her gaze hardens. "You had a chance once to join me, and you betrayed me. For her." She blinks, and her eyes change, soften. She removes the daga from my throat and runs her hand along my cheek.

Then she turns. My door clicks open, then shut again, and she's gone.

When she leaves, I shake. It takes me a moment to realize it's rage.

Bo betrayed us.

CHAPTER 32

AT FIRST, I try to count the seconds in my head, then I lose track. Thoughts intrude. Questions, like where has Karima taken Aliya? And where's Bo?

So I can wrap my fingers around his throat.

I hear sounds in the distance. Moaning or someone weeping quietly. The dank air makes everything sound louder, like every time a drop of water falls from the ceiling and plops into the puddle at my feet. When I hear the sound of sharp, terrified screams, they reach me as clearly as if the torture were happening right in front of me. It takes all my effort not to twist and try to fight my way out of these restraints. I know any movement will just exhaust me further. I'll have nothing left for when they eventually come for me. I need to be alert, on the hunt for any opportunity, no matter how small. I need to rescue Aliya.

The screaming stops. Almost immediately, footsteps splash my way. Louder. Louder. Then I hear the jangle of keys on a ring. My time is coming. I'm trying to stay loose. I know I need to in order to be ready for whatever comes, but my body tenses up. Terror wraps itself tight around me.

The person standing in front of the door to my cell has on baggy clothes that cover thick limbs with a leather apron over the front of their outfit. Their face is obscured by a metal mask with a shield of glass for their eyes to see through. So, Karima uses gear-heads for torture now too. Instead of making auto-mail for half limbs or tinkering with machines, they pull screams out of the queen's prisoners.

I steel myself as my torturer takes the key ring from their waist and, with hands covered in thick leather gloves the same color as their apron, fiddles with the keys. Their steps are non-chalant, like this is business as usual. They try one key, but it sticks in the lock, so they twist and shake it, then give up and try another. This goes on a few times until I hear that click. I get ready to kick out. My masked torturer pulls a tool out from their beltloop and flicks something along the handle. Out of its curved snout comes a jet of flames, and I cry out.

Karima's torturer is on me in an instant and has their hand over my mouth. I gag against the smell and the taste of it.

"Be still." A woman's voice. Deep and commanding. I don't recognize it. "I'm helping you," she whispers into my ear. I can see a blond ponytail spilling out the back of her helmet. "Make a sound, and you will die. Painfully."

She holds me so tightly that my back cracks. Before I can even think to struggle, the flame meets the metal over my hands, warming my fingers until they're on the verge of burning. I grit my teeth against the growing heat until I hear a snap and fall forward, right onto her broad shoulder. She's built like two pillars joined together, side by side, and she carries me with ease as she slips the broken remains of my wall chain through my wrist and ankle shackles, then slides through the door and closes it shut behind her.

I bounce on her shoulder, half of me dangling against her back, while she bounds down the prison corridor and around a corner into a small nook. She sets me on the ground like I'm a bag of farina. Then she gets to one knee. Her tool is uncomfortably close to my face.

"Can you walk?"

"Yes," I tell her.

"Good." And before I can protest or scramble away, she pins me against the wall and puts the torch to my ankles. My teeth chatter, trying to hold back the scream, but then the shackles split apart. I feel a little bit more courage, or at least enough to stick my wrist out for her to break those restraints too. I have to look away, though, because I can't bear to see her slip and burn my hands clean off. "All right," she says when she finishes. "Let's go."

I stand. "Aliya."

"What?"

"My friend. Aliya. They're keeping her somewhere around here."

She balls her fists at her sides, and I can tell she's more annoyed with me than angry.

"Wherever you're taking me, I'm not going without her."

"If you get captured again . . ." she says, then lets out a sigh. "Here, follow me," and she sets off ahead of me, back the way we'd come but down the other end of the corridor. For a while, the only sound I hear is the splash of our feet in the puddles dotting the prison floor. I try not to imagine the people rotting here with no shoes or flats on their feet, forced to stand or lie in this water for however long they've been down here.

This part of the prison is empty, but I can still hear the sounds of torture from earlier—the moaning and the shrieking and the weeping—all in my head again. I'm running so hard that I overtake the gear-head who freed me and round a corner straight into the flank of a sin-lion. I fall back with a loud splash and reach for my daga only to realize that it's gone. I scramble back to my feet, and the lion crouches, then leaps at me, fangs bared. At the last second, the gear-head's hand clamps down on its throat, and she hurls it into the wall with such force that I half expect the prison to collapse on us. I take a step toward the beast and glare at it, forcing it to lie on the ground. Then, slowly, I put my hand to its forehead and watch light replace its shadow-flesh. It grows so bright that I have to shield my eyes, then it bursts apart into a thousand sparks that hiss when they hit the puddles of water at our feet.

When I turn, the gear-head is staring in shock at where the sin-lion had been moments earlier. She's got her helmet over her head, but I can tell her mouth is probably hanging open.

"Should make the whole escaping thing a little easier," I say, and wink at her before hurrying around that corner and down another hall.

I don't know who this person is or why she's helping me. I don't know if she's part of any resistance, if she even knows about the resistance, or if this is all part of some really complicated plan Karima has put together. Make me think I'm going free and that I'm escaping, then flip me just like Wale would and snap the cage shut around me once again. Makes me feel like a rat that has been let out of one cell only to run straight into another. But if this gear-head's helping me for now, I better use her while I can.

Light starts to spread at the end of the corridor. I can hear bootsteps hurrying toward us. The gear-head grabs me by the arm and pulls me into a groove in the wall just as a troop of Palace guards runs by.

They know I've gotten free.

When the hall is clear, we step back out and continue running. This place is like a maze. People used to tell stories of Kosians being locked in here as punishment back when Kolade was king. They'd vanish, and you'd never hear from them again. It was as though they'd never existed.

This next hall ends ahead of us, but to our right is a small, brightly lit cavern. I run toward it and crouch at the base of the wall just by its entrance. Whispered conversation trickles out, something about prisoners and aki and a Mage. I peek over the wall and see guards milling about. Four of them, helmeted and wearing armor plating on their shoulders and legs. They look so different from what I remember. Heavier. More powerful. They each hold pikes. One of them stretches his neck. In the middle of the cavern is a metal table. It looks like it was fashioned out of the armor welded to the inisisa we fought in the forest. There's a shape of a body on top of it. It's covered by a blanket, but I can see tendrils of curly black hair peeking out.

Aliya.

The blanket doesn't move. She's not breathing.

I make a move to leap, but the gear-head grips me by the back of the neck so hard I almost yelp. "Move," she hisses, "make any sound, and I will crush your skull with my bare hand."

More footsteps.

Seeing Aliya like that drains all the energy out of me. All the hope. Stunned, I realize I've started crying.

The look on the gear-head's face changes, turns softer.

I'm too weak to resist, so I just lie limp as the gear-head hoists me over her shoulder again, and I watch as Aliya's covered body grows smaller and smaller. We round a corner, and she's gone.

By the time we stop, the tears are flowing freely. They darken the back of the gear-head's shirt. I'm as limp as a washrag when she sets me down on the floor of the cave. For a long while, I stare at the ceiling, struggling to pull myself together.

Aliya.

Gone.

Even to think those words makes my heart seize up all over again. I don't know how long I lie on the ground like that, but the tears stop, and I wipe the moisture from my eyes and nose and try to gather my wits. I notice the cave we're in is full of people. I can feel them around me, all quiet and staring.

Slowly, I rise and face the people in the cave. Aki, Mages, a few gear-heads.

The gear-head who carried me joins them.

This is it. The resistance.

Noor. Nneoma. Miri. Dinma. And so many others I thought I'd never see again. Aliya never stopped believing they were alive. She was so close.

Torchlight illuminates their faces. Someone steps through the crowd and comes toward me, his face solemn but happy. He looks tired, but there's joy in his expression.

Ras slides his hand out, palm up. "To you and yours, Taj."

I slide my palm over his. "To you and yours, Ras."

He grips my forearm and pulls me into an embrace.

I wrap my arms around him and hold him tight. I don't want to let him go. Ever. I won't let anyone go ever again. All the people here in this cave, the people who have come together to fight for their city—for *our* city—I will never let them go.

Karima will pay for what she's done.

CHAPTER 33

THE OTHERS PAT me on the back and the shoulder and feed me egusi soup and welcome me home. It feels hollow to have made it here without Aliya. We were almost there.

When this is all over, I will make sure she has a proper burial and that people all over Kos know and remember her sacrifice.

A few of the aki and Mages guide the tall gear-head who led me here into a side tunnel. Her gloves are torn. Inside the ripped leather are metal fingers.

Ras is bandaging my wrists and wrapping my hands. We sit on wooden boxes in what looks like some sort of war-planning room. Tables made out of stones and boxes, maps everywhere, things scrawled on walls, then half wiped away, then scrawled again elsewhere.

"Who's that?" I ask him, inclining my head to where they hauled off the gear-head.

He looks to where I mean, then back at my hands. "Name's Chiamaka. Older gear-head from the north. Came after Karima's forces pushed past the mines. Some of us work in the shadows, but others up above, they protest, and they speak out against the royal decrees. And they're punished for it, but many of them are as stubborn as you. There's even the occasional Ijenlemanya." He chuckles. "The parade usually goes a half dozen streets before prelates stomp it out. Anyway, Chiamaka brought a bunch of gearheads with her too. They want to help." When he says that last part, there's a bit of amazement in his voice, almost like he still can't believe it. "They've helped fortify these tunnels. Before, they were just wet stone, but now they have metal supports, and there's less risk of collapse. And we can make new tunnels now too."

"What? How?"

He fishes what looks like a thin cylinder almost as long as his forearm out from his belt. "This. They call it dynamite. The towns up north make it, and it gets shipped to the mines in the northern dahia just below to help with the digging."

I take the thing from him.

"How does it work again?" I ask.

"You put fire to the string," Ras tells me, pointing to the line of thin rope poking out from one end, "then you throw it where you want the explosion. It is like an arashi is trapped in this stick, and when you light it, it comes out."

Then it comes back to me. In the forest, after our escape, we heard explosions coming from the other side of the Wall. From inside Kos. My face blanches. "OK, you take it." I shove the arashi-stick back in his hands as quickly as possible.

Ras fits it back into his belt. "Some people come for the adventure that comes with the fight," he says, and I know he is once again talking about the rebellion. "Some people come because they are bored with their lives. Others want revenge." He looks back to where they took Chiamaka. "That's what it seems like with her. She wants Karima personally. She has never said why, but whenever the queen comes up in conversation, she shuts down and there's a look of hatred on her face like I've never seen before."

I understand. We have all lost something precious. Defeating Karima might not bring it back, but it's something.

I push myself to my feet. My shoulders still burn but less now than before I got here. Maybe Chiamaka knew someone in the resistance whom Karima dragged out onto the Palace steps for a public execution. Whatever her reasons, I'm glad she's with us and not against us.

Ras rises with me. "Come, let's join the others."

The next room is much more organized. A table has been fashioned out of wood and metal supports, and Miri leans over a map of Kos with the dahia spiraling out from the Forum. The others are crowded around her. Everyone looks up when Ras and I enter. Then they bow their heads. Even after all of that time spent in Juba's village, where my sin-spots made people nod their heads at me and clear paths through crowds for me, I'm still not used to this respect.

"Welcome," says Miri.

I nod my head in thanks. "So, what's the plan?"

She grins at my eagerness, as do many of the others. Then she points to one of the dahia. "We begin by liberating the dahia closest to our current location. If we can secure it, we can spread out to the others. We're powerful and skilled, but there aren't nearly enough of us to accomplish a frontal assault on Karima's forces. Each aki here is as strong as five soldiers, especially against the inisisa. The rebellion has hardened us. Which is to say that we can't afford to lose too many of us. Everyone here is necessary."

Not too many moons ago, it would have knocked me senseless to hear a Mage talk about aki this way. About our being powerful and necessary. Now, after everything that's happened, it seems as normal as the way plantains ripen.

"So, we free the dahia from the inisisa guarding them." She frowns. "And that is where you will make your entrance. We need the inisisa on our side."

I shrug. "Done. Easy."

"Taj." There's a warning in her voice. "There are many of them."

"That won't be a problem. I've stopped a whole city of inisisa before." Now that we're actually discussing plans, I'm itching to do something. Anything.

"Taj, that was once, and in the chaos of everything that happened that night, we don't know that we can replicate that situation. There are too many variables. And if it doesn't work, the inisisa will turn on the people of the dahia. They will consume the whole city. All those people will have been Eaten for nothing."

The gravity of it hits me. This isn't just about revenge. This is about saving the city. Protecting people. Keeping them alive.

"And this is how she's able to keep the arashi over the dahia," I say, realizing just as I say it. "By making sure there are enough inisisa to keep them near."

Miri nods. "The arashi are being kept hungry. If they consume enough sins, then their hunger will be satisfied, and they will leave."

"So, we can't kill the sin-beasts, then."

Miri shakes her head. "We need them." She lets out a sigh. "We've been trying to uncover methods for controlling the arashi. We've heard rumors from the Palace that Mages and algebraists have a formula for understanding and commanding the arashi, and it is rumored that that is how Karima is able to hold them in the sky and keep them from feasting."

"Aliya had been working on something like that." I start when I realize I've said that out loud.

Miri looks at me, surprised. "Aliya was working on a proof for the arashi?"

"Yes. She'd figured it out too, but now . . ." I grit my teeth, ball my hands into fists on the table. "Now she's . . ." I still can't say it out loud.

Miri looks away. There's a moment of silence before she continues. "We will have our forces scatter to the dahia simultaneously. We don't have time to move one by one. Karima will discover us and assemble her army in no time. So, we must move as one. Then, when we have control of the inisisa, we will send them toward the Palace."

"And draw the attention of the arashi."

Dinma steps forward from where he had been standing by the

wall. "Our scouts have been doing a regular reconnaissance of Kos. Each dahia has the exact same number of inisisa patrolling it. It is to maintain balance; otherwise, the arashi equilibrium would be disturbed, and she would lose control."

It's a pattern. All those shapes and equations Aliya had written on all those pieces of parchment, all those scribblings in the books in Zaki's home. Aliya knew the pattern.

There's a part of their plan that no one has brought up yet. If the inisisa are all sent to the Palace, the arashi will destroy the Palace and everyone in it. Karima will be gone, but so too will all the algebraists working there, the kanselo, even the servants. Some of them are there by choice, but many of them are not. Maybe Karima has threatened their families, or maybe they are paying off debts, or maybe this is simply the life that has been chosen for them. All of those people will die.

I can tell by the way Miri looks at me that she knows this. And that she's come to peace with it.

If we're going to save Kos, I need to come to peace with it as well.

There's movement from the other end of the room, and light shines in the cave. A Mage stumbles in with Arzu in his arms and rushes past me to lay her on a table. Blood spills over the maps and equation-covered parchments laid out.

In two quick strides, I'm at her side. Her breathing is slow, difficult. I hold her hand and make sure she knows it's me standing over her. Her eyes wander, searching, then her gaze finds my face, and she smiles.

I squeeze. "You found us."

Her smile broadens, then several people push me aside, swarming to attend to her.

I back away, and when I turn, I stop. A figure stands in the entrance to our cave. Someone who makes me forget everything else happening around me.

It can't be. It's like Ras stuck a stick of dynamite down my throat and lit the string. My whole body trembles. There she is, smiling, her smock soaked through, for some reason. The cotton is plastered to her skin, where I see the letters and numbers and symbols sketched in. Patterns. Order. Balance.

I run to her and gather her in my arms. Her body pressed against mine is the greatest feeling. I don't ever want it to stop. Her warmth, the feel of her breath on my shoulder. Her fingers pressed against my back.

Tears run down my cheeks as I pull away and stare at her face, taking in every feature, every curve, every angle. Before either of us can say a word, my mouth is on hers, and once again, it is like she is breathing life right into my body.

Aliya.

CHAPTER 34

ALIYA SMILES. LIGHT pulses beneath her skin. She's the most beautiful thing I've ever seen. As she slowly pushes away from me, I have trouble letting her go. She keeps a hand on my arm as she faces everyone. Dinma comes forward and drapes a woolen blanket over Aliya's shoulders, and Aliya nods her thanks.

Miri stands before the both of us and slides her hand out, palm up.

"To you and yours, Aliya."

Aliya, with a grateful look in her eyes, slides her palm over Miri's. "To you and yours," Aliya says softly.

Then Miri backs away and joins the crowd facing Aliya.

Arzu is standing again, but color has drained from her face.

Aliya scans the room, then steps forward. "They are not hungry for sins." She turns to Dinma. "The arashi do not consume sins. They consume inyo." She looks at her hands. The markings have spread. "When the uncleansed become inyo, they cannot immediately rejoin the Balance. They are an extra unit on our side of the equation." She pulls up a wet sleeve to reveal a dizzying array of numbers and letters. "The arashi terrorize us so that they can gather our souls." The Mages look at her in wonder. Someone gasps audibly. "The arashi balance the equation."

The silence in the room is so sharp you can hear every drop of water in the whole prison. Is she saying the arashi are . . . necessary?

Aliya puts her fingers together, tips pointed to the ceiling, and draws downward. Gradually, a thin stream of water, pulsing slightly, appears like a string out of thin air. Just like when she had that seizure by the river and her spilt water rose from the earth. I've seen her break stones and turn air into fire, and it still kicks the breath out of my lungs to see her do this. Aliya snaps her fingers, and the thread of water bursts apart, evaporating before the drops even have a chance to touch the ground. "Balance is connectedness." Symbols and numbers round her fingers. "For so long, we thought of our skin as a barrier to the world." A smile flits across her face. "Our skin is a vessel for the Unnamed."

A murmur surges through the crowd, but everything quiets when Miri steps out from the group and people see the look on her face.

She is the only one not gawking. In fact, she looks as though Aliya has just committed the most grievous sin and she must hold herself back from caning her senseless. Aliya lowers her sleeve.

"Iragide," Miri says slowly, as though the word is venom rolling on her tongue.

Several people gasp loudly. All heads snap in Aliya's direction. In some of those faces, there's wonder. In others, there's shock, and in others still, fear and horror. Then I remember what Aliya said back in Arzu's village. Iragide is forbidden. Has been since the time of the Seventh Prophet. This must be like seeing someone do something people have only read about for centuries. It's not supposed to be real. Then again, neither were the arashi.

"Yes," Aliya says, straightening. "Know the elements in the air, break them down, and re-form them. We can turn air to water. We can turn it to fire. We can change the face of the earth beneath us."

Several of the Mages hiss and look at Aliya as if she's cursed, and I glare at them, fists clenched.

"Where did you learn this?" asks another from the crowd of Mages. His voice is thick with despair.

Aliya puts a fist to her chest and smiles. She has the look on her face of someone in the midst of a pleasant memory. "A Mage taught me. One as curious to know the secrets of this world as I was. Who loved knowledge and the search for it. His name was Zaki."

Miri scoffs. "The heretic."

"Do you think Karima's Mages and algebraists care that Iragide has been forbidden for centuries?" Aliya shoots back. "That so many call it heresy? Do you think Karima cares when her people are using it to create her army of armored inisisa? The time for worrying about such things is over." Then her voice softens. "We need to save this city. We cannot win by fighting the old way."

"But this is blasphemy!" shouts a Mage from the back. Too much of a coward to show his face.

Aliya puts a hand to her chest. "If it is, then I will answer for it in Infinity. But the Unnamed knows my head and it knows my heart, and it knows that I quest for Balance. And that I will do everything in my power to right the wrong that Karima has committed on our city. On our people. But if we're to make this plan work, I will need all of you."

Everyone is still.

Noor shoulders her way to the front where the Mages stand and stares straight at Aliya. "What is your plan?"

Aliya walks to the map of Kos. The others, staring at her as though she has just fallen from the sky, make way for her. "Taj will control the inisisa, and we will control the arashi, and when the people of the dahia are smuggled safely into the tunnels beneath Kos, we will direct the inisisa in the dahia to the Palace." She draws these motions out with her finger. And even as she points and presses, I see she is making a shape. A pattern. An equation. "The arashi will give chase and destroy Karima and everything she has sought to build since she took the throne. When they are satisfied, they will leave us."

"How will we control the arashi?" asks one of the Mages, an older man with wrinkles at the corners of his snakeskin-colored eyes.

Aliya pauses for a moment, like she's gathering courage, then says, "You will have to be marked. To control the arashi, you will have to be marked like me." She gestures to her left arm.

"This will have to be written on your skin." She gulps, but her face never loses that steely expression of resolve. "We will have to share blood."

A gasp goes up from the crowd.

"Which means there is a chance that you will have to share in the fate waiting for me." She waits for the noise to die down. "Karima binds metal to the inisisa with blood. On every piece of armor they wear, the Fist of Malek is written. Karima needs several Mages and algebraists to etch the proof into the metal and bind it with blood to the inisisa. The proof to do this is written on my skin. And it is written in my blood." Aliya turns my way. I catch her gaze, and I see in her eyes that her mind is moving through the memories of our time in Juba's village. "The secret is guilt. Consequence, as we experience it in our souls. It binds us together through our actions. It is the hurt that governs our relations with one another. Guilt forces us to right wrongs. Guilt brings about Balance. Guilt uncleansed drives us mad. It feeds the arashi. It is what connects us to Infinity. The Seventh Prophet understood this." The look in her eyes changes. "The reason your markings do not fade, Taj, is because you can bear the guilt of so many others. It is now the same with me. The Unnamed has chosen us, and it has written itself in the very cells of our blood."

She's thinking of Bo and how I brought him back to himself. Back to us.

Almost brought him back.

The Mages know what she means. They know she means that they will have the power to control the most powerful beasts

in the Kingdom of Odo. They know she means they may suc-
cumb to the fate that befell the Seventh Prophet: madness and
violent, agonizing death.

Noor considers Aliya's words, then nods. She stands apart
from the crowd until Ras joins her, then Nneoma, then more
and more aki. One by one, the Mages move toward them. But
a few of them remain where they've been standing. Miri is the
most prominent of them. She does not join the others. If anything, the sneer on her face has deepened.

"Miri," Aliya says, and reaches out with her tattooed hand.

Miri was one of the first Aliya had brought me to in the
beginning of the rebellion, back when the plan was to deliver
Kos by capturing King Kolade. Aliya had deferred to Miri, had
made me remember that Miri was our leader, that she was the
architect of the rebellion, the general. There's a part of Aliya
now—I can see it in her eyes—that wants Miri to join her, not
just to confirm that she has the right idea but because it will mean
approval from her mentor. Sometimes, that is more important
than anything else.

"Please," Aliya pleads.

For a long time, Miri stares at Aliya's outstretched hand in
silence. Then she says, "For many, many years, we have been
preparing for this day. We who have known have girded ourselves and studied the Word and practiced our art to glorify the
Unnamed, so that when the day came that we would be called
upon to deliver our city from tyranny, we would be properly
pure. We would not be sullied. We would be as untainted as we

were when the Unnamed raised us out of the ground to which we shall one day return. Now that we are here, at this crucial point, I will not throw all of that away. You speak as if you *are* the Unnamed. You speak of the power to make fire and to break the earth. The Unnamed is what bestows order. The Unnamed determines Balance. Not you, not anyone else. I cannot be a part of your plan, Aliya." With that, Miri bows her head and walks past us to the cave's entrance. Her cape whispers behind her as she rounds the corner. Then she's gone.

Aliya watches her go. Tears pool in her eyes, but they don't spill. All it takes is an instant, but Aliya's face firms. She sniffs once, then turns to the rest of us. "Our plan doesn't change. Anyone with an objection, you are free to follow Miri. You will not be judged. You will not be cursed or spat upon. It is your decision." She looks around, waits.

Then she returns her gaze to the table and the curled parchment atop it. She undoes a scrolled book whose pages are blank, calls for a stylus and ink, and sets to explaining an equation. On paper, it looks like a fountain of gibberish. In the sky, it is the arashi. A piece of Infinity. In the beginning, it was all lahala to me, all harsh consonants and missing vowels, letters and words that made no sense. Now, even though it's still a language I can't understand, there's a beauty to it I couldn't hear before. An order. With stylus in hand, Aliya sketches out a series of algebraic proofs. All numbers and letters crammed together. At the center of her swirling script is a single equation. The Ratio. She then reaches for a stone, and the first of the willing Mages comes to her and rolls up the left sleeve of his robe. Aliya carves. The Mage grimaces, then it is finished, and she cuts a wound in her palm and a wound in the palm of the other Mage.

"To you and yours, Mage," Aliya says, sliding her hand out, palm up.

"To you and yours, Prophet," the Mage says back, grasping Aliya's hand. Drops of their mingled blood splash onto the cave's floor.

CHAPTER 35

WE BEGIN BY sending groups of aki and Mages out through the tunnels and into the dahia. The gear-heads follow, fortifying the tunnels where necessary, creating nooks and hiding places and traps for guards, if they try to follow us. I can't imagine how long some of them have been down here, trapped without seeing the sun maybe for days or weeks at a time. Some of them might have been down here for a whole moon, preparing for just this day. Or night. I can't even tell anymore. But they set about their tasks. I even see some of the aki from the northern dahia where mining is what everyone does working alongside the gear-heads. Some of them are silent and determined, others whistling old songs from their neighborhoods. Some of them converse about the rebellion or about what they'll cook to celebrate when it's all over.

Arzu is to stay behind, resting. She sleeps on the bed that's been made for her, attended to by some of the aki and Mages who remain behind. When she wakes up, Kos will be liberated, I tell myself. And the thought nudges a smile across my face.

I'm to follow Aliya to where she will stand once the preparations have been completed.

The others have found a proper robe for her and have given her the chance to dry off. Before we head into the tunnels, I take her arm.

"Hey," I whisper.

She turns. "Hey," she says softly.

"How did you . . . I thought you were dead."

She faces me fully and puts her hands on my arms. It's the lightest touch, but still, I feel a shiver up my spine. "Arzu and I were separated, but the rebellion is everywhere. We are not alone. The Unnamed is with us, Taj. It spoke to me." She smiles. "It speaks to me still." By now, the smaller groups of aki and Mages are all gone. "Come. Soon, the advance parties will have begun clearing the city of innocents. We must be ready to move as soon as everything is in place."

I nod. Then, together, we hurry into the maze. Aliya doesn't slow down as she leads me through the twists and turns. I concentrate completely on following her lead. Otherwise, I'd easily lose myself in this tangle and get stuck down here with all the action happening right above me and no way to get to it.

After what seems like no time at all, we reach a metal ladder that ends in the ceiling. There are grooves near the top, and I can tell there's movable stone there. "Here, let me go," I say, and climb up first, then try to push the stone aside. When it doesn't budge, I twist on the ladder and push my back against the stone, straining with all my strength until I hear it groan and shift. With one last heave, I get it off to the side, then peek my head through. There's brush and dirt all around, and I shake it out of my face and hair before climbing through and going into a crouch, my daga in hand.

We're clear.

I reach my arm through the hole where Aliya waits. She grabs my hand, and I pull her through. Then, once we're both aboveground, I get down and drag the slab back over, leaving enough space so that it'll be easier to move next time.

It's so dark outside that I can barely see my feet. A starless night with no sound at all, not even the bootsteps of Palace guards or prelates. I don't even hear the wailing of children who have decided they all of a sudden don't want to sleep. None of the hum of conversation that seems to hover over Kos at all hours. Nothing.

Wind stirs our clothes against us, then again. Gusts of it, like something flapping its wings, and I look up, and fear clenches my throat. An arashi, its shape outlined against the sky, circles overhead. It moves in a slow circuit, its tail lashing back and forth. It's high enough that I can see its whole body. It looks like a bat nearly the size of a city, the way its six leathery wings spread out and contract. Lightning courses through it and around it. When it turns, I can even see its face. Sunken eyes and an opened jaw large enough to clench itself around whole houses.

"Taj," Aliya whispers, and that snaps me out of my terror. "We have to go. Quickly. The evacuation should be under way by now."

"Right," I murmur, then she takes me down a street and around another. We thread through alleyways, and then I stop when I see what looks like nothing more than a pile of rubble. Stone and twisted metal, it stretches on, then I see it again to my right as well as to my left. But around it, the homes are untouched. We skirt the destruction, then I see it again only a hundred paces on. Like a pattern. In some places, strange material coats the ground and crunches beneath our feet.

Aliya stoops and picks some of it up. She lets it slide through her fingers, rubbing the tips together, then sniffing. "Gravel," she says, then drops it.

It spreads like ash along all the cleared pathways. And it makes noise every time we step on it, announcing us. Is this part of a trap?

I look around, then I see it. We're in the dahia. This looks like the neighborhood of Arbaa. Before me sits a large pile of shattered stone and clay, like a home in a Baptized dahia. I take my time getting to it because I'm almost afraid of what I'll see, but as soon as I get close enough, I know. It's the marayu. The orphanage where Auntie Sania and Auntie Nawal took so many of us when we couldn't live on the streets anymore. When our eyes had changed and we'd been cast out of our homes or had left on our own. Even after I left the marayu, they watched over me. And so many others. And now this is what's left of it.

I feel a new resolve and follow Aliya to the edge of the dahia, staying close to the sides of buildings and stopping whenever I think I hear something or someone behind us. The air is thick with inyo, and the way around us is so dark it's impossible to know how many inisisa roam about. But I have to hold myself together if we're going to make it.

Memories swim around me like the inyo. Even in the darkness, I recognize where Costa used to have his station. Where we aki would wait in line to exchange our markers for the ramzi we were supposed to be paid. Where we would shout and moan and complain about being shorted while Palace guards waited to bash our heads in. I recognize the streets Omar and I would watch the Ijenlemanya pass through. The drumming, the lines of dancers. The children standing with their parents on both sides of the street, some of them breaking away to dance with the paraders.

Omar and I watched one the day before we gave him his first daga.

This is for him.

We climb farther up a hill, and I start to recognize the shantytown we're in. By the time we get to the top, I'm going too fast, forgetting myself and how quiet we're supposed to be. In that slice between two dahia, where houses leaned against each other and everyone was too close, there was always one building people left alone. A few floors tall, made out of adobe. And it would be stifling in the summers. We had no windows to protect us from the rain, so what blankets we could steal or scrounge would get soaked through. And in the cold season, we had to practically sleep on top of one another for warmth.

Home.

I dash into the entrance on the first floor, not even worrying if there are inisisa waiting for us, and scramble up to the second floor, where our rooms branched out from a main hallway. One of the rooms is bare, and dust high enough to run a hand through coats every surface. When's the last time anyone slept here? I get to my room and remember how it used to be full of stolen plush cushions that I'd drooled on in my sleep. And I see the window out of which I used to watch the city breathe and live and glow with all the jewels everyone wore.

I remember standing here one time with Omar at my side, the both of us watching little kids play on the rubble of what had, earlier that day, been their homes. Their dahia had just been Baptized, and even after having lost everything, they had come together to kick a ball on the broken stones. The memory pains me, and I break away.

Aliya points to the ceiling, and I lead her down the hallway to the room where the others slept. Outside the one window is a balcony, and I help her onto it, then jump and reach for the rusted sheet-metal roof, hoping the rope's still there. My fingers brush against it, and my heart leaps with joy. Still there. I tap it again, and it falls down. A few tugs to see if it still holds, then I pull myself up. The rusted roof sways a little beneath me, but, on my hands and knees, I'm able to keep steady.

I reach my hand and pull Aliya the rest of the way up.

A gust of wind nearly knocks us off. The whole city rumbles. Above us soars another arashi, this one closer than the last one.

From here, we can see most of the city. The Palace estates rise to our left at the top of the hill where all the wealthy of Kos live. Or used to live. Now all the old mansions and courtyards are overrun with vines. Trees grow through whole buildings.

Some of the homes of those kanselo or algebraists or wealthy ministers who used to pay aki to Eat for them before weddings and whenever they needed to have a sin purged are completely covered by overgrowth. They look like they belong in the forest.

Kos lies in darkness. And it's only from this height that I can see the shapes moving in the streets below. The aki are all dressed in black, but occasionally one of them will come out from behind a building and lead a family or a small group of Kosians out of sight and into shelter elsewhere. Other shapes squirm in the inky black below, and I know them to be inisisa. In the darkness, their armor glints.

It's all been made equal. What happened to the marayu has happened to the homes on the hill. Orphans and preachers. Children who had nothing and men who had everything. Both of them have been stripped of what they used to have. This was her plan. This was what Karima wanted. This was what she had promised me on the steps of the Palace. A Kos where all are equal. Except her.

"It wasn't supposed to be like this, Karima," I whisper. I turn to Aliya. "Are you ready?"

She rolls up her sleeves, revealing the ridges of her new markings. Her arms are almost completely dark with them.

"All right."

I close my eyes and concentrate. I've never tried to control this many inisisa before. I'm not entirely sure what to do or what it's supposed to feel like, but I try to let myself loosen up. I think of Arzu's tribe and Juba and the Larada. I think of the open desert plain, and I think of the calm on the faces of all the tastahlik who faced off against the army of inisisa Zaki had called from Bo. I open my mind and feel myself vanish.

When I open my eyes, all of Kos is still. I can see the armor on the inisisa, but none of them is moving. The air just above the rim around each dahia shimmers. Then, so slowly I almost don't notice it, the arashi hovering over the dahia move higher into the sky. On rooftops all over the city, I see Mages with their newly marked arms spread and their faces angled toward the black sky, just like Aliya. And the arashi cease their circling. They hover, then rise higher and higher.

Aliya trembles. I make a move to help her, and she shakes her head. "Don't. I can handle this. Concentrate on the inisisa."

The ground rumbles again. We feel the arashis' growl in the earth beneath us.

Aliya stumbles. "It's not enough." We need Miri and the others.

"How much longer?"

Above us, the arashi start to move faster, more erratically. They're not going to hold.

"Aliya, say something."

She's gritting her teeth. "There aren't enough of us." She collapses to one knee, her arms still raised above her head, as though she's holding the sky on her shoulders.

Then they screech, all at once. The sound is like glass breaking inside my head, and I fall to the roof. Aliya's on the sheet metal at my feet.

"Aliya!" I cry out, picking her up. She's unconscious.

The arashi above us lets out another roar so loud it feels like my head's being crushed. The pain blinds me.

A glint of emerald shimmers in the distance. At the Palace, on the balcony that juts over the Palace steps. She is little more than a speck, smaller than the smallest stone. But I know it's her. She sees us. Karima.

I look up. The arashi has stopped circling.

It's diving down from the sky.

It's coming straight for us.

CHAPTER 36

THE ARASHI FILLS the entire sky above us.

The wind from its wings makes the sheet-metal roof bend beneath us. I have to shield Aliya with my body to keep the stones from the rubble pile from hitting her, and each one thuds into my back until another head-splitting roar cuts through the air. We were so close.

We *are* so close.

The inisisa can't be contained anymore. Below us, the evacuation isn't complete. Armored inisisa corner aki trying to protect refugee families. Already, the fighting has begun. I put my hands to my chest, then vomit a griffin. I need to work fast. The arashi is almost on us. All of a sudden, it's like I've been thrown into a star. My skin is so hot it feels like it's about to start boiling. But there's no time to think.

I grip the griffin's forehead and watch the shadows fall away like scales. Then I hop onto it and soar into the air. The wind whistles in my ears. Faster. Faster. I don't know what I'm going to do or even what I *am* doing. I just know I need to save Aliya. She's the key to all of this.

The arashi wants inyo? It wants sin-poisoned souls? Then it can have me. A quick look behind me and I see that inisisa follow me like a tail. Griffins and eagles and a dragon. They're all flying behind me. I don't have time to gawk. I turn back to the arashi and urge my griffin faster. *Come on, come on, come on!* The arashi opens its jaw wider, and steaming saliva hisses on its long fangs. I shrink myself close to the griffin's back and fly straight toward that open mouth.

This is it. This is how it ends. The world around me slows down. It's the feeling I get whenever I know I'm close to falling before a sin-beast, when it looks like I won't be able to kill it. When I've run out of energy and all that remains is luck. Only, there's no escape this time. This time, I don't get out.

I hope that when they build my statue, it's at least as tall as the statue of Malek that grows smaller and smaller beneath me.

Then we hit the arashi.

Pain rips at every part of me. Like a million hands have dug claws into my skin, every inch of skin, and are pulling as hard as they can in every single direction. Fire slithers inside my head. My eyes burst open with light. Sins. So many sins. Liar. Thief. Murderer. Adulterer. Brawler. Glutton. Thief. Murderer. Brawler. Glutton. Murderer. Over and over and over, as though

I'm glimpsing every horrible act ever committed. A girl in envy over her sister's Jeweling ceremony. A medicine man cheating a father out of money for a cure for his son's sins. A cutpurse plunging a knife into the back of an unsuspecting jeweler. It feels like every sin in Kos is latching on to my heart, squeezing it in its talons. I want to fight it. I want to fight it so bad and beat it all back and remember that the guilt isn't mine, that it belongs to the sinners. That this is simply Balance. The sin is never forgotten; it is just moved. And I let myself go. This is how it's supposed to happen.

I can't imagine a better, nobler, more impressive way to die.

Aliya, remember me.

I'm flying. And the sun is out. And everything smells of smoke. Thick, acrid smoke. This is what I see and feel and smell when I wake up. Then I try to lift my head and realize I'm not flying. I'm falling.

My arms swim through the air. My legs flail. What happened? This isn't how it's supposed to go. I'm supposed to die defending Kos by flying up into the mouth of an arashi, not as a splatter stain on the street. But I'm falling faster and faster, and nothing I do can stop it.

No no no no no no no.

I hit something so hard it knocks the wind out of me, then I'm moving again.

I'm on someone's back. Noor!

"Oga, hold on," she says as she carries me, running, from

rooftop to rooftop, leaping over alleyways and up and down balcony steps. "Are you OK?"

All around us, the clang of stone on metal. Dagas against armor. They're fighting. I spot Palace colors and the Fist of Malek. The guards are out too. Noor's dressed in all black, but now, with the light shining from the sky, she stands out. I can't figure out where the arashi is. Or Aliya.

"Aliya—where is she?"

"Just hold on tight." Noor makes one last leap, and we soar through the air to land in a small copse. I recognize it from earlier. This is where Aliya and I came through to sneak into Kos.

"Wait, Noor. Where's Aliya? We have to go back for her!"

"Oga, come on!" The stone is already open, and she tugs me, then tosses me in and leaps after me.

I land with a thud on the ground, right on my tailbone. Uhlah, such pain. Noor hauls me to my feet, and we start running. I can hear the bootsteps of the Palace guards overhead. As we run, Noor pulls a stick of dynamite from inside her shirt and, with her daga and a stone, sparks light onto it. It sizzles, and I run away from her just to get as far from it as possible. Noor doesn't miss a step as she spins around and hurls the thing back the way we came. Then it dawns on me. We're using it to seal the entrance.

An explosion hurls us forward, and we get to our feet as fast as we can. The cave ceiling falls in a mass of rocks heading toward us, and we run and run until it stops and we have a moment to catch our breath.

It's not long until we meet stranded Kosians. Some of them are gathered into families; others are alone or attended to by strangers. Many of them are wounded, but a few of them just have soot and ash on their clothes and faces. Many of them are coughing or crouching or lying on the ground, exhausted. And more stream in from side tunnels, led by aki dressed exactly like Noor. Aki direct the new arrivals to where there's still space and hand out blankets as well. Some of the new arrivals are directed to what I realize is a sort of infirmary or sick tent, only it's a deeper cave underground, where other refugees, medicine men and women, work on them. I hear crying and screaming and shouting and laughter. Already, some jewelers have crowds gathered around them and have their wares spread out on the blankets given to them for warmth.

The whole city is down here.

We get to the room where we put together our plan earlier, and Aliya leans over the maps and proofs written out on parchment scattered over the table. Tremors ripple through her bare, marked arms. She's surrounded by Mages and a few aki. When Noor brings me in, Aliya looks up, and even though her face is pale and sickly and hollow and her eyes slightly sunken, she smiles. From cheek to cheek.

"Taj, we figured it out." Her words come out weakly, even though she trembles with excitement. "We know how to finish this. We—" She pitches forward. I'm not able to get to her in time, but another Mage nearby grabs her and keeps her from falling. They bring her to a crate, where she sits and bows her head, breathing heavy, slow breaths. She's exhausted.

I kneel by her side, my hand running along her back. She gives me a tired smile.

"What happened?" I ask Noor. "I remember flying into the arashi's mouth, then I wake up and I'm falling and nearly crush you when you pluck me out of the sky."

"Dynamite," Aliya says. "That is our secret."

I look to her. "But I wasn't holding any. I didn't have any with me. Dynamite's the secret to what?"

She puts a hand on my arm to calm me. "I'm saying you're the secret. You cleansed the arashi. You freed the inyo."

"I *what*?"

By now, everyone else is looking our way. There's enough attention to make me uncomfortable. "You rode on the back of a cleansed griffin. And you brought behind you dozens of inisisa, and when you entered the arashi, you cleansed them. And it. Your inisisa, Taj. They are like sticks of dynamite. You bathe one in light and throw it at an arashi, and, well, a chemical reaction follows." She smiles.

"You mean I blew a hole in it?"

"Yes, Taj. You blew a hole in it." She pushes herself halfway to her feet, and I help her up the rest of the way. "I know the composition of the arashi. They are made of hundreds of inyo. Some of them contain thousands. The inyo are the pieces that make them, the way molecules and atoms make us. Their wings, their talons, the saliva that drips from their teeth, all of it is inyo. Sin." She gasps, eyes wide in epiphany. "You are returning guilt to sin. Balance."

She shakes her head, returning from wherever it was she went to just now. "We couldn't hold them." She looks around at the others gathered, some of them covered in dust from barely escaping collapsed hallways and tunnels. The ceiling rumbles over us, and another sheet of dust falls on our shoulders. "Even if all of us gathered here were properly schooled in the art of Iragide, we could not defeat the arashi. You see what it has done to us." All around me are Mages on the verge of collapse, some of them so pale and drawn it looks like they're two steps from joining Infinity. "Karima has hundreds of algebraists and Mages in her employ. It is only because they number so high that she is able to do this."

I curse to myself. If only I'd thought ahead, I could have sent the inisisa toward the Palace. I could have sent them far enough that the arashi would have followed, and everything would have gone according to plan. But it would have meant sacrificing Aliya. I know as soon as that idea enters my head that I couldn't have done it. Ever. Kos is not worth having without her.

"This only means that Mages alone cannot destroy the arashi." Thunder booms around us, and the earth shakes, like the arashi are challenging Aliya. She doesn't flinch or bow her head. "Taj, it is you who can control the inisisa. It is you who have to do what must be done."

I remember the almost unfathomable pain I felt flying through the arashi that last time. Like I was dying in the slowest, most horrible way possible. "H-how many are there?" I manage to ask.

Aliya grimaces. Her face tells me that she feels pain for the hurt I will have to endure.

My courage comes back. If that's how it has to go, then that's how it has to go.

"We must act fast," Aliya says to the Mages and aki gathered. We don't really have a plan, but Aliya talks like we do, and I see the confidence rise in the others. If she believes, then we can too. "The arashi broke free from our hold before the evacuation was complete. There are still civilians trapped in the city. And now they're not only at the mercy of the Palace guards and the inisisa, but also the arashi whose sleep has been disturbed."

One of the Mages says, "But the tunnels are blocked."

"Only the ones that lead to the city," says Noor, still catching her breath from when she led me through the tunnels. "The ones that lead out past the Wall and into the forest are still open."

Aliya looks to Noor. "We will use those to bring the refugees into the forest, then we will scale the Wall to reenter Kos. From the air." The two of them, Mage and aki, nod grimly at each other, and I take a moment to think about how remarkable that sight is. When I was growing up, Mages dragged us from our homes during Baptisms, and they forced us to sleep ten to a room in a slum. They called us whenever rich people needed their sins Eaten, then, when it came time for the aki to be paid, they shorted us. Every time. Now we're all looking at one another as equals. If nothing else comes out of this, I'll at least have witnessed that. And that's more than enough of a miracle.

"We will safeguard the refugees," says a voice from the back. Miri marches forward, and several Mages walk with her. "We will guard the ones you bring to the forest. You needn't divide your forces further in order to protect them. Should Karima's army make it to the Wall or farther, we will battle them however we can. But we will know that if that door opens and we do not see sunlight, then we have lost the city, and it will be on us who remain to keep the people of Kos safe. Rescue our city, Mage."

Miri speaks with such power in her voice that everyone else has grown completely silent. The two of them, Aliya and Miri, stand not ten paces away from each other, and neither of them smiles.

Then Aliya walks toward her former mentor and commander and slides her hand out, palm up. Her back is straight, her head held high. "As you command. To you and yours, Miri."

Miri looks at Aliya's hand, then slides her own over it. "To you and yours, Aliya," she says softly before gathering her group and fanning out to direct the refugees into the forest.

Outside, the Wall towers over us. And for the first time, I let myself imagine what Kos would be like without it. What it would be like to walk through the forest as a wanderer and come and see this magnificent city sprawled out in front of you, waiting to offer you shelter and a new life. I let myself imagine a city that isn't trying to keep people and things out. A city that lets them move freely. When this is over, maybe we can see about bringing this thing down. It's given us more than enough trouble. But the Scribes might get upset that they won't have so big a canvas to paint on anymore. I smile. They'll find a way. They're resourceful like that.

Aki line up on either side of me.

As one, the Mages hold our heads in their hands and murmur their incantations. I close my eyes and open my mouth and let the sin pour forth, a jet that arcs out in front of me, then pools at my feet before turning into a griffin large enough for me to ride. Each aki has one of their own. When we're finished, a few aki stagger, dizzy. A few go down to one knee, and I remember that not all of them are as strong as I've become. So much has happened that now it's almost painless to bring a sin out of me. There's always the sharp hurt that strikes like a needle through the brain and the brief moment of suffocation when I can't breathe because the sin is leaving my body, but I'm able to stand tall at the end of it. For the others, it takes a few moments, but we wait because we need everyone at full strength.

I can hear the arashi roar, and even though the sun sprays light down around them, lightning still strafes the sky and snaps at the ground, sending sparks that set homes and streets and stalls on fire.

Karima's waiting for me on the other side. And so is Bo. And their army of enemy inisisa. Inisisa beyond my control.

But this ends now.

I put my hand to my inisisa's forehead, and the shadows fall off it like a second skin. Its feathers are the color of a sunrise. Light shines through them. The aki gawk as I walk down the line and cleanse their beasts. It brings back memories of how they used to look at me when we were all younger and I was the most skilled aki in Kos. How they would whisper praises about me behind my back! Sky-Fist this and Lightbringer that. When I finish, I mount my griffin, and the other aki do the same. Aliya climbs on behind me, and one Mage joins each aki, and together, we shoot into the sky.

I have to make it to the Palace.

I look to my right, then to my left. Then, when I know we're good to go, I send my griffin onward, and we cut a line straight over the Wall.

Arashi writhe in the air, confused. Inisisa roam the streets below, hunting the aki and the Kosians left behind, and now this new battalion of griffins flies toward them, arcing just beneath the claws and teeth of the arashi overhead. We dip in formation to get out of their reach. They're too slow to catch us. A ray of light shines down on me, and I don't see the catapults lining the outer rims of the dahia until their loads snap forward into the air. I turn on the back of the griffin and shout, "WRECKERS!" just as the first flaming boulders cut through the air. They head straight toward us, and I hear behind me a crash and mingled screams as one of the boulders smashes an inisisa and its riders out of the air. I want to turn and rescue them, but I know that we'll only have one chance to make it to the Palace. The Wreckers farther down, closer to the Palace, are already waiting for us, and we can't give them any more time.

Boulders whistle toward us, but when we try to arc upward, arashi snatch at us. I hear more cries behind me as claws wrap around one of the griffins and haul it and the Mage and aki riding it into its open mouth. We're not going to make it.

Aliya grips me tightly as I bank left, dodging another boulder. This one explodes just above us, and we spin. Aliya slips off and flails in the air. The scream catches in my throat, and I push my griffin into a dive, moving so fast the wind brings tears to my eyes. I catch her just before she lands in the midst of waiting armored inisisa. Flying low, I can see that the street is blanketed with them. Sunlight vanishes, and we're cast in the darkness of the arashi again. I pull us up until we're level with the other aki who remain.

"I have to do it," I tell Aliya.

The look she gives me nearly undoes me. This may be the last time we see each other. While I'm holding on to our griffin, she hugs me tightly and kisses the back of my neck. I can feel her tears fall onto my skin.

Nneoma pulls up beside us. "Let us."

I'm trying to keep an eye on Nneoma while at the same time scanning the horizon for Wreckers. It looks like those boulders are being stuffed with dynamite. So, if they don't hit us, the explosion will kill us. "Let you what?" I ask her.

"Do the dynamite trick," she says, smirking.

"What are you talking about?" I'm getting more agitated, and Aliya puts a hand on my back to calm me. I can't tell if I'm shouting to be heard over the arashi or if it's because what Nneoma's suggesting is making me angry.

"I like this carriage you've made for me to ride through the air, but I think I prefer one made of light." She has the widest grin on her face. "That is how it works, right, Mage?"

Aliya nods. "Once it's turned to light, it can change the arashi." The wind picks up, and Aliya shouts, "But you don't have much time!"

"Well, then, Taj. You'd better hurry up. We'll draw the armored inisisa into the arashi and destroy them." Nneoma points ahead. There are at least several, by my count, swimming in the sky near the Palace. Karima has them guarding her. An emerald in the storm. "Oga, this is the only way. Otherwise, we all die here today."

"But if you go, then *you* will die!"

She straightens on her griffin's back. "And when you tell the story of how we sacrificed ourselves to save our city from a tyrant, you better not mess up any details. Remember, it was Nneoma who gave you this idea and who led the charge." Her smirk widens. "We are here to help. This is for all of us."

I don't want her to do it. I don't want to lose any more people.

"Taj," Aliya whispers in my ear.

I have no choice. "OK. Circle back and tell the others."

Nneoma winks at me. "Oh, they know already. I told them the plan earlier. We just needed your approval. We have already put the Mages on other beasts so that they are safe." She lets out a chuckle and winks again. "Come now, Taj, are we really going to be more prepared than you?" She laughs, and it's enough to make me laugh. I don't care that the sound is drowned out by the exploding boulders around us and the arashi screeching above us.

"OK, then."

She expertly guides her griffin to mine.

I wait until she's close enough, then I put my hand to the forehead of her griffin. It begins to glow, and Nneoma takes a moment to stare in wonder. Then she looks at me, nods, and swoops down into the inisisa-covered streets. She's blazing a trail of light. All the inisisa her beast touches, their armor falls away, and when she pulls back up into the sky, the cleansed inisisa follow her like a shadowy tail, light dripping down to infect all the others. She vanishes into the distance, then a massive burst of light, like a star splitting open, shines in the sky over the Palace. Sparks like comets spill out, and sunlight cuts through that now-clear patch of sky.

Another aki pulls up to my side, looking straight ahead all the while. This one is determined not to let fear conquer him. I touch his griffin's forehead, and he does the same as Nneoma, drawing armored inisisa and bringing them with him into the face of another arashi. Another burst of light, and more blue sky opens up overhead.

Something so beautiful and painful to watch is little more than a chemical reaction. Shapes and elements meeting one another and changing.

"Taj," Aliya says to me before I can mourn the sacrificed aki, "I have an idea." She points to a rooftop down to our left. "Let me down over there."

I trust her, so I bring my griffin to a stop, and she hops off. Inisisa swarm the building below her. I can hear them inside, bounding up each floor.

"I will meet you in the Palace."

I want to ask her how, but she puts her hands to the roof, and out of it springs a bridge made of stone that arcs to the next building, then to the next after that, and the one after that, until she's created a whole walkway leading to the Palace's front steps. It's like when she broke the earth in front of Zaki's home. And like when Zaki formed a bridge to cross that chasm.

"Go!" she says, then sets off at a run.

I shake my head in amazement as my griffin takes me forward. Is there anything she cannot do?

Other griffins let Mages down on rooftops around the Forum, and they make bridges as well. This is it. This is Iragide. Breaking and binding.

I bring the riderless griffins behind me and touch them, one by one, as they pass, then send them like sticks of dynamite into the streets, where they charge through the inisisa and set them alight. The streets glow, as Aliya and the Mages run from rooftop to rooftop.

We're going to make it.

Inisisa swarm the front steps to the Palace. Bears and dragons and lynxes. I may be all alone, but nothing will stop me from getting into that Palace. I urge my griffin to go faster. Faster, faster. I'm almost there.

A sin-falcon crashes into me, hurling me off my griffin. The two inisisa grapple in the air, bursting into sparks of light, and I soar high above the Palace steps, coming down on the back of a sin-dragon waiting for me with jaws open. My flats tear as I slide down its scaled back then leap into the air right at the sin-bear before me, plunging my hands into its forehead. It explodes in a burst of light. The inisisa on the steps all charge at me. I strike right, left, duck beneath the sin-wolf that dives at me. There are so many of them, but I kick and swing and jump, whirling around, battling them all. The Palace entrance is so close.

I grapple with a sin-lynx that has me on my back. Its jaw snaps at me, angling for my neck. Something sharp that glints in the light comes down through its neck.

Bo pulls me to my feet.

"I thought . . ." I say, stunned.

"That I betrayed you?" He smirks, and he's the old Bo again. "I got you past the Wall, didn't I? Come now, you know I need a good wrestling partner." Then the two of us stand back to back. He slices at the inisisa with his good hand, disabling them, and I take their remains in my arms and cleanse them. Light surrounds us. Through the chaos, I see Noor fighting, defending herself against the army of inisisa with a double-bladed staff. They can't touch her, she's so fast.

"Get to the Palace, Taj," Bo tells me. He grabs a sin-spider by one leg with his foot, slices through it, and when it falls, he drives his daga into its back. "Go!" He slips a second daga out of his boot and grips the first one in his teeth. Without looking back, he charges into the fray, slashing and whirling and flying through the air like a madman.

The two of them have cleared a path for me, and I bound up the steps. I take one last look back and see nothing but moving shadows, but then I squint into the distance and see people. They're not marked in any way, but they carry whatever they can. Staffs, kitchen knives, hammers. The people of Kos.

Around them, Mages gather, and the ground beneath them and the stone of the buildings around them break apart and re-form to make walls from behind which the people of Kos can fight.

My heart leaps. The survivors left behind. They fill the streets of the Forum and drive right up to the steps, clashing with the inisisa. They've joined us in battle.

The Palace doors are locked shut. In the midst of the battling citizens and aki and inisisa, I spot the sin-dragon from earlier. That's it.

I run to it, and it lowers its head for me. Once I get on its back, it flaps its wings once, and I soar upward. We land with a heavy thud on the balcony overhead, and before I slip off its back, I touch its forehead. It turns into light, then vanishes.

The large windows before me are open.

Karima steps out of the shadows. Slowly. Her emerald gown shimmers in the light. But its colors change to red. Instead of making her look like some otherworldly blessing from the Unnamed, it makes her look like she's wearing blood.

I shake my head straight. "It's over," I say, loud enough to be heard over the battle below. "You've lost." I gesture to the city. "The people have risen up against you."

She walks toward me without saying a word. Just smiling. And it chills me.

She stops, and the smirk falls from her face.

Shadows dance behind Karima.

Three wolves emerge from the darkness.

"It is just us now, Taj." Her voice is like silk in my ears. "You and me. Balance."

Beneath the sound of her voice, I hear the inisisa growling.

"You can still stop this. All this death. All this destruction. All this Unbalance." The shade of her dress grows darker and darker, shimmers green, then red, then white, then black.

The first wolf leaps for me, and I stick my hand out to press against its forehead, but it barrels me over, unchanged. I need both forearms to keep its jaws from my face. It snarls and snaps its teeth at me. Am I too weak to cleanse it? The wolf squeezes the air out of my lungs. Silver dots pop up before my eyes.

"Karima," I hiss between gritted teeth.

I hear her footsteps until I can see her slippers right beside me. "Karima!"

I feel myself slipping away. To my right lies my daga. Just out of reach.

The inisisa's jaws get closer, then suddenly, it stops. Like an obedient dog, the wolf steps off my chest and backs away. The others join it. I cough as I push myself onto my knees, and that's when I see Bo standing on the balcony. His eyes have a glazed cast to them. He's Crossing.

The inisisa all turn in Karima's direction.

For the first time, I see genuine fear on her face.

Bo takes his second daga from his mouth, then holds both his dagas between his knuckles. "This is what you've done. This is what your magic has made." His skin is covered almost entirely in shadows. They sizzle on his flesh. "And now it has returned to you. Balance." His chuckle sounds like rocks grinding together.

"Bo," I call out, coughing.

But he doesn't turn my way. "I am your weapon. I have killed for you. Slaughtered for you. I have darkened the air of entire villages with inyo. For you." He points his dagas at Karima. "I thought I was done killing. But I have one more yet."

"Bo!" I scream. I rise to my feet. Everyone looks my way. I can feel it pulsing like lightning beneath my skin. Rage. It was the sound of her voice. How she can describe everything that has happened as though it is simply the regular order of things. The executions. The demolitions. "You feel no guilt."

She says nothing, but she sees the look in my eyes, and it frightens her.

"You feel nothing for all the sins you have committed." I stalk toward her. I feel alive with anger. "You will feel them now." Then I'm upon her. I have her head in my hands. Her eyes grow wide with fear.

"Taj," she whimpers. "Taj, please. Don't."

But then the first sins choke the rest of her words in her throat. I grip her head tightly as ink spills out of her mouth. Her dress changes colors so fast it's like Gemtown during the day. She pitches forward, but I hold on to her head. Her body convulses, and ink spills and spills and spills like a waterfall onto the floor. We're both on our knees, and it hasn't stopped. She tries to raise a hand, to beg me to end it, but I grip her head tighter. Even as some of the ink molds itself into inisisa, more and more pours from her. Tears run down her face. But I tell myself it's not from guilt. It's from pain. Well, if she can't feel guilt, then she will at least feel pain.

After what feels like forever, she dry-heaves, then falls out of my hands. Her hands and knees splash in puddles of sin as she tries to get away from me, but each place in the pool that she touches turns into another beast. A snake, a lynx. Behind her, a bear and a dragon. Her dress is so black it matches the lake of sin she crawls through.

But when she turns and looks up, she sees me standing over her.

The floor groans beneath the weight of all these inisisa. They fill the room entirely, the necks of the taller ones bent against the ceiling. And they all, as one, look down on Karima.

"Taj, change them."

Even now, she commands me. I try to steady my breathing, but I can't. My arms and legs tremble. I can't change them. To do that would mean I'd have to bring myself to forgive her. And I can't.

"Change them, please."

My face turns into a mask. I can feel my features freezing into that same expressionless look I saw on Juba's tribespeople. Whenever emotions warred within them, they would put it on. I don't know what exactly my face looks like, but it's enough for Karima to gaze at me in horror. "You will pay for your sins. You are just like your brother, Kolade. Do you remember him?" I step toward her. "Do you remember how you cursed him for casting the burden of his sins on others? For painting his sins on us because he could not be *bothered* to live with his guilt?" I'm shouting now. The refugees. The families split apart. The shattered marayu. The aki who died fighting back. "You are no different. But where he escaped punishment, you will not." I step away from her. "Your sins will eat you alive." I finally still the tremors that wrack my body. Then I close my eyes and connect with every inisisa in the room. This is it. This is how it will end.

"Taj!"

The voice snatches me back. I turn, and the inisisa part to give me a straight line of sight to Aliya, who now stands next to Bo at the large balcony entrance to the room. Her robe hangs in shreds and tatters about her, but she walks with strong, determined steps. Arzu is there too. They all survived.

The door connecting this room with the rest of the Palace bursts open, and the heads of the inisisa turn to see Chiamaka leading a group of aki and Mages and Kosians into the room. They stop in their tracks when they see the beasts that fill nearly every inch of this chamber.

Fine. Karima's death will have an audience.

But the look that Aliya gives me stills me. "Taj, don't."

I clench my fists. "Why not?" After all she did . . .

"Because that is not Balance."

I point to Karima, who lies on the floor at my feet. "You want me to forgive her? Aliya, I tried, and I cannot. She feels no guilt! Even now, with all of her sins staring down at her, she feels no guilt! Nothing!"

Now Aliya is close enough to touch. "The other side of guilt is forgiveness."

"But it isn't fair." I know I sound like a child, but that is how this feels. It feels like what it meant to be born aki in this city, where people kicked you in the street and used you like a dishrag until they couldn't anymore. It feels like playing a game you were never meant to win.

Her hand alights on my shoulder. Patches of soot mar the markings on her arms and fingers. "Fairness and Balance are two separate things." She squeezes. "Killing her will not save Kos."

I simmer. "And you, Arzu?" I snap. "You would forgive her too? After what she did to your family?"

Arzu says nothing.

"Aliya, I can't," I tell her, even as tears spring to my eyes.

"Let me." Bo's voice cuts through the air. Suddenly, he moves.

"Bo, wait!" But it's not enough to stop him from slicing at the inisisa, toppling them one by one. He dances through the shadows, and the ink spins and twirls and swims around him until every inisisa in the room is a puddle of ink again. I know what he's doing, and pain lances my heart so swiftly that I drop my daga.

When he's done, he stands in the middle of the room, surrounded by onlookers. He stares straight at me. And smiles. "Taj, when you bury me, bury me close to our home. And if the flowers on my grave are not regularly tended to, I will haunt you." He winks, then opens his mouth and closes his eyes as all of Karima's sins arc into the air in slick, black streams and dive down his throat.

Tears run freely down my face.

When it is over and the room has been emptied of sin, Bo pitches forward, and I catch him just in time. I try to see if there's any of him left, but his limbs have already gone cold and his eyes have already gone blank. He's Crossed.

Suddenly, Aliya's at my side. She comes down to her knees and wraps her arms around both me and Bo. It feels as if I've been reunited with my missing parts. The poems on our skin meet one another.

"Arzu?" The gear-head has her mask off, her blond hair tied in a ponytail over her shoulder.

Arzu freezes when she sees the woman. Chiamaka. The half-limb from before. Arzu looks at Chiamaka as though nothing else in the world exists.

The two women stand there, paralyzed, frozen in disbelief. Tears begin to leak from Chiamaka's eyes.

"By the Unnamed," she gasps. "I thought you were lost."

"Mama?" Arzu whispers. "Mama, is that you?" Before she can get an answer, Arzu runs into the woman's embrace.

Chiamaka takes her daughter's face in her hand and says, "Yes, my daughter. It's me."

Outside no longer sounds like chaos. It no longer sounds like screeching. Like thunder. Like death.

It sounds like cheering. And weeping. The good kind of weeping.

The joyful kind.

"Taj, look." Aliya points out toward the balcony. On the ground, Kosians stand or kneel, hug themselves or weep over the fallen, but some of them are shouting. Some of them are even singing.

Night has fallen.

Red glows under the clouds. Dark, purplish red. Like a bruise on the sky. It rises in rays and sways. Stars begin to shine through the tides of light.

"Ụtụtụiụ n'abalị." Aliya is breathless when she says it. "Falling red flames."

The light turns into glowing curtains. Blue joins the red, then columns of green waver in the curtain of color.

The gemstones. People are wearing them, tossing them into the air, holding them in bundles toward the sky. The aki, faces wide with smiles, are bathed in colors.

My city glows with light.

ACKNOWLEDGMENTS

Preparing a book for the wild a second time has only been more surreal than doing it the first. All throughout, however, I had help. I thank my publisher, Razorbill, and specifically #TeamBeasts: Ben Schrank for his wisdom and deadpan humor; my associate publisher, Casey McIntyre, for her superlative organizational skills and tireless advocacy for Taj's story; my agent, Noah Ballard, for his reassurance when I stood in the quicksand of doubt, and for the sandwiches; my copyeditors for their superhuman skill; and, of course, my editor, Jess Harriton, for her enthusiasm, her patience as the book endured its seismic changes, and her certainty that, all the while, I was heading in the right direction.

I thank every Bookstagrammer, every blogger, every person who shouted from the rooftops that Taj's story was worth reading. And I thank every person who thanked me for writing it.

I give thanks to Nigeria for giving me its history, my history, and its sense of humor, now, to an extent, my sense of humor. Wrapped in that green and white flag, we are alchemists.

Finally, I must thank my Penguin Sister Julie C. Dao, whose steps have mirrored mine, whose shoulder is likely soaked through with my tears, and who has been among my loudest cheerleaders and most beloved confidants. You have my heart, Sis. See you at Denny's.

219823191197842